NIGHTMARE

Abby Jaquint

PAGE PUBLISHING, INC.
New York, NY

First originally published by Page Publishing, Inc. 2017

ISBN 978-1-63568-353-0 (Paperback)
ISBN 978-1-63568-354-7 (Digital)

Printed in the United States of America

I don't know what I'm doing with my life. I never really have known. Everything just kind of happened, and I went along with it. That's all I could really do. I'm a firm believer that you can't control what happens in your life. Whatever comes your way, you just have to deal with it. Obviously, if I'm thinking things like this, I'm not feeling very great. And sitting out in the cold isn't making me feel any better about myself. I should go back in. I should apologize to everyone for being a drag. Instead, I take my phone out of my coat pocket and call the only person I can think of calling. Valentine is the only person in my life that might be able to understand me.

"Hey, Keyon," he answers the phone after the first ring. "You good? I thought you were out with Grace."

"I was," I say. "And Nelson. And Hayden. And Andrew. And Mercedes. And all of her friends apparently."

Valentine laughs. "Sounds like absolute hell, if you ask me. What happened to it just being you and Grace?"

"No idea." I sigh. I should go back in. I shouldn't be on the phone right now. Not after how I left it in there."

"She decided she didn't want to be in a bar alone with you?" Valentine laughs again.

"Apparently. So much for us going out, huh?" I look up at the sky.

"Hey, man, it could still work out. Why aren't you with her anyway? Or them, I guess."

I take a deep breath. "Got a little defensive."

"Here we go again." Valentine sighs. "About what?"

"Don't worry about it. It's nothing."

"Are you sure? Because you don't sound sure."

"I'm sure," I say as a few cars drive past.

"So why are you calling me, exactly?"

"I hate to interrupt whatever it is you're doing."

"Keyon, it's fine. I'm never doing anything anyway." I hear him laugh.

"Can you come get me?"

"Anything for you. It's that place at the end of Fifth, right?"

I smile and sit down on the bench behind me. "Yeah. That's the one."

"Alright." Valentine sighs. "Be there in five. Try your best to avoid everyone. And you'd better not be crying when I get there."

"No promises."

I hang up and think about my life choices. All I can think to do is slam my head into a wall about a hundred times. A few minutes later, I hear a door open next to me.

"Thanks for that," Grace says as she walks up next to me. Great.

"I'm sorry," I say.

Grace rolls her eyes and crosses her arms. "You kind of ruined this for me."

I stand up and say, "No offense, Grace, but you kind of ruined this for me too. You invited a bunch of people I've never met."

"I've told you about all of them."

"You didn't say they were going to be here." I take a few steps forward and get close enough that she can hear me speak softly. "I thought this was just going to be the two of us."

Grace sighs and looks around. When we make eye contact again, she looks somewhat distressed. "I think we need to talk about that," she whispers.

"Talk about what?"

"About us." Grace sighs again. "I just don't think . . . I don't know. I just don't think I feel the same way anymore."

This has happened many times before. I know that nothing lasts forever, so I'm not surprised when she says this to me. I guess I just hadn't expected her to say it so soon. I probably should've prepared myself for this day.

"Are you"—I laugh a little—"breaking up with me?"

"Yeah," she says.

I think about this. "I guess that makes sense," I say quietly.

"I'm sorry. I know you thought this was going well."

"Yeah," I say.

We stare at each other. "Do you need someone to take you home?" she asks.

"No. Someone's getting me."

"Val?"

"Yeah."

Neither of us is looking at each other now. I think about slamming my head against the wall again.

"I think I should go back in," Grace says.

I nod. We look at each other for a brief moment before she heads back inside. I sit back down and put my head in my hands. This isn't how I thought my day was gonna go. About a minute later, I get the feeling that someone is in front of me.

"What did I say about crying?"

I look up and see Val. His bright-blue eyes staring down at me.

"I'm not crying," I say as I stand up.

Val laughs and puts his hand on my shoulder. "You should probably talk to Grace." He flashes me a smile.

"Just did." I sigh.

"And?"

"We broke up," I say.

Val's eyes widen.

"Well, no. She broke up with me. I guess." I shake my head and look at the ground.

"Hey." Val takes his hand off my shoulder. "Some things just aren't meant to be. And you can do better than her anyway." He smiles.

"Yeah," I say. "Maybe."

"You good, though?"

I sigh. "I think so. Not like we were together that long anyway."

"I don't know, man. Three months is pretty long. For you at least." Val puts his arm around me as we start walking toward his car.

"I was going to tell her when we got back to her place tonight." I look down at the ground as we walk.

"Tell her what?"

"That I love her."

Val stops in front of his car and lets go of me to get into the driver's seat. "Fuck, man. I'm sorry."

I get into the passenger's side and nod my head. "It's all good. Doesn't matter now anyway."

Val sighs and backs out into the street. "That's what I hate about you. You're too damn depressing all the time," he says.

I can tell that he's joking, but I get offended anyway. "You do realize I was just dumped by a girl I was in love with, right?"

"Alright, alright." Val waves his hand at me. "I guess being depressed makes sense. Just don't stay that way for too long."

I smile a little. "I'll try not to."

"You were only at that bar for half an hour. You drink anything?"

"If you count water, then yes."

Val laughs as he pulls into the parking lot outside of our apartment building. "You know that's not what I meant. Let's go in and actually have something."

I sigh and get out of the car as soon as Val parks. "I don't need to drink, Val. I'll be fine."

"Hey," he says as he walks next to me. "Maybe you don't need it, but I sure as hell do."

"I'm beginning to think you have a problem." I smile at him. He smiles back at me and follows me up a couple steps to our building. We head inside and go up the three floors to our apartment. Val unlocks the door and immediately walks over to a high cabinet in the kitchen. "Fuck, I forgot to buy anything after last Saturday," he says to himself.

I smile and go sit down on the couch. "Nothing for you then," I say.

Val walks over to where I'm sitting and plops down next to me. "Probably a good thing," he looks up at the ceiling. "I think you're right about me having a problem." We stay on the couch for the next four hours, watching the Spider Man movies. I think about Grace the entire time. Lovely.

"Jesus Christ, it's almost midnight," Val says.

"And?"

"And I have a class at eight in the fucking morning." He leans forward and rests his elbows on his knees, putting his head in his hands.

"Well," I say as I stand up, "your fault for signing up for a class that early."

"I know." He stands up as well. "I'm an idiot. I get it. And you're an asshole for reminding me. I'm going to bed."

"I might do the same thing." I follow him down the short hallway of our little apartment. "See you in the morning then."

"You're getting up at the same time I am?" Val asks from where he's standing in the doorway to his room.

"Work, remember? Some of us have jobs." I smile.

Val smiles back and shakes his head. "Go to bed," he says. He closes his door, and I walk into my room next to his. I shut my door gently and sit down on my bed. I look in front of me at the mirror I have hanging on the back of my door. I look tired. My skin seems paler than it usually is, my eyes more of a dull gray than my regular chestnut color. I sigh and shake my head at myself. Thinking about Grace again, I lie down. Stupid. I'm so stupid. What did I think was going to happen with us? There had to have just been something wrong with her. That was it.

I get up at six and take a five-minute shower. After taking a quick look around the kitchen, I decide that one of us needs to go grocery shopping. I make myself a bowl of cereal and eat it slowly at the table for fifteen minutes. I look at my phone and see that I have to be at work soon. Val probably isn't up yet, so I try to put my dishes away as quietly as possible. But seeing as how I am a moron, I drop everything into the sink, probably waking up everyone in the building.

"Jesus, what are you doing?" I see Val standing at the end of the hallway, rubbing his eyes.

"Sorry," I say. "I didn't mean to wake you up."

He waves his hand at me and walks into the kitchen. He opens the fridge and sighs. "Gotta go fuckin' grocery shopping too. Gotta go to an eight a.m. class. Gotta live the worst life ever."

If there's anything that I've learned about Val in the past ten months of living with him, it's that he is definitely not a morning person.

"You don't need a ride, do you?" he asks me, running a hand through his blond hair.

"No, I can walk," I say as I head toward the door.

"Alright," Val sighs. "See you when I see you."

I go outside and wait until I hear Val lock the door behind me. My first class of the day isn't until two, so I need to be back by around one thirty. Time for six hours of brutal labor. I take my time walking. Something about walking around downtown in the cold makes me feel good. I try to think about nothing as I make my way to work. I almost manage to get Grace out of my thoughts. Almost.

I try my best to sell tea to people. This isn't a hard job; I just have to stand outside the shop and get people to buy our stuff. Maybe this would be easier if I was a little more charismatic. I'm giving some teenager a sample of a tea made out of flowers or something when I see her. We make eye contact. I don't want to talk to her. I don't think she knows that I'm thinking this, because she is walking over to me.

"Keyon," she says. "I didn't know you worked here."

"I've worked here for the past year, Erica. And I'm not really supposed to just stand out here and socialize," I say in a tone that I wouldn't exactly call friendly.

"Not going to make an exception for me?" Erica smiles.

"Nope." I smile back. I walk past her and offer a sample to an older woman. She says she'd love to try some of our stuff and follows me into the store. I don't look back to see if Erica is still there. It's not like I would care if she is.

Five hours later, work is over, and I'm finally allowed to go back home. I text Val and see if he's at the apartment. He doesn't respond, so I just start to walk back. I make it there in about fifteen minutes, still no response from Val. When I walk up to the building, I see Grace sitting on the steps outside.

"Hey," I say as I shove my hands into my pockets.

"Where's Val?" Grace looks up at me. I feel a little offended that the first thing she asks about is Val.

"I don't know." I shake my head. "Why?"

"I got some texts." She looks down at her phone. "Did he text you anything?"

"No."

"He said he didn't know who to talk to."

I stare at her. "Okay?"

"I'm just saying that I think there's something wrong with him."

"I'll go inside right now. See if he's in there."

"Mind if I come with?"

I look down at my shoes then back up at her. "Kind of."

"Oh," she says, pressing her lips together.

"Sorry," I say. "I'll tell you what I find out."

I leave Grace standing on the steps as I go inside. I kind of feel like an asshole, but I'm sure I'll get over it. I make my way up the stairs until I get to our front door. It's unlocked. That's definitely unusual. Once I'm inside, I look around the living room and the kitchen.

"Val?" I call out as I walk into the kitchen. I notice that there's a knife missing from our knife block. I know it could just be in the dishwasher or something, but I'm still worried. "Valentine, seriously," I say a little bit louder. I walk down the hall and over to Val's room. I try the door handle, but it's locked. I knock a few times but don't say anything. A second later, I hear the lock click. I take a deep breath and open the door slowly. In front of me, I see Val standing near his bed, holding the missing knife in front of him.

"Whoa," I say as I put my hands up.

"Fuck, man," Val says as he lowers the knife. "It's you."

"Yes. It is me," I give him a quizzical look.

"I totally just—" Val sighs. "I have no idea, dude. I have no idea what is wrong with me. I swear to god I heard someone talking a little while ago. I swear to god I did. Thought you were just home early, but when I walked out to the living room, you weren't there. I have no idea what was wrong, I just knew, Keyon. I knew it wasn't—"

"Hey," I put my hand on his shoulder. "What are you talking about?"

"I'm just fucking paranoid. It's stupid. Whatever. Sorry you thought I was gonna, like, murder you." He looks at the knife in his hand.

I sigh. "Let's just put that away, okay?" Val nods and follows me out of his room and into the kitchen. I take the knife out of his hand and put it away. I sigh again and turn around to look at Val, where he's now sitting at the kitchen table. "You alright?" I ask.

"Yeah," he says this quietly, like it's a secret.

"So," I sit next to him. "You texted Grace?"

"Well, I couldn't exactly text you. I thought you were in the fucking apartment."

"But Grace?" I'm almost offended that he didn't think to text me. I decide not to say anything about it, though.

"First person I could think of, I guess." He pauses. "How did you know that I texted her?"

"Oh." I stand up. "She was waiting outside the building. I said I would go find you."

"God." Val puts his head in his hands. "I didn't think she'd get so worried that she'd actually show up here." He stands up and walks into the living room. He shakes his head a few times and looks over at me. "Alright. Let's stop worrying about me. Did you tell Grace she could go home?"

"I can text her right now."

"Okay." Val sighs. "Shouldn't you go to class?"

I take a deep breath. Val looks so shaken up there's no way I can leave him alone. I think about what might happen if I decide not to go to class. Nothing too bad hopefully. "I think I'll be okay if I skip today."

"Hey." Val gets a few steps closer to me. "You don't have to stay here because of me. I'm not scared." He stands up a little straighter as if to prove his point.

"You sure?" I raise my eyebrows. "Because two minutes ago, you were locked in your bedroom with a knife."

Val laughs a little at this. "I guess you're right," he says. He sighs and sits down on the couch. I do the same and text Grace that Val's alright. I let her know it's okay for her to leave.

"I think I need to stop reading so many scary stories." Val laughs and leans back.

"Yeah, probably a good idea." I smile at him.

"I'm serious, though. I'm fine. You can go to class. Wouldn't want you failing."

"Val, if I were you, I wouldn't want to be alone right now."

"Alright, fine." Val sighs. "You're right. I don't want to be alone. But I don't want to think about my day. How was yours?"

I roll my eyes and lean back with him. I'm glad that we can talk to each other normally again. "Saw Erica at work today," I say.

"Like, 'marry me' Erica?"

"That's the one." I nod.

"You say anything to her?"

"Not really. She said she didn't know that I worked at the mall or whatever, and then she asked if I'd break the rules to talk to her."

"Did you?"

I laugh. "No way. You think I'd still want to talk to her?"

"I don't know. I mean, you were going to marry her." Val smiles.

"Stop, don't even say stuff like that. Worst idea I've ever had."

"Who even gets married at twenty-two?" Val turns sideways and lies down.

"I don't know. But I guess I wanted to."

"Was she the one that tried to kill you?"

"No." I shake my head. "That was Audrey. Erica's the one that totaled my car."

"I think you need to just stop dating forever." Val closes his eyes and smiles. "Nothing good ever happens with these girls."

"Hey, nothing bad has happened with Grace," I point out.

"True." Val opens his eyes and looks at me. "Did you text her?"

"Yeah. She knows you're good."

"What did you tell her?"

"What did you want me to tell her?"

Val sits back up and leans toward me. "No, seriously. What did you tell her?"

"I told her you thought there was someone in our apartment."

Val lies back down. "I feel like a crazy person right now. You know what I mean? Ever feel like you're seeing or hearing something?"

"I guess." I shrug my shoulders.

Val sighs. "You don't know what I mean, do you?"

"Not at all."

"Man, whatever. I need a hug."

I hold out my arms.

"Not from you." Val laughs and lightly pushes my arms away from him. He stands up and walks into the kitchen. "I'm gonna go out. I think. So you can go to class and stuff. I told you I don't want you failing on me."

I smile and stand up. "Fine. I'll go. Where are you headed?" I start to walk toward my room.

"Oh, you know," I hear Val say.

"I don't know!" I yell back so he can hear me.

"I think I might possibly have a date."

"Nice," I say as I walk out of my room, holding my laptop. "Who's the girl?"

"Well." Val scratches the back of his head. "Don't, like, freak out or anything."

I freak out anyway. "Jesus, don't say you're going out with Grace or something."

"What? Keyon, no. I'm not going out with Grace."

"Then why would I freak out?"

"It's kind of a guy."

"It's kind of a guy," I repeat him.

"Yeah. I wasn't sure if I was ever going to tell you."

"Why not?" I'm genuinely confused about this. I'm not a judgmental person. I don't think I am, at least.

"Last roommate I had was a little weirded out by it. Didn't end so well." Val sighs.

"You thought it was going to be the same way with me?"

"Kind of. I mean, I don't really know how you feel about that kind of stuff. You know?"

"Yeah." I walk over to him and put my free hand on his shoulder. "Don't even worry about it. It doesn't bother me."

Val smiles and looks down at the ground. "Thanks." I take my hand off him and walk toward the door. I haven't had the chance to take my shoes off, so I'm already ready to go.

"How'd you plan a date that fast anyway?" I ask before opening our door.

"Oh, no. We planned it last night. I just have to, like, get actual nice clothes for it. So I should probably go do that."

I nod. "What's this guy's name?"

"I don't wanna jinx anything." Val shrugs. "I'll tell you when I know we're official." He smiles at me then looks away. I smile too and walk out the door. I wait until Val locks it behind me, then I head downstairs. Honestly? I'm a little upset that Val hadn't told me sooner. You live with someone for ten months, and you learn absolutely nothing about them. Nothing important, at least.

The rest of my day is uneventful. Class is boring. I grocery shop. The walk back home is boring, and the rest of my night I just sit around watching Netflix because of how dead tired I am. Thinking about what happened earlier, I start to wonder if Val is actually okay or not. I'm still sort of confused about what exactly it was that he was talking about, but whatever the case, I'm still scared for him. I don't want there to actually be something wrong. I look at my phone and see that it's almost two in the morning. Val isn't home yet. I can't help it; I start panicking. Just as I'm about to call him, the door to our apartment swings open.

I see Val walk in, and I start talking. "Hey—"

"What the fuck is wrong with me?" Val puts his hands in the air.

"What?" I ask him.

"Never mind. Don't even answer that. I know what's wrong with me."

Val takes off his shoes and undoes the top two buttons of his shirt before lying facedown on the couch. "Everything. Everything is wrong with me."

I sit down on the floor next to him. "What happened?"

"I hate him, Keyon. I hate him so much."

"What did he do?"

"You know that stereotype that all guys want is sex?" He turns his head to look at me.

"Yes." I nod. "I believe it to be true, mostly."

"Well, there ya go." Val puts his face back onto the cushion.

"So he didn't really like you?"

"Apparently not."

"That doesn't mean anything's wrong with you," I say.

"That means everything's wrong with me, man. Fucking everything."

I pat his back a few times. "You'll be okay."

"How do you know?"

"How many times have I had relationships not work out for me?"

Val laughs. "A lot of times. I'm sorry."

"Hey, I should be the one saying sorry. It sucks what happened."

"Yeah." Val turns to lie on his back. "It really, really does."

"You want a drink?" I ask as I stand up.

"You bought some stuff?" Val sits up and looks at me.

"The only kind I like." I smile.

"Fucking Ciroc, man." Val lies back down and covers his face.

"So you don't want any?"

"I never said that."

I laugh as I pour us both a glass. "Jesus, you're gonna drink that much?" I turn around to see Val standing behind me.

"It's as much as you usually have."

"Yes," Val says as he picks up his glass, "but I am the most unhealthy person I know. I am also insane. So I'd recommend that you never drink as much as me." He smiles as he takes a sip. I smile back and drink some of mine.

"God, this is the worst idea I've ever had."

"What do you mean?" I ask.

"I've already had way too much today."

"Wait, what?" I grab his glass out of his hand. "Didn't you drive home?"

"Yeah. Like I said, I'm insane."

"That's not being insane, Val. That's being stupid."

"I get it, okay? I wasn't being very smart. I was just having a not-so-great time, and I'd love it if you didn't get pissed off like this."

I roll my eyes. "I'm not mad at you. I just don't want you to die because you decided to be an idiot."

Now it's Val who's rolling his eyes. "Not like I'm planning on doing it again. I'm not that stupid." He hits me lightly on the arm. "Now give me my drink back."

I hesitate to give it to him, but I do it anyway.

"You really don't have to drink it if you don't like it." I smile.

"What, and let you drink alone? I could never."

We laugh and talk about better things. By three thirty, most of the bottle is gone, and we're sitting on the floor.

"It just doesn't make any sense," I say. "If you're going to kill someone you know is stronger than you, why try and choke them? Aren't there better ways to get the job done?"

"No, no." Val shakes his head at me. "She wasn't going for that classic crazy ex-girlfriend thing, you know?"

"Classic?"

"Yeah. They always go after you with a knife or do some crazy torture shit on you. You get what I'm trying to say? Audrey wanted to be different."

"I can't believe I put her in jail, Val."

"Jail is just a room," Val says.

"Exactly." I nod. "Exactly. Do I have class tomorrow?"

"Tomorrow's Saturday, man."

"Fuck," I say.

"Whoa." Val drinks straight out of the bottle. "Listen to you. Swearing and everything. Never thought I'd hear you say anything like that. I should get you drunk more often."

I laugh and lie back on the floor. "I'm really going to regret this tomorrow."

"You and me both, Keyon. You and me both."

I laugh, then I shut myself up. I hear crying coming from underneath me. I flip over onto my stomach and put my ear to the tiles. "You hear that?" I lift my head up to look at Val. He sets the near-empty bottle on the ground. "I do," he says as he lies down next to me. We look at each other and listen to the crying.

"What should we do?" I ask.

Val nods a few times before he sits up. "We need to make them okay."

I sit up as well. "We what?"

"We gotta go check on them, Keyon. Do you want to listen to this all night?"

I shake my head no.

"Alright." Val claps his hands together and stands up. He holds out a hand for me. I take it, and he pulls me up just a little too roughly.

"So what do we do?" I ask as he drags me toward the door leading out of our apartment.

"We just go down and knock. Simple as that."

I nod and follow him down the steps and onto the second floor. The first door on the right doesn't have a knocker on it or a name plate. The crying is still audible. I look at Val, but he isn't looking back at me.

"I don't wanna knock," he says.

"Well, I don't either."

"Please?" Val looks at me. "I've had a bad day."

I roll my eyes and knock a few times. The crying on the other side stops, but no one opens the door.

"Guess they don't want to talk to anyone." I shrug.

Val sighs and knocks on the door. "Hey," he says loudly. "We heard you, man. We wanna help."

I reach out to grab Val's hand. "Val, I don't think we should—" He shakes my hand off him and knocks again. That's one thing Val has that I'll probably never have. An outgoing personality. I don't think I could ever see myself being as extroverted as he is. A few seconds later, the lock clicks, and the door opens. I look down and see a twenty-something-year-old girl in pajamas standing in front of me. She doesn't say anything; she just stares at us. Val talks first.

"We heard you crying," he says.

"Wow, way to be straight up with her." I look at him. He ignores me and looks at the girl. She still doesn't say anything. "Are you okay?" Val tries again.

The girl sighs. "Yeah. Sorry to wake you up, I guess." She rolls her eyes.

"Don't worry, you didn't wake us up," I say. "We were already up."

"What do you guys want? Really?" the girl asks.

"I'm Valentine." Val holds out his hand. She takes it and sighs. "Weird name," she says. "I'm Quinn." She glances at me and looks me up and down. "And you?"

"Keyon," I say.

She nods and looks back and forth between the two of us. "So you just wanted to confront me?"

"Basically." Val nods.

Quinn looks down at her feet then behind her and into her apartment. "Well, since this is already weird enough, come on in," she says.

Val smiles and follows her inside. I open my mouth to object, but it's too late now. I walk in and shut the door behind me.

"Whoa, looks just like our place," Val says as he sits down at her kitchen table.

"That's usually how apartments work when they're in the same building," Quinn sits down next to him. "They all pretty much look the same." She looks up at me now. "You joining us, or are you just going to stand there awkwardly?"

"I, um—"

"Dude, sit down," Val says.

I nod and join them at the table. "So," Val says cheerfully. "Why the tears?"

"Stupid girl problems, trust me."

"Does it have to do with a guy?" Val asks.

"Yes." Quinn sighs. "It does."

"Tell me about it." Val puts his elbows on the table. "I bet you anything I can relate."

Quinn rolls her eyes.

"No, for real," Val says. "Just tell me." She looks at me and raises her eyebrows. I nod at her.

"Fine," she says. "His name is Aiden, and he kind of just let me go. Like, an hour ago. We'd been dating for two years and everything. He proposed to me last month, but I guess for some reason he didn't think things were going that well anymore. So he basically just broke up with me."

"Well." Val looks down at the table then up at me. "Keyon, any words of wisdom?"

"Guys suck," I say.

Quinn rolls her eyes for the third time tonight. "Yeah, no shit." She looks over at Val. "Can you relate to this?"

"I have had many men break up with me, yes. But I've never dated anyone for as long as two years. And no one has ever proposed to me. So I can't *exactly* relate. But I do agree with my friend here on this one." Val looks at me. "Guys do suck."

Quinn laughs a little and looks at me. "You look sad too," she says.

"I do?" I turn to Val. He tilts his head and sighs. "You do," he says. "Keyon here got dumped yesterday by the love of his life."

"She wasn't the love of my life," I say.

"You loved her, though." Val points a finger at me then looks back over at Quinn. "And I sort of broke up with someone, like, four hours ago. So I think we all can relate to each other a little bit." Val laughs.

"Are you two high or something? Who comes down to see a random neighbor they've never met before just because they hear crying?"

"Not gonna lie to you, we had a little bit to drink," I say.

Quinn raises her eyebrows and nods slightly. She turns and looks behind her. When she turns back toward us, she looks worried. "I'm almost glad you guys are here, actually."

"You are?" Val asks.

"Yeah. Call me crazy, but I've been hearing noises all night. It's nice having other people here. Even if you are"—she looks at both of us for a few seconds—"younger than me? Older than me? I can't tell."

"We're four years apart." Val gestures to me. "Keyon here just turned twenty-three last week." He puts his hand on my shoulder and smiles at me. He looks back at Quinn. "What about you?"

"Twenty-nine," she says.

"Damn." I raise my eyebrows. Quinn gives me a look.

"Sorry," I say. "It just slipped out."

"Wait a second." Val takes his hand off my shoulder and leans forward toward Quinn. "Did you say you've been hearing voices?"

"Noises," Quinn says. "Have you been hearing voices or something?"

"What?" Val looks at me then back at Quinn. "No. Why would you say that?"

Quinn looks over at me and raises her eyebrows. I just shrug and shake my head.

"No, guys." Val lays his hands down flat on the table. "Quinn, tell me about the noises."

"Um, I don't know." She shakes her head. "I guess it just kind of sounds like someone else is in my place. Like there's someone else living here. I know it's ridiculous."

"It doesn't sound ridiculous at all," Val says seriously. "I heard the exact same kind of thing earlier today."

"Walked in on him holding a kitchen knife." I nod my head.

I notice that Quinn is starting to seem a little uncomfortable.

"Okay." She stands up slowly. "You guys seem really nice. I mean that. But I think I need to be alone for a little while."

"I thought you said you didn't want to be alone?" Val stands up as well.

Quinn takes a step back. I can tell that she really doesn't want us here anymore. I decide to try to save her.

"Come on, Val." I grab on to his sleeve. "We should probably get going. I mean, it's getting really late." I give him a look and hope that he understands what it is I'm trying to do.

"Yeah." Val nods. "You're right. We should leave."

I give Quinn a nod, while Val gives her a small wave. She does nothing in return; she just closes the door loudly behind us.

"I think having two drunk guys in her apartment alone late at night scared her a little," Val says to me.

"You think?" I smack him on the arm as we make our way back up to our apartment. I think about how stupid we are for doing what we just did. I don't think I'd want to talk to two drunk guys this late either. I think a little more about stupid things I've done before Val starts talking again.

"Hey." He pulls on my arm before I have a chance to unlock the door. "Do you think we can just, you know, stay up for a little while longer? Maybe pull an all-nighter?" He smiles at me. I give him a small smile back. "Sure."

We finally go inside and sit down together on the couch.

"Any particular reason we're doing this?" I ask. We do this a lot, but I ask anyway. I never really know exactly what's going on with Val.

"Just had a rough day, I guess." Val shakes his head.

"Seems like that's been happening a lot lately."

"It really seems like that?" Val looks over at me.

"Yep," I say.

Val laughs then sighs. "I guess I have been having a few bad days here and there."

"That's your own fault, though," I say, stupidly.

"What?" Val raises his eyebrows at me.

"You never have a positive attitude about anything that you do. Like, ever. I think that has something to do with your bad days." I'm not exactly sure what is coming out of my mouth right now, but I know that this conversation is probably not going to end so well.

"Are you being serious?"

"Why wouldn't I be being serious?"

"Because you seem like you're the one who's never positive about anything." Val sounds like he's getting close to being angry, but not quite.

"I'm just saying it's nobody else's fault but yours," I say calmly. I still don't know what I'm saying.

"What the hell are you even talking about?" Val is raising his voice now.

"Nothing. I don't know."

Val stares at me for a few seconds.

"What?" I ask.

He just shakes his head. "Sometimes you just act like you know everything, and it kind of pisses me the fuck off," he says.

I laugh a little. "What?" I repeat myself.

"You heard me. And you know it's true too."

"I really don't think it's true at all, actually."

Now Val is the one laughing. "Are you fucking kidding me?" He glares at me.

"Val, I have no idea what you're talking about."

"You think everything is about you. Always. It doesn't matter what's going on, somehow it always relates right back to you. Have you never noticed that?"

This sets me off.

"What is wrong with you right now?" I stand up from the couch.

"What's wrong with *me*? You started this."

"*I* didn't start anything," I say.

"God, Keyon. That's another thing I can't fucking stand about you. You can never blame yourself, can you? It's always someone else's fault, isn't it?"

I stare at him for a moment. I'm not entirely sure what it is that he's talking about, but I do know that I'm mad now. "You know, I've been so worried about you. So worried about you, Val. And this whole thing about you hearing things or whatever really has me scared. But right now I'm kind of wishing there *was* someone in our apartment. You're better off dead anyway."

Val looks at me then down at his hands. Then he almost whispers, "Keyon, I—"

"Just forget it," I say as I turn toward the hallway.

"We can forget this ever happened," Val says.

"Whatever." I walk down the hall and into my bedroom, slamming my door behind me. I realize that I wasn't just being a horrible person; I was being a horrible friend. Why had I said that? Any of that? I lie down and think about what Val said. Maybe he was right. But it's a little too late now.

———————————•◆•————————————

I do not want to get out of bed the next morning, so I don't. It's almost three when I finally decide that I'm hungry and that I need to get out of my room. But I still don't want to leave. I don't want to have to see Val. I know I have to apologize; I'm just not sure how. I open my door and walk quietly through the hall. I'm surprised when I find that Val isn't here. I look back and see that his bedroom door is open. He's not home. Heading into the kitchen, I notice that there's a sticky note on the fridge. It says, "*Left at 11, not sure when I'll get back. Don't forget you have work today.*" And then I panic. I did forget. I look at my phone and realize that I'm exactly three hours late. No point in going now, I guess.

I make myself a bowl of cereal then go back into my room and try to do some homework. It's pointless, seeing as how I can't focus on anything. I'm thinking about how I'm still in love with Grace. I'm thinking about what happened with Val and how I acted toward him. I'm thinking about how I'm probably going to get fired for this, since this isn't the first time this has happened. I think about how in the world we're supposed to pay for everything if that happens. Then I think about how in the world I'm supposed to act around Val now. Do I just do what he suggested and pretend like nothing happened? I go back out to the kitchen and pick up Val's sticky note where I left it on the counter. I flip it over and it says, "*I'm sorry.*"

This makes me feel awful. I want to tell him I'm sorry too, but I decide that if I'm going to apologize, I should do it in person. I need to go outside. Get some fresh air or something. I put on my shoes and a coat and get out of the building as quickly as possible. I almost trip over someone sitting on the steps outside I'm going so fast.

"Keyon?"

"Oh." I see Quinn sitting on the steps, smoking a cigarette. "Hey."

"You okay?" She sounds uninterested, so I lie to her.

"Yeah," I say. "I'm good."

"Heard a couple door slams in your apartment last night." She raises her eyebrows.

"Oh, um, yeah."

"You sure you're okay?" She sounds a little more sincere this time.

I sigh and sit down next to her. "No. I'm an idiot." She sighs too and turns to look at me. "What'd you do?"

"I got in a fight with Val."

"You mean Valentine? Your friend?"

"Yeah." I look out at the parking lot.

"So you started the fight?"

"Basically." I sigh.

"Well, what made you think that was a good idea?"

"I don't know, okay?" I say loudly.

"Just a question, kid."

I almost say something about how I'm not a kid, but I keep my mouth shut. Instead, I sigh again and look down at the steps. "Sorry. I'm just a little on edge."

"I understand. I've definitely been on edge all day."

"Why?"

"You know those noises I told you about?" She looks away from me.

"Yeah."

"Thought I heard something again this morning. Right outside my door. Really been starting to freak me out. Makes me feel like I never want to go back inside."

"Maybe you should tell someone," I say.

"Probably." She smashes her cigarette into the cement beside her then flicks what's left of it into the grass. She stands up and looks down at me. "Talk to him," she says. "It'll be okay, alright? Don't worry about it too much." Then she goes inside.

I think about this and look up at the sky. It almost seems like it should be night. There's so many dark clouds I almost can't see anything. Don't worry about it too much. Yeah, right. Like I could do that. I worry about almost everything. How could I not worry about something like this? I'm deep in thought when my phone rings. I look at the caller ID and see Grace's name. I really don't need this right now.

"Hello?"

"Keyon? Are you okay?"

"Yes?"

"Val told me that you two are having problems."

"What's up with you two talking all the time now?" I ask her. I'm interested to know, but I'd also like to talk about anything else besides my problems. I especially don't want to talk about them with her.

She ignores the question completely. "What's the problem?"

"Grace, I really don't want to talk about this with you." I sigh. Might as well tell her how I really feel.

"I just wanted to see if I could help at all."

"Why do you even care?"

"You think I suddenly just stopped caring about you?"

I sigh again but say nothing.

"Did you stop caring about me?" she asks.

"No." I shake my head even though she can't see me.

"Then why am I not allowed to care about you?"

"I'm sorry," I say.

"For what?"

"I don't know. I'm sorry, I really have to go."

I don't wait for her to say anything else; I just hang up. I put my phone back in my pocket and sigh, putting my head in my hands. I decide that I need to go inside and that it's too cold to be out here anyway. I head back in, and once I make it upstairs, I stare at the door for a few seconds. For some reason, I don't want to go in. I think about what Quinn said about the noises and not wanting to go inside. I think about what happened with Val the other day. There has to be something going on. But I don't believe in ghost stories, so I unlock the door and walk in.

It's cold, and I don't want to take my coat off. I put my shoes by the kitchen table and go into my room. I work on writing the paper I had started that morning. I make myself lunch then bring it back to my room. It isn't until seven that Val gets back. I hear him open our front door and go into the kitchen. I figure it's now or never, so I open my bedroom door and walk down the hall.

"I'm sorry," I say. Val says nothing. He just kind of looks at me. "I, um, got your note. So I thought I should say sorry. Or something."

"Apology accepted." Val sighs. "I'm sorry too." I'm surprised. I didn't think he'd forgive me this quickly.

"I don't want this to be weird or anything," I tell him.

"It won't be," Val assures me. He smiles at me then walks out of the kitchen and down the hall into his room. I sigh and look down at the ground. There's no way things aren't going to be different now. But I figure I have to at least try to get past this. I sit on the couch and turn on the TV. A few minutes later, the power goes out. I panic for a second then turn on the flashlight on my phone and stand up. Val walks into the living room with his flashlight on as well a few seconds later.

"What happened?" he asks.

"Don't know," I say.

"You guys got power up there?" we hear someone yell from beneath us. It takes me a minute to realize it's Quinn.

"Nothing!" I yell back.

"Good thing I bought all those candles you made fun of me for." Val smiles at me.

"No one needs that many." I smile too as Val walks into the kitchen. He sets his phone down then opens a cabinet and pulls out about a dozen candles. He opens one of the drawers and grabs a lighter. "I got this," he says. He lights all of them then motions for me to come over. I help him spread the candles around the two small rooms evenly.

"Now what?" I ask.

"I suppose we just sit here until the power comes back on."

"I suppose so," I say as I walk back over to the couch. I sit down and lean my head back.

"So." Val walks over and sits down next to me. "How was work?"

"Oh." I sigh. "I missed it."

"You missed it?" Val raises his eyebrows.

"Yeah. Stayed in bed till about three."

"You didn't call your boss to say you weren't coming?"

Val doesn't sound angry, just a little disappointed. I shake my head no.

"And they didn't wonder where you were?"

"I don't really think anyone there cares." I laugh a little.

"Well." Val sighs. "As long as you don't get fired, right?"

"And if I do get fired"—I look over at him—"maybe someone else can get a job?"

"I had a job," Val says.

"Six months ago."

"Do I really need a job, though?"

"You don't think you do?"

"No." Val shrugs.

"You're twenty-seven."

Val points a finger at me. "Don't bring age into this." I laugh and look up at the ceiling. I really hope I don't get fired. I'm not the best at getting people to hire me."

"Hey," Val says.

"Hey," I repeat him.

"Do you think I'm crazy?"

"No?" I turn my head to look at him. "Why would I think that?"

"Just wondering. I was just thinking about some stuff today."

"Where were you today anyway?" I ask.

"Doesn't matter," Val says quickly. "I was with some people, but I felt like there was someone watching me the whole time. You know?"

"I guess."

"What do you think that means? Am I going fucking insane or something?"

I lean forward and sigh. "I don't think you're going insane. I just think you're a little paranoid."

"Well, what's making me paranoid then?" Val holds up his hands.

I shrug. "I don't know. Could be anything, I guess."

"I hate myself so much right now," Val says as he leans his head back. I do the same and laugh.

"Don't say stuff like that," I tell him.

"I'm getting my laptop." Val stands up, completely ignoring me. "I'll be right back."

I nod, and Val walks down the hall. It's silent for a few moments, then I hear a scream. I immediately think that it's Val. Then I realize that the scream didn't come from down the hall; it came from beneath me.

"Keyon?" Val yells before he runs into the living room.

"You heard that?" I ask.

"I heard it. You think it was Quinn?"

"Who else could it have been?"

I give Val a look and head toward the front door. I don't bother to put on my shoes; I just walk out, phone in my hand. Val follows me and shuts the door behind us. We make our way down to the second floor, and I knock on Quinn's door a few times. "Quinn?" I yell. Two more people come out of their apartments to see what's going on. They're both using their phones as flashlights.

"Everyone okay?" a guy probably younger than me asks.

"We don't know," Val tells him.

I knock again. "Quinn, open up," I say even louder. I have no idea what's going on, but I'm worried. What could have happened?

"Check the handle," the kid in the hall says. I nod at him and grab the door handle. It opens as soon as I push. We all stare into the apartment for a few seconds before anyone says anything.

"I'm calling the police." A girl in the hall presses some buttons on her phone. Val says, "Good idea." He looks at me and raises his eyebrows. He wants to know if we should go in or not. I shrug and hold my phone out in front of me.

"Quinn?" I say quietly. I walk into her living room and look around. I don't see anything, so I look over into the kitchen. I turn around and see Val and the two others behind me. Val nods at me. He wants me to keep going.

"I feel weird just kind of walking into her place," the younger kid says.

"Maybe we should wait until the police show up." The girl looks at me.

"I think we should look around. We all heard that scream, right?" Val holds his hand out.

"I agree," I say. I turn back around and walk down the small hallway to where the bedrooms are. I get to the first room and turn back again to look at Val. He takes a deep breath and walks up toward me.

"You want me to look?" he asks.

I nod. Val nods back at me and takes a few steps forward. I almost reach out to stop him. I don't want to know what happened. He puts his hand on the door handle and takes another deep breath. He looks at me one more time before throwing the door open. He shines his light inside and looks around. "Nothing," he says. I close my eyes and nod. Everything is fine for now. I turn to look at the others.

"I really think we should leave," the girl says to me. I'm starting to think we should listen to her.

"Val, maybe she's right." I turn and put my hand on his arm.

"Can't we just check the other bedroom?" he asks.

"I guess." I sigh.

What happens next happens quickly. It's hard for me to process exactly what it is that goes down. Val opens the door, and I see him put his hand up to his mouth.

"You okay?" I hear the younger guy ask. Val doesn't say anything. I don't want to know what it is that he is looking at. But apparently, the girl behind me wants to know, because she pushes past me and stands behind Val. "Oh my god," she whispers. I do not want to know what's going on. I walk out of Quinn's apartment just as the lights turn back on. I walk all the way down the stairs and outside into the parking lot. I hear Val running down after me, calling my name, but I don't turn around. He puts his hand on my shoulder, and I look at him.

"What did you see?" I ask him.

"Keyon I think we should just—"

"Tell me what you saw," I say. "Please."

"I really think we should just go back to our apartment and wait until the police get here."

I stare at Val for a few seconds, then I hear sirens. Val looks over my shoulder and starts to walk away from me. I take a couple of steps back and sit on the steps outside of our building. A few people from inside come out and walk past me and over to where Val is waiting for the police. An ambulance pulls up first, and I look at the ground. I don't want to know what happened, but in a way, I feel like I understand.

⚊⚫⚊

"Do you think we should move out?" Val asks me a week later.

"I was kind of thinking we should," I say.

Val leans against our kitchen table and sighs. I'm worried about him. I can't help but feel like it's my fault he's even more paranoid now than he was before. I shouldn't have let him look inside Quinn's room. I should've stopped him when I had the chance. I should've just gone in myself.

"You alright?" Val walks over and sits down on the couch next to me.

"Yeah," I lie. "Are you?"

"I guess." Val sighs. "Just freaks me out a little every time I come back home. You know?"

"Yeah."

"Jesus, Keyon." Val stands back up and paces around the living room. "I just can't believe someone was actually fucking murdered. Someone we knew too. Can you believe that? Because I can't believe it."

"I can't believe it," I say.

"You know what I've been thinking about?" Val sits back down next to me.

"What?"

"How both of us had been hearing noises and shit. How both of us felt like we weren't the only ones in our apartments. You know what I mean?"

"Your story was a little different than hers, though. You said you heard my voice."

"I thought it was yours. It could've been anyone, though. If you think about it. But anyway, what's been going through my head is that maybe I'm next. Or you're next. Or something."

"What?" I ask him. "Why would either of us be next? Why would you even think about that?"

"I have no idea, man. But think about it. Really think about it. Quinn and I were both hearing shit, and next thing you know, she's dead. She's fucking dead, Keyon."

"I understand that." I nod once. "But that doesn't mean we're in any danger."

"Alright, but how do you know?"

I think about this. "I guess I don't really know."

"You see?" Val holds his hand out. "Exactly. We don't know. I think we need to leave."

"You just got a job down here," I point out.

"I don't care about my job." Val rolls his eyes. "I care about not getting stabbed to death."

Now it's my turn to roll my eyes. "Don't say stuff like that. We'll be fine, Val. Seriously. We don't have to go anywhere." Val looks at his phone then back up at me. "Well, you have to go to class in twenty minutes," he says. I sigh and stand up. "I guess you're right."

"Be careful, alright?" Val looks at me closely.

"I will. What do you think is going to happen?"

Val raises his eyebrows. Now I feel stupid. Of course I already know what he thinks might happen. I wave him off as I walk out the door, hoping that he'll forget I even asked.

A little while later, I'm walking back from my second class of the day when I'm stopped by someone pulling my arm.

"Grace?" I say as I turn around.

"Keyon, hey. Sorry. Didn't mean to scare you or anything," Grace says to me. She tucks a stray strand of hair behind her ear and presses her lips together. She seems nervous. I don't know why.

"Don't worry. It's okay," I say. "So, um, what's up?"

"I heard about what happened with that girl in your building."

"Oh." I nod. "Yeah. Really freaked Val out."

"It didn't freak you out?"

"Well, I mean, it did, but it freaked him out more. I'm just worried about him, I guess."

"You think you guys should move out?"

"I don't know. Val seems like he wants to leave, but the more I think about it, I don't really see how moving out would help us."

"I get it. Val told me he wants to leave." Grace nods. "I'm just a little concerned. Worried about Val." She pauses. "And you."

"Seems like you and Val are getting close," I say.

Grace shakes her head at me. "I gotta go, Keyon. I'll see you around." I watch her walk off in the other direction, and I sigh. Part of me wishes she'd stop talking to me. The other part of me wishes that we could talk all the time. I'm not going to lie to myself; I'm still in love with her. And I can't help but get the feeling that she isn't completely over me. Although I can't help but wonder why she keeps popping back up in my life. That has to mean something.

"Hey," I say to Val as soon as I get back to our apartment. He's sitting on the floor with his research papers scattered around him.

"Hey," he replies. He's typing something on his laptop, and I can tell he's not really going to pay any attention to me, so I decide I can say whatever I want.

"I was talking to Grace today, and I know for a fact that I'm still in love with her."

Val nods but doesn't look my way. "Uh-huh," he says.

"Yeah. And I think that she might still have some feelings for me. But that's just me trying to be optimistic."

"Really," Val says.

"Yes. Really. And she also told me that you had been talking to her more. About what happened. You told her you wanted to move out."

Val turns and looks at me now. "Yeah?"

"Why are you talking to Grace?"

"I don't need your permission to talk to people you know."

I sigh and sit down on the floor next to him. "I get that, alright? It's just that I'm a little mad at you."

Val raises an eyebrow. "For what?" I don't want him to get upset, so I try to get him to stop asking about it.

"Nothing. It's stupid."

Val shuts his laptop and looks back at me. "I'm sure it's not."

"It just seems like she wants to talk to you more than she wants to talk to me."

"Well." Val sighs. "I hate to say this, Keyon, but she might not be in love with you anymore. She might have really moved on."

"In a week and a half?"

"Maybe she—"

"Never loved me at all?"

Val gives me a sad smile and sighs. "I didn't want to be the one to say that might be a possibility." I pull my knees up to my chest and take a deep breath. "What's wrong with me?" I look over at Val.

"Nothing's wrong with you."

I shake my head. I think about how I could bring up what he said during our little altercation. How apparently there are several things wrong with me. But I keep my mouth shut. I look back at Val and sigh. "I've been thinking about what you said the other day."

"What?" Val asks.

"What you said. Saying how I always blamed other people or whatever."

"Keyon—"

"Let me finish." I hold up a hand. "I think you're right. I've never even considered that I'm the problem."

"That's not what I—"

"I think that it's kind of my own fault what happened with Grace. And with basically everyone else."

"Keyon, you know I didn't mean any of the stuff I said," Val says sincerely.

I sigh. "I guess. But I've just been thinking about it a lot. And another thing, I feel like I didn't give you a very good apology."

"Well, to be honest, you didn't." Val presses his lips together. "But neither did I. So I'm sorry. I'm really, really sorry."

"I'm sorry too," I say. "I mean it."

It's silent for a minute before Val says, "So now what?"

"I don't really know."

"I gotta get to work soon," Val says while looking at his phone. "Should probably go get ready. You good alone for a couple hours?"

"Why wouldn't I be?"

Val shrugs. "I don't know. Just checking." He stands up and walks down the hall into his room. I stay sitting on the floor and think about everything that's happened. And for some reason, all I can think about is Quinn. I'd only known her for two days. That's it. I'd barely even known her at all, and now it was impossible for me to ever see her again. I thought about moving out. I'd really thought about it. Val and I could find a place somewhere else, maybe even closer to our school campus. Someplace better. But then again, I couldn't think of any reason for us to move out. We were both just scared. Val even more than I. But we couldn't just up and leave because we were afraid. That didn't make sense to me.

"Okay, what do you think?" I look up and see Val standing in front of me, holding two different ties. "Black or gray?" He holds them up to his neck one at a time.

"Gray," I tell him.

"Why are you still on the floor?"

I sigh and shake my head. "No idea." Val smiles and holds out his hand for me. I take it, and he pulls me up. "Okay," Val says. "Help me." I laugh and take the gray tie out of his hand.

"I still can't believe you don't know how to do this." I smile as I wrap the tie around his neck.

"I'm stupid, I know." Val smiles back at me. I tie his tie then step out of the way so Val can get to the front door.

"Good luck," I say.

"Thanks." Val keeps smiling and heads outside. I sigh and stare at the door for a few seconds. I think back to our earlier conversation. What if Val was right? What if we were next? But who would do that? And why?

I walk over to the door and lock it. There was no way I was going to let anything happen to Val or myself. But I was starting to feel a little bit more like him. I was completely paranoid. Mainly about Val. He didn't have to walk to work like I did, so that made me feel a little better. But still. Anything could happen to him. Or me. I now find myself thinking about Grace. She could be in trouble too. Even if she didn't live in our building. I decide that I need to call her and talk to her about this. I take out my phone and scroll through my contacts until I find her name. It only rings once before she picks up.

"Keyon?"

"Grace, hey," I walk slowly around the living room.

"Hey," she says. "What's up?"

"I've been thinking a lot about Quinn."

"Okay?"

"Yeah. I really just can't stop thinking about her."

"Why are you telling me this?" Grace asks.

"Because I'm worried."

"I would be too." Grace sighs. "I honestly think you guys should move out."

"Well, I wouldn't go that far. I don't think we should move just because we're scared. Doesn't that seem kind of stupid?"

"Not really. If someone was murdered in my building, I'd never go back in."

"Yeah," I say. "I guess."

"Is this really what you wanted to talk to me about?"

"What?" I walk over to the couch and sit down.

"I don't know. You don't usually call your exes to talk about murder."

"I guess that isn't normal, is it?" I laugh a little. Grace laughs too.

"No, not really," she says. "But seriously. You're not calling to try and take me back?"

"What? No? Unless you want to get back together," I say, stupidly.

"Sorry, Keyon. I don't think that's a good idea."

"Why not?" I don't know what I'm doing. I realize that I need to just shut up and hang up, but for some reason, I am still trying to get her to say she isn't over me.

"I just really don't think that it's going to work out. I mean, we can both agree it didn't work out last time, right?" she says.

No, Grace. I don't think we both can agree on that. "Yeah," I say.

"So yeah."

There is a long silence.

"Well," I speak up, "I have a lot of stuff to do, so I should probably go."

"Yeah. Me too."

We do not tell each other good-bye; we just hang up. I lean forward and put my head in my hands. What am I doing? I decide I need to get out and do something. I put on my shoes and coat and leave the building. I don't know where I'm going; I just know I can't stay in the apartment any more tonight. About fifteen minutes into my walk, I find myself somewhere called Sunset Drive. It's basically just a line of houses, but for some reason, being here makes me feel safer and also makes me feel a little happier. I see a couple of kids playing around outside, and one of them waves at me. I wave back and smile. A parent out on the front lawn nods toward me. I nod back at them and keep walking.

I really need to start doing this more often. I need to get out more. I need to do things on my own. I rely too much on other people. I walk a little farther down the road I'm on before I come to a park at the end of the neighborhood that surrounds me. I take a couple more steps forward until I'm standing in front of a bench. I walk around it and sit down, staring straight ahead. I don't even know what I'm doing right now. Then again, I never really know what I'm doing. I decide to ignore this thought and think about something else. After a while, I start to feel a lot better about everything.

I get so lost in my thoughts that it's not for another half an hour that I look at my phone. I have seven missed calls from Val. I do not feel so good anymore. I call him back as fast I can and wait for him to answer.

"Pick up, pick up, pick up," I say to myself as I turn around to start walking back home.

"Keyon. Where are you?" Val definitely sounds upset when he answers.

"I'm walking back home right now. What's wrong?"

"I just left the library."

"The one by where you work?"

"Yeah," Val says. "It happened again."

"What do you mean?"

"I mean, another person we know is dead."

I stop walking. "What?" Val doesn't say anything.

"Tell me who it is," I say quietly. Val is still silent.

"Just meet me at home, alright? I'll tell you then," he says after a minute. I tell him I'll get there soon, and I hang up. I walk quickly until I finally make it back to the apartment. I run up the stairs and fumble around with my key until I get our door open. Val is sitting on the couch, and when I come in, he looks up at me.

"Jesus Christ, are you okay? Is everything alright?" I ask as I walk over to him. I sit down on the couch next to him and look him up and down. "Nothing happened to you, right?"

"I'm fine," Val says. "Really, I am. The only thing I'm worried about is how you're going to be after I tell you what happened."

I think about who it could've been, who had been killed. Only one name pops into my head.

"Please don't tell me it's—"

"It's not Grace, if that's what you're thinking," Val assures me. I let out a sigh of relief.

"Okay." I nod. "Then who—"

"It was Erica."

I take a minute to process what it is I've just been told. "What?"

"Yeah." Val looks down at his hands.

"Erica. Like, the one that I used to—"

"Yeah. Her."

I have no idea what to say. It's not like I'm sad, but I'm certainly not happy either. At one point in time, I had been in love with her. We met almost two years ago, and we were together for seven months. I loved absolutely everything about her. Until she seemed like she didn't love everything about me. She was constantly putting me down, making me feel like everything was my fault. But I didn't care. I still loved her, and I still wanted to marry her. But one day she just snapped. No, she didn't do anything to me; she did something to herself. This is the part of the story I hadn't told anyone, not even Val. Yes, she crashed my car. But not because she was mad at me or anything. She had done it to try to kill herself. I, of course, freaked out. I saw her at the hospital and tried asking her if she was okay. She didn't tell me that she was okay. She told me it was all my fault. She had done this because of me.

I started to think about my fight with Val again. How he said I never blamed myself. Maybe that whole Erica experience changed something in me. Maybe because of it, I had some stupid mentality that I could never be to blame for anything ever again. After Erica had told me that it was my fault, I went crazy. I yelled and yelled at her. I don't even remember what I yelled at her about. But I was mad, and I started to hate her. For no reason, really. I just didn't want to be blamed for something that was definitely my fault. Back then, I tried to imagine what life would've been like had she actually succeeded in killing herself. I remember thinking that if she had, my life would've been over. I'd have nothing to live for anymore. I realize that you can't have one person be your only source of happiness, but that's what she was for me. She used to be, at least.

"You okay?" I hear Val's voice and remember that I am not alone.

"Yeah. I think so."

"Are you sure? Because if you're not, you can tell me."

"I'm alright," I say. "How did you know it was Erica?"

"There were a bunch of sirens outside, and I was getting off of work early, so I went out to see what was going on. There were a shit ton of ambulances and police cars outside the library, so out of curiosity, I walked over to find out what had gone down. Walked up to the first guy I saw and asked him what happened. He told me he'd been out wandering around when he heard a guy scream. He told me some guy was yelling that his sister had just been stabbed. Then the guy I was talking to pointed to the closest ambulance, and I saw the girl they were carrying in. And I knew who it was. I'm so sorry, Keyon. I don't even know what to—"

"It's okay," I tell Val. "I'm really okay. When I saw her last week, that was the first time I'd seen her in almost a year. It's not like we were close anymore."

"I know." Val sighs. "But still."

"I just can't believe this even happened," I say.

Val sighs again and stands up to walk into the kitchen. He comes back with some paper towels in his hand. He sits back down next to me and says, "Here." I didn't even realize that I'd started crying.

"Thanks," I say quietly.

"What are we supposed to do?"

"What do you mean?" I ask.

"Like, what are we supposed to do, you know?"

"I don't know. This doesn't really affect us, does it?"

"I guess not." Val laughs a little. "Guess I'm just scared. That sounds stupid, doesn't it?"

"It doesn't." I give him a small smile.

"You're just saying that." Val smiles too and leans back on the couch.

"I'm not," I tell him. "I'm scared too. Especially now."

"Don't worry about it. We'll be fine."

"I don't know if I believe you," I say. "This morning you seemed pretty worried about something happening to one of us."

"Sorry. I didn't mean to, like, you know."

"Uh-huh." I nod. "Totally. I know exactly what you're talking about."

"Shut up." Val laughs. "You know what I mean."

I stand up and throw the paper towels away in the kitchen. I sigh before looking back at Val. "I think I'm gonna go to bed. Sleep everything off."

"Good idea." He stands up. "I think I might do the same thing." The two of us walk down the hall and over to our rooms. I walk into mine and sit down on my bed, taking off my shoes. I notice that Val is still standing in my doorway.

"Yeah?" I look up at him.

"You sure you're alright?"

"Yeah." I smile at him even though I am not alright.

"A'ight." Val nods a couple of times before giving me a small wave and going off to do his own thing.

I stare at my hands for a little while, and I start to feel like a complete idiot. Too scared to even want to stay where I lived. If that isn't the dumbest thing I've ever heard, I don't know what is. I take off my coat and throw it on the floor. Lying back on my bed, I try really hard to think about whether or not there is a connection between the two murders. Quinn had been stabbed multiple times, and according to Val, Erica had been stabbed too. But that doesn't mean that they are related to each other. That kind of stuff happens to people all the time, right? Although, it does seem a little odd that it is two people that Val and I both knew. I had met Val around the same time that I'd met Erica. We'd been in a study group together for a couple months. But that still doesn't mean anything. I think about this until I check my phone and see that it's almost four in the morning. I sit up in bed and put my head in my hands. A few moments later, I hear a knock at my door.

"Yeah?" I say weakly. I look up and see Val open the door.

"Hey, sorry. I don't know why I, you know. I shouldn't have woken you up."

"It's all good. I was already up." I sigh. "You too?" Val says as he walks over to sit down on the edge of my bed.

"Why were you up?" I ask.

"Why do you think? I've been pondering life and death all night."

"I've been trying to connect these murders, if I'm being honest."

"Trying to connect them?"

"Yeah. I haven't come up with anything yet, though."

"All I've got is that we both knew them. But that probably has nothing to do with anything. I'm sure a lot of people knew Quinn and Erica. Small town, after all." Val lies back on my bed.

"True," I say. "You know what? I did something stupid today."

"What'd you do?"

"I called Grace."

"What about?"

"I don't even know." I sigh. "I was freaking out about Quinn. But she just seemed confused. She just wanted to know why I was telling her about her."

"Did she know her?" Val raises his eyebrows at me.

"Did she know Quinn?"

Val nods.

"I don't know. She didn't ask who she was when I said her name. So maybe. I guess." I shrug.

"Huh." Val looks up at the ceiling.

"So," I say as I lie down, "should we, like, try to get some sleep or something?"

"I don't have class tomorrow. Or work." Val turns his head to look at me. "So no. I think it'd be okay if we stayed up."

I laugh. "I have class, Val."

"Fuck, that's right. You want me to get outta here then? Leave you alone?"

"Nah," I say. "Not really feeling the whole 'sitting alone with nothing but my thoughts' thing."

Now Val is laughing. "I feel that, man. I really feel that. Let's talk about something else. Unless you want to keep talking about murder. And Grace. Both things that we need to forget about for now."

"We probably shouldn't talk about any of that." I sigh. "Tell me something."

"What?"

"Just, like, tell me something. About your day or whatever."

"Oh. Okay." Val takes a couple of deep breaths. "Well, I got up, got ready, then I talked to you. Then after you left, I went out with Hadlee and just, like, talked about school or whatever you're supposed to talk about with your friends. I never know what to say around her. You know?"

"She's a little hard to talk to sometimes, I'll give you that," I say.

"Exactly." Val nods. "But anyway, after that, we just kind of walked around town until I remembered my research paper was due in, like, two days. So I went home, then you came back. And I think you know pretty much everything else. Wasn't a very interesting day. And I'm probably boring you to death right now."

"No." I shake my head. "You're not. Tell me something else."

"Like what?" Val looks at me.

"I don't know. I have a question, though. Well, I guess it's not a question. It's just kind of something that I wanted to know, and I've been thinking about it and—"

"Keyon," Val says. "Just say what you wanna say."

"I feel like I don't really know you. I mean, I get we're good friends or best friends or whatever, but I don't know. Do you know what I'm talking about?"

"I think so."

"Okay. Good. Because I don't think *I* know what I'm talking about."

"Alright." Val laughs. "Let's do something."

"What?"

"What's your favorite color?"

"My what?"

"Keyon, shut up." Val laughs. "Just answer the question."

"Orange," I say. "What about you?"

"Blue. Okay. Your turn."

"For what?" I look at him.

"To ask me a question, dipshit. We're getting to know each other."

I laugh. "Okay? What's your middle name?"

"You don't know what my middle name is?" Val raises his eyebrows at me.

"Do you know mine?"

"Pierce."

"What the—" I turn on my side to look at him. "How'd you know that?"

"You told me, like, a year and a half ago. I don't forget important stuff like that." Val smiles and shakes his head. "It's Cole, though. Because you wanted to know."

"That doesn't seem right for you," I tell him.

"Right?" Val turns on his side as well. "I feel like I need something more unique."

"You do," I say.

"Alright. My turn. Tell me about high school you."

"That's not exactly a question," I point out.

"Sure it is. Go."

"Um, I don't know. Pretty normal experience, I guess."

Val rolls his eyes. "Wow, thank you for that incredibly detailed description."

"Whatever," I say, laughing. "What do you want me to say?"

"I don't know. Just tell me about it. I didn't know you then. Surely you must've been different than you are now."

"Not really," I say. "I guess I was a bit more social."

"Seriously?" Val looks at me and smiles.

"Yes, seriously. I wasn't always this introverted."

"Weird," he says. "Couldn't imagine you any other way. It's your turn now."

"Okay." I sigh. "If you weren't majoring in biochemistry, what would you be doing instead?"

"Hard question." Val hums. "Probably, like, criminal law or something."

"I like that," I say. "It's very you."

"What do you think about Jared?"

I look at him. "Who?"

"Jared Davis. We met him at that thing at Hadlee's last month."

"Oh, yeah. I think I remember him," I say, even though I have no idea who he's talking about.

"What do you think of him?"

"Is this your next question for me?"

"Yes."

"Well, he seems like a good guy. Why?"

"I've been seeing him sort of." Val sighs.

"Really?" I keep looking at him, but he won't make eye contact with me.

"Yeah. I'm not sure how I feel about him, though. Wanted to ask you first."

"You need my opinion on a guy?"

"Yes. I do. And what better time to ask about it than four thirty in the morning?"

I laugh. "Alright. Well, if I'm being honest, I don't remember this guy at all."

"I was thinking we could go out and do something. The three of us."

"You want me to third wheel with you two?"

"It won't be third wheeling since we're not actually together. You'll be fine." Val yawns.

"Alright." I yawn as well and close my eyes. "Sounds like a plan. But I think it's definitely time for us to sleep."

"Don't take this the wrong way, but is it cool if I just stay in here? I don't feel like getting up," Val says quietly.

"It's cool." I yawn again.

Five hours later, my phone buzzes, and I know that I need to get up and go to class. I get out of bed carefully, really trying not to wake up Val. I get ready in about fifteen minutes and head out the door. I have a boring day, but all I hear anyone talk about is Erica. I'm walking back from my second class of the day when I hear someone calling my name. I turn around to see one of my few friends, Hadlee, coming up to me. I smile at her but say nothing.

"How are you?" she says as she approaches me.

"I'm alright," I say, shoving my hands in my pockets. "You?"

"Doesn't matter how I am." She gives me a small smile. "I'm sorry about what happened."

I sigh. Everyone knows. "It's alright. We weren't that close anymore."

"Still," she says as we start walking. "You're absolutely sure you're alright?"

"Yeah. Absolutely sure."

She laughs a little. "You know I never believe you when you say that."

"I know." I smile.

"So," she says, "any plans for this weekend? After work, of course."

"I think Val wants me to go with him to meet some guy he's seeing. Jared Davis."

"Who?"

"No idea." I shrug. "Apparently I met him at your party last month."

"I don't even remember him." Hadlee laughs. "So it's just going to be the three of you?"

"I guess. Unless you want to come with me?" I look at her and smile.

Hadlee laughs again. "Sure. Would Val be okay with it?"

"I could text him, but I doubt he's up yet."

"It's four in the afternoon."

"We stayed up until five last night," I say.

"Why?"

"Just talking, I guess. I don't know. Wasn't a very good idea. I swear I almost fell asleep walking here this morning."

"How's he doing?"

"Weren't you with him yesterday?" I raise my eyebrows.

"Yeah, but I feel like he's not telling me something."

I think about this and take a deep breath.

"Did you hear about the girl in our building?" I ask.

"What girl in your building?" Hadlee looks at me.

"Maybe about a week and a half ago, we met this girl Quinn whose apartment was underneath ours," I sigh. "She was murdered in her bedroom."

"Oh my god." Hadlee puts a hand to her mouth. "Seriously?"

"Yeah. That's probably what Val's been thinking about. He's worried that we'll be next or something."

"Keyon, wow. I had no idea. Have you guys, I don't know, considered moving out?"

"We have. But I think it'd be kind of pointless." We stop at a crosswalk, and I look down at her. "I think it's stupid that we're too scared to even want to stay in our own place. You know what I mean?"

"Kind of." Hadlee sighs. "But really. If I were you, I wouldn't want to stay there." We walk across the street quickly.

"I don't know. Doesn't seem like it's too safe anywhere else, either," I say.

"I'm still so sorry about that. Erica didn't deserve that."

"Yeah, well. It's what she wanted."

As we approach my apartment building, Hadlee finally comments on what I've just said.

"What do you mean that's what she wanted?"

"You didn't have to walk all the way over here with me," I say.

"Keyon, seriously. What are you talking about?"

I sigh. "I'm going to tell you something I've never told anyone."

"Alright?"

"Remember when she crashed my car?"

"Yes."

I take a moment to gather my thoughts.

"She was trying to kill herself," I say.

Hadlee looks at me for a few seconds. "What?"

"Yeah." I nod.

"That's—" Hadlee shakes her head. "I don't even know what to say. I had no idea she was feeling that way."

"She said she did it because of me." We stop walking once we reach the steps outside the building.

"Because of you?" Hadlee looks up at me. "Why?"

"I don't know." I shrug. We stand outside for a few minutes, neither of us saying anything.

"I should probably go check on Val," I say.

"Probably." Hadlee sighs. "I'll see you later, alright? Tell me if we ever figure out any plans."

"You got it," I say as I give her a small wave. She smiles at me before I go up the steps and inside.

When I get into our apartment, there aren't any lights on. It doesn't look like anyone's touched anything all day. I take off my coat and shoes before walking down the hall and into my bedroom to see that Val is still fast asleep. I sigh and lean into the doorframe. I stand there for a couple minutes, debating whether or not to wake him up. I finally decide not to, and I close the door quietly and make my way back out into the living room. I lie facedown on the couch and sigh. Once again, I start to think about everything that's happened. I still can't believe any of it. It just seems so surreal. I'm thinking about Quinn. And Erica. And Grace. I just can't get them out of my head. I remember that I have some work to do, but I don't care. I don't think I could focus on school right now if I tried.

An hour later, I'm still lying on the couch, and Val has finally woken up.

"Morning," he says as he walks out into the living room.

"It's not exactly morning anymore," I say. Val yawns and looks at his phone. "Jesus," he says. "You let me sleep for twelve hours?"

"You seemed like you needed it."

"Why do you seem all depressed?" Val asks as he walks into the kitchen.

"Just thinking about death."

"Wow. Wasn't really expecting you to say that." He comes back into the living room with a glass of water in his hand.

"Yeah, well." I sigh. "I talked to Hadlee today. Told her you wanted me to meet that guy you were talking about."

"Jared?"

"Yeah. Him. And I gotta ask, is it okay if she goes out with us? I know you said I wouldn't be third wheeling, but it kind of feels like that's exactly what I'd be doing."

Val laughs as he moves my legs so he can sit down at the end of the couch. "Yeah, that's fine. I don't care if she goes."

"Cool." I sigh again.

"So," Val says. "When you say that you're thinking about death, what exactly does that mean?"

I sit up and crack my neck. "What do you think it means?" Val just shrugs.

"I'm still thinking about Erica and Quinn," I say. "I literally cannot focus on anything else."

"Yeah. I get that."

"You do?"

"Someone in our building and someone I was friends with were both murdered within a week of one another. How am I not supposed to think about that?" Val looks over at me.

"Sorry. I didn't mean to—"

"No, Keyon, seriously. It's alright."

I look at him for a few seconds before I say anything else. "We need to get out of here."

"What?" Val raises his eyebrows.

"I know I've been gone all day, but I think both of us should just go out. We gotta get our minds off of this."

Val nods a few times. "You're right. Where should we go?"

"You know that little picnic area that Hadlee always takes us to?"

"Yeah?"

"You ever just walked around there? Besides just around the pavilion?"

"No." Val shakes his head. "What's around there?"

"Nothing," I say. "That's the good part."

"Let me get ready." Val stands up and stretches. "We can go in a few minutes."

I nod my head and put my shoes and coat back on while I wait for Val. But for some reason, it takes Val much longer than a few minutes to get ready, so I'm stuck standing by the front door for about fifteen minutes.

"You ready?" I ask Val when he finally comes out of his bedroom.

"Yeah. Let's do this. We're not walking there, are we?"

"Unless you want to." I shrug.

"Not really. You want to drive then?"

"You trust me with your car?"

Val looks at me for a few seconds. "No. I don't. I'll get my keys."

"That's what I thought." I laugh a little.

We make our way out of the building and over to where Val has parked his car. We get inside, and I sigh. "I can't wait till I get another one of these."

"Why don't you?" Val starts up the engine.

"Maybe someday when I get a real job." I smile.

Val laughs and pulls out of the small parking lot. "So we're doing what, exactly?"

"Walking," I say.

"Walking," Val repeats me. "Seems kind of late for that, doesn't it?"

"They've got streetlights all over that place. We'll be okay."

We drive for about five minutes until we get to our destination.

"So," Val says as he turns off the car. "We're walking."

"Yeah," I say as I get out. "Fresh air and all that."

Val gets out of the car as well and slams his door rather loudly. "I really hope this helps," he says.

"What do you mean?" I take a couple steps forward until I'm standing on a dirt path surrounding a pond. Val makes his way over to me, and we start to walk.

"I mean"—Val sighs—"I hope this actually does help me to get my mind off of things. I'm so fucking stressed, man."

"I can tell," I say, putting my hands in my pockets.

"I thought you said there'd be streetlights?" Val looks at me.

"Well, I thought there were. But I think we'll be okay. We're walking through a park, not a dark alley."

Val laughs at this and looks down at his feet while he walks. "Yeah. I guess that's true." We walk in silence for several minutes. I finally decide that I'm sick of the quiet, and I start talking.

"So," I say. "I've been meaning to ask you about something."

"Well, this can't be good." Val laughs a little. "What have you been meaning to ask me?"

"Nothing serious. I just want to know more about this Jared guy."

"Oh." Val smiles but doesn't look my way. "What do you want to know?"

"What's he like?"

"Why do you ask?" Val looks at me now.

"I don't know." I shrug my shoulders. "Guess I just want to know a little about him before I meet him. Don't want to go into this knowing absolutely nothing."

"I don't know." Val shakes his head. "I'm not very good at talking about stuff like this."

I nod my head in understanding. "It's alright. You don't have to tell me anything."

"Alright." Val looks up at me. "What about you?"

"What about me?"

"We talk about me too much. Tell me something."

"God, we're not doing that question thing again, are we?" I laugh.

"No." Val laughs too. "I'm just, like, asking about your day, I guess."

"Well." I sigh. I can't figure out whether or not I want to tell him about my earlier conversation with Hadlee. About Erica, I mean. I feel like I need to tell him the real story. Although I also feel like he'd be a little more than unhappy if I told him I had been lying about the whole 'crashing my car because she was insane' thing. But then I remember the whole reason we left the apartment to come out here. To get our minds off stuff like that. So I lie.

"Nothing really interesting happened," I say.

"I feel that." Val nods. "Seems like there's so much going on, but at the same time, I feel like my life is more boring than ever. You know?"

"Yeah," I say. "I know."

We talk for another two hours, just making laps around the pond. And for a while, I forget about most of my problems. It's nice. Pretending like your life is completely normal.

"Jesus, we've been out here for almost two and a half hours." Val stops walking and looks at his phone.

"I guess we have, haven't we?" I pull out my phone as well.

"We should probably go back."

"Probably. I don't really feel like going back to the real world, though."

Val laughs. "This isn't the real world?"

"Does it feel like it is to you?"

"I guess you're right." Val turns around, and I follow him as we head over to his car. "Doesn't feel like the real world at all. Kind of felt like life was simple again. Nothing too crazy going on."

"Well, it was nice while it lasted, right?" I laugh. Val laughs too.

"Yeah. It was."

We drive for a couple minutes until we get back to our building. Val parks the car but doesn't get out.

"You good?" I ask him.

"Yeah." He nods a couple of times before he looks at me. I raise my eyebrows at him. He just continues to stare at me.

"You sure you're good right now?" I ask, because he certainly doesn't seem like everything's good.

"Yeah." Val turns his head away from me and opens his door, stepping outside. I sigh and do the same. We walk inside in silence. I take off my coat and shoes while Val stands in our hallway.

"Seven," he says.

"What?"

"On Saturday. Me, you, Jared, and Hadlee. Seven. That place you like at the end of Fifth."

"Okay," I say. "I can do that. I'll text Hadlee."

"Good." Val nods a couple of times before walking down the hall and into his room. I sigh and look down at my feet. Going out didn't help as much as I thought it would. All my thoughts about the murders are coming back to me. Then I feel a stupid, stupid emotion. Guilt. This doesn't make any sense. How can I be guilty about something I didn't cause? I sit down on the couch and lean my head back. I just had to make it until Saturday. Then I'd be back to doing normal things, living a normal life. Maybe by then these thoughts will have finally subsided.

At around six thirty on Saturday, I am definitely distracted enough to forget about my problems for a little while. Val has been talking nonstop the entire car ride to the restaurant we are currently on our way to. I'm not even sure what he's talking about. He's just talking. And since it seems like he has a lot on his mind, I just let him talk. It doesn't bother me that he's the one making most of the conversation. I don't mind it at all, really. I like listening to other people. Especially now that I'm trying desperately to get my mind off the things I keep thinking about. I realize that I've been kind of zoned out for a little while, so I try to focus on what it is that Val is saying.

"So he told me we could just finish it together at his place, and I figured that meant more than he was suggesting, you know?"

"Uh-huh." I nod.

"Yeah, so we were at his place. Sorry I didn't tell you where I was that day. Wasn't sure if I should tell you yet."

It takes me a second to figure out that he's talking about Jared.

"It's alright," I tell him. "We don't have to tell each other everything."

"Right. Yeah. You're right. Anyway, we spent the whole day together, and I thought maybe he did want to just be friends, then he asked me to dinner and I kind of, you know, had to ask him what exactly he was doing, and he said he wanted to get to know me better because he really liked me or something. So that's how that happened. I seriously think you'll love him. I love him." Val grips the steering wheel tightly and laughs a little. "Wow. No. No, I don't. Not yet at least. I'm just excited. Are you?" He glances over at me for a quick second. I can tell that this means a lot to Val, so even though I'm not necessarily excited, I still tell him I am.

"Yeah," I say. "I think it'll be really fun." I smile. I see Val smile too.

"It will be," he says. "Can you check my phone?"

I nod and pick up his phone out of the cup holder between us. I turn it on and read the messages to him.

"Hadlee says she's already there. You have an e-mail from one of your professors, and you just got a text from Jared that says he's a little nervous, lol."

I see Val try to hold back the smile that is slowly spreading across his face. "Alright," he says.

"Want me to text them anything back?" I ask.

"Yeah. Just tell both of them we're about five minutes away."

"Gotcha," I say as I start to type the first message to Hadlee. "How do you want me to text Jared?"

"What do you mean?"

"Should I put hearts at the end or something?"

"What the hell, why would I *ever* do that?" Val laughs.

"I don't know," I say defensively. "Maybe he'd think it was cute."

"Oh, yeah. I'm sure he would."

I laugh and put a heart at the end of the message even though Val will probably kill me once he sees it. We drive into an almost-empty parking lot and get out of the car. I see Hadlee waiting for us next to where she's parked. She gives us a small wave, and Val and I wave back at her.

"Felt kind of awkward just standing inside the restaurant by myself." She smiles. "So I decided to come back out here. Are we ready to go?"

Val looks at his phone after it goes off. "Yeah," he says. "Jared got here a little while ago. We can go inside." Hadlee and I nod and follow Val across the street and into the restaurant. I don't know what I thought Jared would look like, but I'm surprised when I see him. He's tall, *really* tall, with dark-brown hair that cuts off just below his ears. I notice that his eyes are two different colors, and he has sleeve tattoos on both of his arms. He smiles at Val as soon as he sees him. "Hey." He gives Val a quick hug. Val says something quietly to him, and they both laugh.

"Right?" Jared says. He then turns to face me. "You must be Keyon." He smiles at me. He holds out his hand, and I take it. "I'm going to assume you're Jared?" I smile back at him. He laughs a little and nods. "Heard a lot about you," he tells me. "It's nice finally being able to meet you." He turns to Hadlee now and smiles at her the same way he smiled at me.

"Haven't seen you in a while." Hadlee grins at Jared. "How've you been?"

"Never better," Jared says. "You?"

"Same as always." Hadlee laughs.

I wonder how she knows how to act like she remembers him. Seeing as how she told me that she had no clue who he was.

"Should we go ask for a table?" Val looks around at us.

"I already got one for us." Jared smiles. "I was just waiting for the rest of you."

One of the waitresses walks up to Jared and asks if he's ready to be seated. Jared nods and smiles at her. Now I can understand why Val likes this guy so much. He's probably the most charismatic person I've ever met. We follow our waitress to our booth, and I slide into the seat next to Hadlee. Jared seems like a great guy and everything, but I don't think I want to sit next to him in a booth just yet. And it seems like Val wants to sit by him anyway.

"So, Jared," Hadlee says. "Still studying history?" She saves us from an awkward moment of silence. She also must've remembered knowing Jared if she knew what he was majoring in.

"I've moved on to psychology, actually," Jared says. "Much more rewarding."

"He doesn't actually know if he likes it or not." Val smiles. "Only been in one class for about a week."

"Whatever." Jared rolls his eyes, but he's smiling. "I'm pretty sure I'll end up really liking it."

"Keyon." Hadlee turns her head to face me. "You took a couple of classes like that last year, didn't you?"

"I did." I look at Jared. "Not really my thing." I laugh a little. Jared smiles at me and laughs too. "What are you studying now?" he asks.

"Business," I say. "Marketing and all that."

Jared raises his eyebrows at me. "Interesting," he says. I can tell that he's genuinely impressed with what I've told him. We talk about this for a little while longer. What we've been studying, what jobs we think we could have in the future, what we wanted to be when we were younger, etc. I learn that Hadlee and Jared both wanted to be doctors, while Val and I share that we bonded based on the fact that both of us used to be interested in teaching.

The conversation stays casual, and for the first time in a while, I feel at ease. We laugh and talk about our lives, Jared and myself (surprisingly) making up most of the conversation. By the time we get our food, I take out my phone to text Val. I tell him that I like Jared. He has my blessing. Val looks at his phone then smiles at me from across the table. We stay where we are for about three hours, talking about anything and everything. Hadlee looks at her phone and tells us that it's almost ten.

"Wow." Val laughs. "I didn't think we'd be here that long."

"I should probably get going home," Hadlee says. "But this was really fun. We should do it again soon."

"Definitely," I say. Val reaches into his pocket to take out his wallet, but Jared grabs his hand to stop him. "I've got it." He smiles. Val smiles back at him and puts his hands in his lap. Hadlee looks at me and gives me smirk. I give her a smile in return and laugh silently. After Jared has paid for all of us, we stand up and make our way back outside.

"Thank you, Jared," Hadlee says sweetly.

"It was my pleasure." Jared smiles at her. Hadlee waves at the three of us and walks over to her car.

"It was really nice meeting you," Jared says to me.

"You too." I nod my head. I notice the way that Val and Jared are looking at each other and take that as my hint that I need to leave them alone.

"I'll meet you back at the car." I smile at Val.

"Here. Val hands me his keys. "This doesn't mean you're driving. It just means I'm not going to make you wait out in the cold." He smiles at me. I salute him and walk off toward his car. Once I'm inside, I insert the keys and start up the engine. A rush of warm air surrounds me, and I sit on my phone for about ten minutes before Val finally gets inside with me.

"Well?" he turns to look at me. "What'd you think?"

"Why did I have to wait for you for ten minutes?" I smile.

"That's not important." Val points a finger at me. "Did you like him or not?"

"Yeah. You guys are perfect for each other." I laugh.

"Whatever." Val smiles and backs out of the parking lot.

"That was actually a really nice time."

"Yeah. Not awkward like I thought it'd be."

"For someone who said he was nervous, Jared did an amazing job talking to all of us," I say.

"Yeah, he's kind of incredible like that."

As soon as Val says this, I find myself thinking about Grace. Again. She's moved on from me, why can't I move on from her? I'm beginning to think that Val was right when he called her the love of my life. Val notices my lack of communication with him and clears his throat. "You alright?" he asks. I decide not to bother him with my problems, so I lie to him.

"Yeah," I say. "Why wouldn't I be?"

Val raises his eyebrows at me but says nothing. I know he doesn't believe me, but it's not like I'm going to annoy him with my problems, which it seems like I've been doing a lot of lately. We drive home and talk about a few of the things that were said at dinner. After a few minutes, my phone makes a noise.

"Who's texting you?" Val asks me.

"Grace," I mumble.

Val looks at me for a brief moment and sighs. "What does *she* want?"

"She said she saw us at dinner."

"So she saw us, but she didn't say anything? That's not like her. Usually she'd be all over you."

"All over me?" I look at Val. "What does that mean?"

"Not like that. I just meant it seems like she tries to talk to you every chance she has. You know?"

"Weren't you the one that said she was probably never in love with me? Why would she be trying to talk to me?"

"You haven't noticed that you've been talking to her a lot recently?" Val raises his eyebrows at me.

"Well," I say, "I guess I have been. But that doesn't mean anything."

"You know how she's been talking to me a lot?"

"Yeah."

"Half of the time she's talking about you."

I turn in my seat. "Seriously?"

"Seriously." Val nods as he pulls into the parking lot in front of our building. "Did you text her back?"

"No," I tell him. "I don't really know what to say to her."

"I wouldn't say anything. I feel like something's different about her." Val shuts off the car.

"What do you mean?"

"I don't know. She just isn't the same as she was when she was with you."

I think about this. Val isn't making a lot of sense to me. He *had* told me that she'd moved on. That she didn't love me anymore. That she never loved me at all. So why was he saying she seemed different because she wasn't with me? Or that it seems like she wants to talk to me? I'm confused. Val sighs before unlocking the doors and stepping out of the car.

"You coming?" he asks me. I nod and open my door. It's colder outside than I remember it being, so I walk quickly to the main door, Val trailing behind me. We finally make it up to our apartment, and I rub my hands together before taking off my coat and shoes. Val runs his fingers through his hair and looks at his phone. I notice that he's holding back a smile, and I shake my head.

"Let me guess," I say. "Jared?"

Val rolls his eyes at me and waves me off before putting his phone up to his ear and walking down the hallway into his room. I laugh silently to myself and make my way over to the bathroom. I shower, brush my teeth, and get into bed. I have a dream that Grace and I are back together, and she's over at Val and mine's place. Nothing is said in the dream, but I know that we're trying to figure out who killed Erica and Quinn. Grace doesn't like that I'm talking about girls other than her, so she gets upset with me and leaves. Val gives me a look that lets me know he's thinking about what he told me. That she was never actually in love with me. I have no idea what any of this means, but I wake up distressed. I sit up in bed and lean back against the headboard.

Letting out a sigh, I reach my hand behind me and knock on the wall a couple of times. I wait a minute before I decide I'm being stupid and lie back down. As soon as I do, I hear knocking coming from the other side of the wall. About a month after I moved in with Val, he discovered that I was incredibly prone to having nightmares. So we came up with this plan that if I ever needed to just talk it out or anything like that, I'd knock, and hopefully he'd wake up. Usually it would make me feel better just knowing that I wasn't alone, but occasionally Val would go the extra mile and actually come over and talk to me. This was one of those times. Even though it wasn't necessarily a nightmare that I'd just had, I still wanted to talk to someone.

After about thirty seconds, Val comes into my room and turns on the light. He doesn't say anything. He just walks over to me and sits down on the edge of my bed. I take a deep breath and shake my head.

"Wasn't even a nightmare," I say.

"You still knocked."

"I know." I sigh. "I'm sorry."

"You shouldn't be," Val looks at me with sincerity in his eyes.

"I guess everything is just kind of getting to me."

"Yeah. I know."

"You know?"

Val presses his lips together and nods. "It's getting to me too."

"For some reason, I thought I'd feel better after today. After going out and doing something. Didn't really help as much as I'd hoped."

"What was the dream about?" Val asks me.

"I don't really know," I say. "You, Grace, and I were trying to figure out the whole double murder thing, but she got mad at me then left. Then I knew she didn't—"

I decide not to say anything else. It's better to just leave it at that. Val will understand what I was going to say anyway. I'm not trying to get emotional on him. He'd already woken up in the middle of the night for me, why make him do anything else?

"You can go back to your room if you want," I say.

Val shakes his head. "I'm not just going to 'leave you alone with your thoughts,' as you put it. I'd like to think I'm a better person than that." He smiles.

"Thanks." I smile back.

"Want to talk about something else? Besides murder and Grace? Like I keep saying we need to stop talking about?"

I laugh a little at this. "Yeah. Okay. Anything else. I'm good with whatever." Before Val can say anything, my phone buzzes on my nightstand.

"Who's up texting you at three in the morning?" Val questions.

"No idea." I pick up my phone and unlock it. I have a message from Grace. "Grace just texted me."

"This late?"

"This late."

"Here we go again." Val lies down backward on my bed. "What did she say?"

"She says, and I quote, 'Really need to talk to you.'"

"Oh god." Val rolls his eyes.

"What?"

"I'm sorry, but she isn't my favorite of all the girlfriends that you've had. When I said you could do better after she broke up with you, I meant it. I really, really meant it."

"I thought you'd been talking to her a lot. Why would you talk to her if you don't like her?"

"She's alright." Val sighs. "She just seems off. You know?"

"Well," I say, "this is a little weird. Should I text her back?"

"Go for it. I'm not stopping you."

I look at my phone for a few seconds before typing out my reply. I ask what she needs to talk about. Val and I sit in silence for about a minute until Grace responds.

"She says we need to talk in person." I look over at Val.

"Well, tell her she just woke you up and that you need to go the fuck back to sleep."

I roll my eyes. "Great idea, Val. Before I do that, why don't I propose to her?"

"Shut up." Val smiles. "Just tell her not right now."

"Obviously not right now," I say. "I'll tell her we can talk tomorrow or something."

"What do you think she actually wants?"

I shrug. "Who knows. Could be anything, I guess."

"Maybe I was wrong."

"Wrong about what?"

"About her not being in love with you anymore. Maybe she still is. Maybe she wants you back."

I laugh. "I *highly* doubt that."

"Why?" Val looks genuinely confused.

"She told me she didn't feel the same way anymore. I think you were right to say that she doesn't love me."

Val sighs and sits up. "This is getting depressing, Keyon. What did I tell you?"

"No murder talk and no Grace talk," I say.

"Exactly. And what are we doing right now?"

I roll my eyes. "Alright, alright. We won't talk about her anymore. Do you want to go back to bed?"

"Do you need me here?"

"I think I'll be okay." I give him a small smile.

"If you say so." Val stands up and walks toward the door. Before exiting the room he says, "Just don't think about things too much." I nod at him, then he shuts the door. I decide to try to take his advice. I clear my mind of basically everything before I attempt to fall back asleep.

The next morning (more like one in the afternoon), I walk out into our living room to see Val sitting on the couch with Jared.

"Oh," I say. "Hey, Jared."

"Hey." Jared smiles at me.

"Sorry I didn't tell you he was coming," Val says. "Didn't wanna wake you up."

"It's all good," I tell him. "What are you guys doing?"

"Nothing, really." Val shrugs and then smiles at Jared. He then looks back at me. "You got any plans for today?"

"Um." I scratch the back of my head and take a seat at the kitchen table. "Yeah. Grace, remember?"

Val rolls his eyes. Jared looks at me and furrows his brow. "Grace?"

"His ex-girlfriend," Val tells him. "Who we're *not* supposed to be talking about." Val glares at me.

"I told her I'd talk to her today. I can't just not see what she wants."

"Yes." Val nods. "Yes, you can. You don't have to talk to her."

I sigh and stand up. "I'm taking a shower. Then I'll get out of here. You guys can be alone all you want." I smile. I walk down the hallway and hear Jared yell out, "Good seeing you!"

"Nice seeing you too," I say before I walk into the bathroom.

An hour later, I'm sitting inside Grace's favorite coffee shop, waiting for my green tea strawberry lemonade. And surprisingly, I have nothing on my mind. I'm not even thinking about Grace. And I'm not panicking like I thought I'd be. The door to the shop opens, and Grace walks inside. Long dark hair pairing flawlessly with dark skin. Now I'm panicking.

"Hey." Grace smiles at me as I stand up. I'm not sure if I should hug her or not, so I just hold out a hand. Thankfully, Grace just laughs and takes my hand in hers. "You order already?" she asks. All I manage to do is nod. She tells me she'll be back in a second, and I sit down. I think about every possible reason as to why Grace would want to talk to me. All I can really come up with is that she wants to get back together, which definitely freaks me out even more. I pull out my phone and turn on my front camera. Sweet Jesus. Grace actually saw me like this? I ran my fingers through my hair a few times and sighed. Not much I could do now.

Grace walks back over to where I'm sitting, two drinks in hand.

"This yours?" She holds out a cup.

I nod and take it from her.

"Wow." She laughs as she sits down. "You're very talkative today."

"Sorry." I laugh too. "If I'm being honest, I'm actually kind of nervous."

Grace raises an eyebrow. "Nervous?"

"Yeah. Um, never mind. You wanted to talk?"

"I do." Grace takes a sip of her drink. "I figured it would be better to do this in person than over the phone. It might be a little awkward, but overall, I think it'll be better."

"Okay?"

"I've been thinking a lot lately."

"Okay?" I say again.

"Like I said, I've been thinking a lot. And I love you."

I blink a few times and try to breathe. "You do?"

"Yeah. Sorry if that was a little too soon. I don't want to—"

"No, no." I shake my head. "I mean, I love you too. I was going to tell you before, but then you—"

I don't say anything else, but Grace nods her head in understanding.

"Yeah," she says. "I know. It was stupid of me to think I didn't want to be with you. Because I do. I do want to be with you."

She smiles at me and I smile back. We talk for an hour and a half, and everything feels good again. When Grace says she needs to leave, I nod and lead her outside to where her car is parked.

"This was fun," she tells me.

"Yeah." I smile. "We should do this again. You free Tuesday?"

Grace laughs and leans up to kiss me. "Yes," she says when she pulls away. "I am. I'll see you then. Can I call you tonight?"

"Of course." I keep on smiling.

I immediately tell Val when I get home.

"Jesus, Keyon," Val says from where he's lying on the couch. "You've been gone for, like, three hours."

"Where's Jared?" I ask as I sit down at the kitchen table to take off my shoes.

"He left about a half an hour ago. What did Grace have to say for herself?"

I smile and look up at Val. "She loves me." His mouth falls open, and he sits up.

"She did not seriously tell you that."

"Yeah," I say. "She did."

"Isn't she the one who broke up with you? That doesn't make any sense."

"Well, sure it does."

Val rolls his eyes. "How?"

"Maybe she just wasn't sure how to express her feelings or something."

"That sounds likely."

"Why are you so against her?" I stand up and walk toward where Val is sitting.

"Why am I so against her?" Val scoffs. "She broke your heart, man. And you know I've never liked her anyway. She's never even liked me. So why can't I be against you guys being together?"

"Are you serious?" I raise my eyebrows and cross my arms. "You don't want us to be together? That's what this is about?"

"Keyon." Val actually looks kind of hurt. "I just told you I've never liked her. You know that. Why are you getting all worked up about it now?"

"Because I love her, Val." I'm raising my voice, but I can't help it. "You know that. You don't get to hate her."

"So, what? I'm not allowed to have my own opinions of people?"

"How do you think you'd feel if I said I hated Jared?"

Val is standing now. "I never said I hated anyone. And don't you dare bring Jared into this."

"You know what," I say as I put up my hands, "I don't want to fight with you. You know neither of us like doing that. So let's just not, okay? I'm sorry I yelled. I'm sorry I got mad. It's whatever."

I turn down the hall but not before I see Val bring his hands up to his face.

"Keyon, come on," he says quietly.

"I told you," I say before opening the door to my bedroom. "It's whatever."

I quit my job the next day. It had nothing to do with the fight between Val and me. I just don't feel like I can handle work right now. I skip my classes on Monday and Tuesday. The only thing I'm really looking forward to doing is seeing Grace. I arrive at her house Tuesday night, absolutely exhausted from doing absolutely nothing. When she answers the door, I think I may have actually stopped breathing. I swear she gets even more beautiful every time I see her. She smiles at me as soon as she sees me. Grabbing on to my hand, she pulls me inside. I lock the door behind me and turn to face her. She put her hands around my neck and takes a step closer to me.

"You look nice," she says. I kiss her and then smile.

"Not as good as you," I say.

Grace laughs and pulls me into her living room.

"Are we the only ones here?" I look around the room.

"Yeah. Tasha and Alexis aren't here. It's just us tonight." Grace winks at me and drags me over to the only couch in the room. We sit down, but I don't say anything else.

"Hey." Grace puts her hands on top of mine. "You okay?"

"Yeah," I say.

Grace raises an eyebrow. I sigh.

"Alright." I shake my head. "No. I'm not. I skipped class the last two days, and I quit my job. Plus, I haven't talked to Val since Saturday."

"What? Keyon, none of that is good."

"Yeah," I say quietly. "I know it's not. I don't even know what I was thinking."

"Why haven't you talked to Val?"

"I think we got in a fight."

Grace almost smiles at this. "You think?"

"Yeah. Maybe. It felt like a fight."

"What started it?"

"Well." I sigh. "I guess it started when he got angry that we got back together."

Grace puts her hands in her lap. "He was angry about that?"

"Yeah. Which doesn't make any sense. I thought you guys were friends."

"I thought so too." Grace sighs. "Did he say why he was upset about us being together again?"

"Not really."

"Did he have a problem with us before?"

I think about this for a minute. "No. I don't think so. So I don't know why he's upset now."

Grace looks down at her hands and furrows her brow. "I don't know why either."

"It's fine, though." I try to smile at her. "We don't care what he thinks, right?"

Grace looks up at me and smiles. "We?"

"Well, I mean, yeah. Do you care?"

"Kind of." Grace shrugs. "Why don't you? Don't you want his approval?"

"I don't need anyone's approval." I shake my head.

"I'm not talking about need." Grace's smile fades. "I said want. Do you *want* his approval?"

"Yeah," I say. "I do. But it looks like we aren't going to get it. So don't you think we should just forget about it?"

"You seem upset today." Grace frowns at me.

"I told you earlier I wasn't exactly okay."

"Why did you quit your job?"

"What?"

"You told me you quit your job, did you not?"

I nod. "I did."

"Well." Grace sighs. "Why?"

"I don't really know. I just feel like I can't do it right now."

"You can't?"

"Yeah. I don't think I could deal with it with everything else that's happening."

Grace raises an eyebrow. "You mean the murders?"

"I guess. I don't know."

"I think that's something you should forget about." Grace sits up straighter.

"What?"

"The murders. You should forget about them."

I laugh a little. "It was a girl in my apartment building, plus a girl I was going to marry. I don't think I could just—"

"Keyon." Grace takes my hand. "It's not good for you. You have to forget about it."

I stare at her. "I really don't think it's something I can just forget about."

"Why do you say that?"

I raise my eyebrows. "Are you serious?"

"Sorry." Grace sighs. She pulls her hand away from mine and wipes underneath her eyes after taking a few deep breaths. "I just don't like that all of this is happening. I hate that it's making you so upset, and I just don't know what to do to help you."

Grace is crying now, and I feel incredibly guilty. This is what I get for talking to someone about my problems.

"Grace." I sigh and put my arms around her. She leans her head onto my chest, and I can hear her unsteady breathing. "It's alright, okay? Just talking about it helps enough. You're not doing anything wrong."

"I feel like I am."

"You're not," I say. "I can understand that you're upset, but really. You don't have to be sad for me."

"How can I not be?" Grace pulls away from me. "If you're upset, then so am I. If you're happy, then so am I."

This is starting to sound all too familiar. I think back to when I was with Erica. Her sadness was my sadness. Her happiness was my happiness. I can't let Grace get attached like that. She would only end up hurting herself. I don't know what to say.

"Grace, please don't talk like that. I don't want you to have to feel what I'm feeling. You don't deserve that."

"Well, you don't deserve to feel this way either." Grace looks up at me.

I sigh. "What do you think we should do then?"

"You're upset about your fight with Val, right?"

"Right."

"And he's upset about us being together?"

"Yeah?"

"I think you should move out. I'll move out too. We can get a place together."

I almost laugh. "Really? You want to do that?"

"Of course I do," Grace says seriously.

"I can't just leave Va—"

"Why not?" Grace interrupts me.

"He's my best—"

"And I'm your girlfriend. The one you're in love with. Right?" Grace says softly.

I stare down at her and take a deep breath. This is not making me feel any better. I do love Grace. More than anything. But there's no way I can leave Val.

"Right?" Grace says again.

I nod. "Right. I love you, Grace."

"I love you too." She puts her arms around me and sighs softly.

The only thing I'm feeling now is guilt.

I get back to the apartment at around ten thirty. Val is sitting on the couch, and he looks up at me when I walk in. He doesn't say anything. We basically just stare at each other for about a minute.

"Hey," I say awkwardly.

Val raises his eyebrows at me.

"Um." I scratch the back of my head. "I know we aren't exactly on the best terms right now, but I think we need to talk."

"About what?"

"Well," I say as I sit down next to him. "First, I want to apologize. I messed up. Big time. I'm really sorry, Val."

Val sighs before looking down at his hands then back up at me. "I'm sorry too. And apology accepted. Is that all you wanted to talk about?"

I press my lips together and look at him.

"Keyon?" He raises an eyebrow.

"Grace wants me to move in with her."

Val blinks a couple of times before turning his head away from me and leaning back. "Wow," he says.

"Yeah."

"And what did you tell her?"

"I told her I'd need to talk to you first."

"First?" Val looks back over at me. "You mean before you move in with her? You already said yes?"

"No, no." I shake my head. "I didn't say yes. I'm not even sure what I want to do. I mean, I want to move in with her, but I don't exactly want to leave you."

"Oh."

"That's all you have to say?"

"Well." He sighs. "I don't want you to move in with her. For selfish reasons. It's not because of how I feel about you two, I just want you to stay here. You know?"

I nod at him.

"Fuck, wow." Val runs his fingers through his hair. "I'm getting sappy. Sorry. Fuck."

I laugh a little and lean back on the couch. "It's alright," I say. "I don't think I'm going to move in with her anyway. Not sure I'm ready for that."

Val laughs and looks my way. "Good. I mean, bad for Grace, but good for me. Thank you."

"You don't have to thank me."

"Well, you know what I mean. Thanks for not leaving me alone."

"God." I bring my hands up to my face. "Grace is going to be so upset."

"Yeah." Val sighs. "Probably. When are you going to tell her?"

"I don't know. Tomorrow after class, I guess."

"Speaking of class, have you been going? Because I don't think I've seen you leave the apartment."

I put my hands in my lap and shake my head. "No. I've skipped the last two days."

"What?" Val raises his eyebrows. "Why?"

"Felt like I couldn't do it."

"Shit, this isn't because of me, is it?"

"What? Val, no. It's not because of you."

"You just . . . ?"

"Felt like I couldn't go. Yeah."

Val sighs and closes his eyes. "Understandable."

"I swear it wasn't because of you."

Val opens his eyes and looks over at me. "I believe you," he says.

"Good," I nod my head. "Now, what am I supposed to tell Grace?"

"I don't know." Val shrugs. "Just tell her that you're not ready or something."

"She'll see right through me."

"How do you know? Just tell her."

"I don't think I could do it in person."

Val sighs. "Then call her. Sleep on it, then tell her in the morning."

"Yeah." I stand up and run my fingers through my hair. "Alright. Yeah. Good idea."

I feel a little like dying right about now. I'm not good at making decisions. Especially not big decisions like this. I put my hands up to my face and rub my eyes.

"You good?"

I remember that I'm not alone and look down at Val.

"Yeah," I say. "Can we, like, talk about something else?"

"Maybe you should just go to bed."

"Do I look that tired?"

Val shrugs. "Little bit."

"You're probably right." I wave my hand at him. "I'm out. You staying up much longer?"

"Probably. Not feeling like I could sleep tonight. You know what I mean?"

"Yeah." I nod. "I know what you mean. See you in the morning then?"

"See you in the morning." Val smiles.

I smile back before turning around and heading down the hall into my room. Closing my door, I suddenly feel like everything is falling apart. I know it isn't, and I know things are going to be okay, but I can't ignore the small part of me that's telling me everything sucks. I don't even make it to my bed. I practically fall to the ground as I start to cry. I'm trying to be quiet, but I'm in no way succeeding. Less than a minute later, I hear my bedroom door open and see Val sit down next to me. He doesn't say anything; he just sits there until I've finally stopped crying. Once I'm silent, I hear Val sigh, and he looks over at me. I look back at him and shake my head.

"I don't even know why I'm doing this," I almost whisper.

"So it's not about Grace?"

"No. At least I don't think so. I guess it's just kind of everything lately."

"Yeah." Val nods. "I understand. Anything you want me to do?"

"No, I mean, I don't know. I'm sorry. I don't want to be annoying."

Val rolls his eyes. "You're not annoying."

"Yeah, okay."

"Don't get all sarcastic with me." Val gives me a small smile.

I laugh a little and look down at my hands. "Sorry. Couldn't help it." Neither of us say anything for a little while.

"You alright?" Val finally says.

"I think so. Thanks for being here."

"I live here. I kind of have to be here." Val smiles.

I laugh and shove him lightly. "Shut up. I'm going to bed."

"Okay." Val makes a noise as he stands up. He runs his fingers through his hair and yawns. "I might just do the same thing."

"I thought you weren't going to have any luck sleeping?"

Val shrugs. "You never know what could happen." He waves at me and walks out of my room, shutting the door behind me. I stare at the door for a few seconds after he walks out. Every time I tell myself I'm not going to think about things, it never works. I don't know why I thought it would work this time around. Sleep doesn't come easy to me. Never really does. But tonight? I fall asleep faster than you can turn out a light.

I have a dream that I'm sitting inside Quinn's apartment, in her bedroom. Erica is there. She tells me that she knows she's next, and she says that she needs to go to the library. I tell her that it's a bad idea, that she needs to stay home and not go out. She shakes her head at me, then she stands up and leaves. I'm left alone in Quinn's room. I know I can leave; I don't have to be here. But for some reason, I stay. I've never been in here before. I've never even seen the inside of her room. I know Val's seen it. I know Val's seen Quinn dead too. Maybe that's why I'm here. I look to my left and down at the ground. There's blood surrounding me, but I'm not fazed by it. A minute passes. Then two. Then three. I don't know how long I stand here.

When I wake up, I'm standing in my living room.

"Well, this isn't right," I say to myself. Must have sleepwalked out of my room. I make my way back to my bed and lie facedown. After a couple minutes, I turn on my side to check my phone. It's three twenty-five, and I have a couple of unread messages. One from Hadlee, two from Grace. My first message from Hadlee was sent at about eleven, but I wasn't awake then. She wants to know where I've been because she hasn't seen me around lately. I don't answer her. I doubt she's still up. Wouldn't want to wake her.

I check my messages from Grace next. Both sent from only half an hour ago. In the first message, she tells me she can't stop thinking about me. In her second message, she tells me she loves me. I don't answer her either. It's probably better just to forget about everyone for now.

———•———

"I'm glad you finally texted me this morning," Hadlee says as we sit on one of the benches at the nearest park.

"Yeah," I say. "Sorry if it seemed like I was ignoring you. I swear that wasn't my intention."

"It's alright. You going to tell me why I haven't seen you on campus?"

I sigh. "I don't have a very good answer." Hadlee looks at me and raises her eyebrows.

"I just kind of felt like I couldn't go." I shrug.

"I understand." Hadlee nods.

"You do?"

"Yeah. I think everyone feels that way sometimes."

I look down at my hands. "I guess you're right."

"Are you and Val okay?"

"What?"

Hadlee sighs, and I can still feel her eyes on me. "He told me that Grace wanted you to move in with her. He didn't seem too happy about it."

"Well, I'm not moving in with her. I'm staying with him."

"Val made it sound like you weren't sure what you were going to do."

"Grace really wants me to be with her, but I just don't think that's a good idea right now."

Hadlee looks away from me. "Have you told her you're staying with Val?"

"No. Not yet. I seriously have no idea how I'm supposed to tell her. No matter what I say about it, she's going to be upset. And I mean, I don't want her to be angry with me or anything. So I don't know how to tell her without breaking her heart."

"You could say you're not ready for that kind of commitment."

"That would make her upset." I look over at Hadlee.

"How?" She raises an eyebrow.

"Not ready for that kind of commitment? That's going to make her think that I don't see us having a future together. If I'm not ready now, I never will be."

"You really think she'll think that way?"

"I know she will," I say. "That's just how she is. And I know if I tell her anything other than 'Yes, I'll move in with you,' she's going to get upset. She'll probably cry if I'm being honest."

Hadlee sighs. "Kind of sounds like she's guilt-tripping you into moving in with her."

"What?" I raise an eyebrow. "What do you mean? It's not guilt-tripping me if she's actually upset about it."

"Yeah. I guess you're right. I just don't want you making the wrong decision."

"You think living with Grace is the wrong decision?"

"I never said that."

"Alright, well, I already told you I'm going to stay with Val."

Hadlee shakes her head.

"What?" I ask her.

"Nothing. I think it's good you're staying with him. He's been kind of depressed lately. I think he needs someone with him."

"What do you mean by depressed? He seems fine to me."

"Well, with Jared and everything, he's been really upset."

"What?" I blink a few times. "What happened with Jared?"

Hadlee looks up at me. "He didn't tell you?"

"Val and I just started talking again yesterday. He hasn't told me anything at all."

"Oh." Hadlee presses her lips together. "Well, Jared's in the hospital. He's really sick. Family came to visit him and everything. He's been in there a couple days, and Val's just been worried about him."

"Wow," I say. "I had no idea. I know I'd be upset if something like that was happening with Grace."

"Yeah." Hadlee nods. "Why weren't you and Val talking?"

I sigh. "Stupid reasons. I guess we kind of got in another fight."

"Another fight?"

"Yeah. We got into it a little while ago when we were drunk and pissed off at each other for no reason."

"Wow." Hadlee presses her lips together again. "Sounds like your friendship is going well lately."

I laugh a little. "Oh, yeah. I think he'll get over it, though."

"*He* will?"

"Jesus. No. *We* will. God. That's another reason why he's right."

"Right about what?"

"He told me I never blamed myself or something. That it was always someone else's fault. Do you think I do that?"

Hadlee shrugs. I sigh and look down at my hands.

"I mean, he's right," I say. "I really don't ever blame myself."

"You blame yourself for Erica."

I look over at Hadlee. I did blame myself for what happened to Erica. If I had just stayed with her, if I had just done a better job of protecting her, she'd still be here. It *was* my fault that she was killed. "How do you know that?"

"Well, didn't she tell you that it was your fault she tried to kill herself?" Hadlee raises her eyebrows at me. "You kind of seem like you blame yourself for that."

Hadlee and I weren't thinking the same thing. She was talking about Erica's suicide attempt, and I was thinking about her death.

"Oh," I say. "Yeah. That. I don't know. How could it not have been my fault? If she said she did it because of me, then that probably means she actually did do it because of me. She wouldn't have any reason to lie about why she tried to do what she did."

"You're right." Hadlee nods. "But I don't know what happened between you two."

"So what you're saying is that you can't really say if it was my fault or not?"

Hadlee gives me a small smile. "I don't know how else to say it. So yeah. That's what I'm getting at."

I laugh. "Thank you. You know, for being honest with me."

"I couldn't lie to you even if I wanted to." Hadlee smiles for real this time.

I pull my phone out of my pocket and look at the time. "Val's getting off work right now. I think I need to go and talk to him about some stuff."

"We can do this again soon, though, right?"

"Yeah." I smile as I stand up. "We can. I'll text you later?"

Hadlee stands up too and walks in front of me. "Okay." She looks at me with an expression that I can't quite describe, then she hugs me tightly. "Don't be too hard on yourself, Keyon," she says. I sigh and tell her that I won't be.

Val gets home fifteen minutes after I do. He walks in and takes a deep breath before lying down on the couch next to where I'm sitting. With his face in a pillow, he says, "I hate work. I totally understand why you quit."

"It can't be that bad." I smile.

"Oh, it can be. How was your day?"

"Fine," I say. "Talked to Hadlee for a little while about a bunch of stuff. How was your day?"

"Shitty," Val says as he sits up. "What'd you talk to Hadlee about?"

"Well, Grace. And Jared. And you."

"What about us?"

"She doesn't want me to move in with Grace, and she told me what's been going on with Jared. And I'm not mad that you didn't tell me. We weren't talking, so I understand."

Val sighs. "Alright. What did you say about me?"

"I think we need to talk."

Val laughs. "It sounds like you're getting ready to break up with me."

"Don't worry. That's not what I'm doing." I smile. "I just want to say I'm sorry."

"I thought both of us apologized already?"

"We did." I nod. "But I'm apologizing for something else."

Val raises his eyebrows at me.

"I've been a horrible friend."

"You have?"

"Yes. I have."

"I don't think I know what you mean." Val shakes his head.

"I just think I need to say that you're an amazing person. I seriously mean that."

"Okay," Val says slowly. "Where are you going with this?"

"I want you to know that I understand that I'm not the best friend sometimes. I know I can be somewhat moody, and I can get angry easily, and I can get annoying, but somehow you still want to put up with me. So I'm sorry I suck, but thank you for not thinking so."

Val laughs. "Jesus, what? What is wrong with you?"

"What?" I raise my eyebrows. "What do you mean? What's wrong with me?"

"You're so stupid." Val keeps laughing. "Apology accepted. I think. And you're welcome. You're so fucking sappy, man. I hate it."

"Sorry for being a good guy." I put my hands in the air.

Val smiles at me and shakes his head. "You're fine, Keyon. I'm going to do some school stuff. You have stuff to do too, remember?"

"I do?"

"Grace?"

"Oh yeah. Grace."

Val stands up and pats my shoulder a few times. "Let her down easy, good guy."

"I'll try my hardest."

I talk to Grace an hour later at her place. Let's just say she doesn't take it very well.

"You're fucking kidding me," Grace says as she stands up from her couch.

"Grace." I stand up as well and try to grab on to her arm.

"No, Keyon." She shakes my hand off her. "You're seriously picking him over me?"

I think about the advice Hadlee gave me. "I just don't think I'm ready for that kind of commitment."

"Oh, that's fucking great." Grace laughs as she walks into her kitchen. "So what you're saying is you can't commit yourself to me?"

"Grace, seriously," I follow her into the other room. "You know that isn't what I meant."

"Really? That's not what you're saying? I still just can't believe you actually led me to believe you were going to pick me over Val."

"Okay, I'm not picking one over the other. And I don't think that I led you to believe anything. I'm just saying that I don't think I'm ready to just drop everything I know to go move in somewhere with you. I really think I should just stay with Val for now."

"For now?"

"Yes. For now. I told you, I'm not saying that I'm never going to want to move in with you."

Grace sighs and looks down at her kitchen counter. I think I've succeeded in calming her down. Just a little.

"Alright," she says.

"Alright?"

"I understand. We haven't been back together that long, and I was probably rushing into things. I get it."

"You do?"

"Yeah." Grace runs her fingers through her hair. "I get it. I'm being a bitch right now anyway. I'm sorry." She brings her hands up to her face and takes a deep breath.

"Grace, it's okay." I walk over to where she's standing and wrap my arms around her from behind. "I don't want you to blame yourself for anything."

"God, it's just that I know everything is my fault."

"What do you mean?"

"I don't know. I'm sorry."

She turns around and hugs me tightly. I rest my chin on the top or her head and sigh. I'm not sure what to say to her. I'm not really sure about anything anymore. Somehow, things have changed. There really isn't any way to describe it. Everything is just kind of happening too quickly. And everything is just too stressful. Way too stressful. Now I'm thinking about something I know I shouldn't be thinking about. I have no idea what I'm doing with my life. I honestly have no idea what I'm doing right now. Nothing is making any sense. I think about every conversation I've ever had about Grace. Why *did* she want to get back together with me? Wasn't she the one who broke up with me? Wasn't *I* the one who wanted us back together?

"Keyon?"

I back away from Grace and look down at her. "Yeah?"

"What are you thinking about?"

I stare at her for a few seconds. "You know what? I can't even remember."

———◆———

"So you guys are okay?" Val looks at me from across the table we're sitting at.

"Yeah." I nod my head. "I mean, I think so. She's not mad or anything."

"I think you did the right thing," Hadlee says.

"Yeah," I say again. "I think I did too."

Val smiles at me then turns his head and smiles even wider when we all hear a familiar voice.

"Sorry I'm so late." Jared smiles as he sits down next to Val. "Might have slept in a little."

"Good," Hadlee says. "You need all the rest you can get. Are you feeling any better?"

Jared shrugs. "Mostly. I'm just happy to be out and doing things again. After spending three days straight with only my family to keep me company, I was starting to go a little insane."

We all laugh, and Val shakes his head. "God, I know what that's like."

"What, being with your family like that?"

"Yeah." Val nods. "Horrible. Every time."

"I don't think I've actually met any of your family," Jared says. "Do they live around here?"

"They do. But I don't know if you'd want to meet them."

"What? Why not?"

Val looks at Hadlee and me for help.

"They're kind of strange," Hadlee says. "No offense, Val."

"None taken." Val shrugs. "But yeah. They're different."

I laugh. "Yeah. You could say that." Val laughs with me and sighs before turning to look at Jared. "Last Christmas, we had this little get-together, and my grandma was absolutely convinced that Keyon was my brother. She really believed he was her grandson."

"I felt very loved," I say.

Jared laughs. "That doesn't sound too bad, Val."

"No, trust me." Val gets closer to Jared. "They're horrible around new people."

"They really, really are," Hadlee chimes in. "They ask all the wrong questions as soon as you start talking to them."

Jared is about to say something, but I distract him when I get out of my seat.

"Keyon?" Hadlee looks up at me.

"I think that's Emmett," I say.

"Who?"

Emmett walks into the restaurant cautiously, like he's afraid of what might happen. We make eye contact, and he blinks a few times before he starts to walk over. I step out of the booth we're all at and walk over to him. We don't say anything for a few seconds.

"Keyon," Emmett says. "I haven't seen you in a while."

"Yeah." I nod. "Haven't seen you in a while either. How are you?"

"I'm okay. How are you? I mean, since—"

"I'm probably in the same place you are right now."

"I can believe it," Emmett says.

"Um, hang on." I turn around and walk Emmett a few steps closer to my table. "Guys, this is Emmett. Erica's brother."

I'm pretty sure that Val has told Jared about Erica, but his and Jared's faces show that they aren't exactly sure what to do. Luckily, Hadlee is amazing at this kind of thing. She stands up and takes one of Emmett's hands with both of her own. "It's good to meet you." She smiles politely. "I'm Hadlee." Emmett smiles back at her and nods. "Good to meet you too," he says.

Jared is the next one to react to the situation. He stands up as soon as Hadlee sits down and holds out a hand. Emmett takes it and smiles. "Emmett." He nods once. Jared smiles brightly and shakes Emmett's hand. "Jared," he says. "So nice to meet you." He sits back down and looks to Val. Val nods at Emmett and gives him a tight-lipped smile.

"Valentine," Emmett says. "Good to see you again."

"You too." Val keeps the same tight smile.

"So." I look at Emmett. "Do you want us to pull up—"

"I'm alright. I'm actually meeting someone here." Emmett gives me a small smile. He puts a hand on my shoulder, and his expression makes me so sad that I want to give him a hug right then and there. "It was really nice seeing you again. Take care of yourself." He pauses. "And be careful." I nod at him before he walks away. Hadlee lets out a low whistle.

"Well, that was interesting," she says.

"That was probably the worst possible way we could have reunited," I say as I sit back down.

"How's he doing?" Jared looks at me.

I shrug. "He said he was okay. Not sure if I'd be okay in his situation, though."

"I just can't imagine losing your sister like that." Hadlee shakes her head.

"Maybe we shouldn't talk about this," Val says.

"Good idea." I nod.

We change subjects and talk for another hour. Although I can't help but notice how forced Val's smiles seem. I don't say anything about it at breakfast, though. I don't want to make him the center of attention, and I don't want to bring any of us down. Thinking that I should ask about it sooner rather than later, I suggest that all of us head out and go home. Everyone agrees with me, and we go our separate ways. When Val and I get back to the apartment, he goes and locks himself in his room. I don't try to get him to talk to me; I just leave him alone. I keep my shoes and coat on and go out to the coffee shop Grace and I always go to. Only this time, Grace isn't with me. I'm only sitting in the place for about ten minutes when I hear my name being called. I turn my head to see Jared walking over to me.

"Hey." He smiles at me. "I didn't know anyone else knew about this place."

"Neither did I," I say. I nod toward the chair in front of me. "Want to sit?"

Jared responds by smiling even wider and taking a seat in front of me. "So," he says. "Come here often?"

I laugh a little and take a sip of my coffee. "Nice way to start the conversation. But yes, I do. I come here a lot with Grace."

"Your girlfriend?"

"Yeah," I say before sighing.

Jared raises an eyebrow. "You okay?"

"Yeah, it's just, like we were talking about earlier, I feel like we're kind of in an awkward spot in the relationship right now."

"Because of the whole moving in thing? Val told me about it."

I nod. "I mean, don't you think it's a little early? Like, I've known her for a while, but we've only been dating for three and a half months."

"It does seem like she wants to rush into things." Jared nods back at me. "You're sure she's not upset that you wanted to stay with Val?"

"Well." I sigh. "She said she's not upset that I don't want to move in yet. I'm not sure about the Val part."

"What do you mean?"

"I told her I wasn't picking one over the other, but that's exactly what I did. I picked Val over her, and she knows it. There's no way she isn't upset about that."

"Seems like she's quick to get upset," Jared says. "If I asked Val to move in with me after barely three months and he said no because he wanted to stay with you, I'd understand. You guys have been closer longer. Does that make sense?"

I nod again. "It does. So you think that Grace should just calm down?"

"Basically." Jared shrugs. "But I think you could use some calming down as well."

"What?"

"You're a little bit worked up over this."

"Yeah." I laugh. "Just a little bit."

"But you talked this over with her, right?"

I nod and take another sip of my coffee. "I did. But what does that mean?"

"That it's over. You've talked about it already. You don't really have a reason to be upset about this anymore."

Normally, if someone said this to me, I'd be getting a little more than angry. But the way Jared says it, it makes me believe him. He's completely right. I shouldn't stress out about this anymore. But with me being me, I know I'm not going to forget about it anytime soon. I need a distraction.

"Do you want to get out of here? Do something else?" I ask Jared. He raises an eyebrow at me.

"Such as?"

"I have no idea." I shake my head. "I was hoping you'd think of something. Actually, I think I know a place. You willing to drive?"

"Where exactly are we going?"

"Just trust me."

"Well, how am I supposed to know where I'm going?"

I roll my eyes. "We're going to a park."

"A park?"

"Yeah. There's one down by our apartments that Hadlee showed us a little while back."

"Alright. Let's go then."

Fifteen minutes later, we park in the lot closest to the pavilion and get out of Jared's car. Jared stands there for a moment with his hands on his hips. He takes a couple of deep breaths and nods at nothing in particular. "This is good," he says. "I need to get out more."

"We all went out this morning," I say.

"I meant get *out*." He gestures to the all of the trees surrounding us then at the pond a little farther ahead. "I need to get *out* more." He turns his head to look down at me. "You know what I mean?"

I nod. "Yeah. Follow me." We walk about twenty steps forward until we make it to the track around the pond.

"Now what?" Jared asks.

I shrug. "We walk. It's what Val and I always do."

"Oh." Jared looks almost distraught. "Well, I wouldn't want to change that."

"What do you mean?"

"It's not *our* thing." Jared gestures to the both of us. "It's *your* thing. You and Val. Does that make sense?"

"So we can't walk around in the park because Val and I usually do it?" I raise an eyebrow at him.

Jared lets out a sigh. "Sorry. You're right. I'm being confusing. Let's go." He smiles at me. I smile back, and we start to walk.

"So," I say. "I think we've talked enough about me for today. Anything you want to say?"

Jared shoves his hands into his pockets and looks up at who knows what. "I don't know. Besides you all being upset, I think my life is actually pretty uneventful right now."

"Seems like you've been hanging out with Val a lot." I shrug. I see a smile slowly spreading across Jared's face.

"Yeah." He nods. "It's nice. He's nice." Jared laughs and looks over at me for a second. "Sorry." He laughs a little more. "It's probably weird talking about your best friend like that."

I laugh and shake my head. "No worries. You should hear the way he talks about you." I see Jared's head snap toward me faster than I can blink. "What? What does he say about me?"

I smile at him and laugh. "Only the good stuff. All I really know is that he likes you. A lot."

"Oh, well, that's good." Jared smiles. He looks away from me and down at the ground as we walk. "I think I'm in love with him."

I raise my eyebrows. "Really?"

"Really. I know it's sappy or whatever, but I don't think I've ever felt this way about anyone before. Do you know what I mean?"

"I do." I nod. "That's how I feel about Grace. Never felt this way about anyone before."

"Can I ask you something?"

"Sure."

"When you mention her name, it seems like it makes Val and Hadlee uncomfortable. Why is that?"

I sigh. "No idea. Val's never really liked her. I don't know why Hadlee would get that way. I guess it's probably just because Grace can be a little intense. Or she makes things tense. If that makes any sense." Jared nods, but he doesn't say anything. I let myself keep talking. "She just comes off kind of strong. I think you'd understand if you met her."

"I think I would." Jared nods again. "But you love her?"

"I do," I say. "But seriously. We don't have to talk about me. Tell me something about you."

"What do you want to know?"

"You have any family out here?"

"I do. Almost all of them live in the state. My mom and dad live a little further south, my brother lives with them still, and my sister used to live with them too."

"Where is she now?"

I see Jared tense up. "She actually committed suicide last year." I take a deep breath.

"I'm so sorry," I tell him.

"Thank you."

"What was her name?"

"Leah."

Since I can't really think of anything to say, I tell him, "That's a beautiful name."

"It is." Jared nods. "She didn't like it, though. She always went by her middle name."

I pause for a moment. "And what was that?"

Jared smiles a little. "Valentine."

I can't help but smile too. "I like that," I say.

"Yeah." Jared sighs. "Me too."

We talk for a while after this. I learn about how Jared's always grown up here, how he's the middle child, how he doesn't have any cousins, and then it's my turn to talk. I tell him about my family. I say that I lived with my dad most of my life since my mom died when I was eight. I tell him that I'm an only child. I also tell him some stuff I haven't even really told Val about my childhood. I never really had a best friend the first twenty-one years of my life. It didn't ever bother me, but I realized how much more I enjoyed life when I had other people to enjoy it with me. Jared says that he was a bit of a loner growing up too. I don't believe it, but he tells me that it's true. He had a best friend named Nathan up until he turned sixteen. Then Nathan's parents decided to move down South to Mississippi. He tells me that he was pretty much alone after that. He says that Nathan and him had always made plans to meet up again, but Jared can't bring himself to get out of Wisconsin.

"I've been here my whole life. Never even left the state," he tells me. "I just can't leave it. It's my home." He shrugs, and I nod.

"I get that. I don't ever see myself leaving. I've been here since I was nine years old. Besides, everything I need is pretty much here. Well, every*one* I need. You know?"

Jared laughs. "Yeah. I know. Where did you live before this?"

"Utah."

"Wow. What made you come out here in the middle of nowhere?"

"When my mom died, my dad thought we should move. He didn't like being in that house anymore. But I was little, right? I didn't want to leave my friends or anything. After another year, though, I don't think my dad could take it anymore. Too many memories of her there. So he got some job across the country, and here I am. And I guess I just got so used to the state and the people that I never wanted to leave."

"I understand completely," Jared says. "I wouldn't want to leave the people here either."

"Never? Not for anything?"

"Not for anything. I wouldn't change any of this. Don't you feel the same way?"

I want to answer him, but I hesitate.

"Yeah? How was that?" Val looks over at me where I'm standing in the kitchen. I open the refrigerator and sigh. "Fun, actually. You picked a good one, Val. Jared's really great." I look past the open doors and see

Val smiling to himself. "Yeah," he says. "He is. I think I might have to tell him I love him."

I take a bottle of water out of the fridge and close the doors. "Go for it. He feels the same way."

"What the hell, Keyon? You aren't supposed to tell me if he does."

I raise an eyebrow. "I'm not?"

"No, dumbass. You're not. I'm just supposed to take the chance and figure it out on my own."

We're silent for a moment.

"Did he really tell you that?" Val says quietly. I laugh.

"He did."

"Well, fuck." Val puts his hands in the air. "Maybe I should've gone on a walk with him instead. I'm feeling a little left out, honestly."

I laugh again and walk into the living room to sit down next to Val on the couch. "What have you been doing all day?"

"Absolutely nothing. It's been amazing."

"Sounds amazing." I nod. "You want to do something later?"

"Wow. You're really putting yourself out there today, aren't you?"

"Yes, I am. What are you up for?"

"Fuck, you know what I really want?"

"What?"

"Waffle House, man."

I laugh. "Isn't that more of a morning activity?"

"Do you know nothing about the Waffle House? It's more of a three in the morning activity, if you ask me."

"Okay." I roll my eyes. "I guess I'll see you at three then."

"Wait." Val grabs on to my sleeve as I stand up. "Where are you going?"

"Oh," I say. "Grace wanted to see me." Val lets go of my sleeve and nods. I nod back at him and give him a small smile. He smiles back before waving me off.

Grace is happy to see me when I show up at her house. I tell her about my day, and she tells me about hers. She says that she met some new people at work and that she'd love for me to meet them. I, stupidly, tell her that that sounds like a wonderful idea. And the next thing I know, we're out and about looking for a dress for her to wear at the dinner party she decided to have on Saturday that morning. I sit outside of one of the dressing rooms in the store and play a game on my phone. A guy next to me laughs, and I look up.

"You here with your girlfriend or something?" he says to me.

I nod and laugh with him. "I am. I'm going to assume that's who you're with as well?" The guy rolls his eyes and smiles at me. "Her name's Macey. We're going to some dinner party on Saturday. She met some girl at work today and got invited. Crazy how fast people can become friends."

"Wow," I say. "That's coincidental. My girlfriend, Grace, is having a dinner party Saturday for the people she works with."

"Your girl work at United?"

"Yeah." I nod. "I'm gonna guess that yours does too?"

"She does." The guy holds out his hand. "Jeremy," he says. "But my friends call me Bud. Long story behind that one." I take his hand, and we shake. "Mckeyon," I tell him. "But most people just call me Keyon."

Just then, a girl, whom I'm assuming is Macey, walks out of the dressing room in front of Bud wearing a shiny silver dress.

"What do you think?" She poses for him. Bud puts two fingers in his mouth and whistles loudly.

"Stunning." He smiles at her. Macey laughs, and I can't help but smile with them. "Doesn't she look amazing?" Bud looks over at me and gestures to Macey. Unsure of what to say, I agree with him. "She does." I nod.

"Who's this?" Macey smiles at me.

"This is Keyon," Bud says. "He's dating the hostess of the dinner we're shopping for."

"Oh." Macey keeps on smiling. "Grace is amazing. You're lucky you're dating her." I nod and smile before Macey says, "Well, speak of the devil." I turn to my right and see Grace standing outside of her dressing room. I swear to God I feel my heart stop. She looks at me and smiles, tight black dress clinging to her in all the right places.

"Hey, Macey." Grace looks to her friend, then turns back to look at me. "What do you think of this one?"

I struggle to get any words to come out of my mouth. Bud laughs and stands up to walk over to me. He pats his hand on my back a few times and smiles. "Poor boy's all choked up," he says. "I think he likes the dress." I finally manage to speak and clear my throat.

"You look beautiful," I tell Grace. She gives me a smile that makes my heart speed back up.

"Do you think I need to try anything else on?" she asks me.

I shake my head no. Bud and Macey laugh. Grace just smiles at me and goes back into the dressing room. Bud whistles again and looks down at me. "Your girl's really got you excited."

"Yeah." I laugh a little. "I guess she does."

We leave the store a little while later after we say our good-byes. Grace takes me back to my apartment but grabs on to my arm before I get out of the car.

"Saturday at six, alright?"

"Alright." I smile. I kiss her lightly then smile again. She waves before she drives off. I sigh and try to hold back yet another smile.

Val and I talk for a few hours once I get back inside. Once Val decides that it's late enough, we get outside and hop into his car, taking the five-minute drive to Waffle House. Val says that he guarantees he can eat more waffles than I can. I tell him there's no way. He bets he can do five. I bet six. We shake.

Two waffles later, I'm laughing about something Val is telling me until he stops right in the middle of his story.

"You good?" I ask as I take a sip of my coffee.

"Okay, remember that guy that broke my heart, like, a month ago?"

I nod. "I remember this. Yes."

"Well, don't look now, but he just walked in."

"What is he doing here at one in the morning?" I turn around in my seat before I feel Val smack my arm.

"Keyon. What the fuck. Literally what do you not understand about 'Don't look now'?"

I shrug, but I'm already making eye contact with the guy that just walked in. He's pale, with long blond hair that reminds me of a surfer. Not Val's type at all. At least, I don't think so. He ignores my gaze and looks past me at Val.

"Fuck," Val says as he looks down. But it's too late. The guy walks over to us and smiles. Val gives him a tight-lipped smile back.

"Hey, Val," the guy says.

"Nathan," Val answers him.

Nathan turns his head to give me somewhat of a dirty look. "And you are . . . ?"

"Keyon," I tell him.

The look goes away as soon as I say this. "Oh." Nathan relaxes. "The roommate."

"Yeah," I say flatly.

"Well," Nathan looks back and forth between Val and me. "I'm not interrupting anything, am I?"

"You kind of are." Val gives him the fakest smile I've ever seen.

"Oh." Nathan raises his eyebrows and points two fingers at us. "So you two are . . . ?"

"No," Val says. "But even if we were, why would you care? We didn't exactly have a 'connection,' as you put it. Did we?" I raise my eyebrows and look up at Nathan, who is clenching his jaw. I almost laugh, but I manage to control myself.

Nathan licks his lips and looks down at the table. "Good seeing you again," he says before walking away. Val and I look at each other, then both of us burst out laughing.

"Dear god," I say. "Now I know why you two didn't work out."

"He's awful, right?" Val laughs. "Jesus. What is wrong with me? I swear he wasn't like that when I met him. I don't know what happened."

"Seriously? I can't imagine that guy being nice."

"Yeah, I can't imagine it now either."

We spend another two and a half hours at the place, talking about whatever. Val mostly talks about Jared the whole time, but I don't mind. Whatever makes him happy.

"Hey," I say.

"Yeah?"

"Do you think Grace would mind if I asked you and Jared to come to this dinner thing she's having on Saturday?"

"Dinner thing?" Val raises an eyebrow.

"Yeah. It's just for us and some people from her work. Would you be up for that?"

Val shrugs. "If Grace says it's okay, then I'd go. And I'm sure Jared would love that kind of thing."

"Alright, good. I was kind of freaking out about having to go to a party where I don't know anyone."

"Isn't that kind of why you broke up, though?"

"What do you mean?"

Val sighs. "You know when you were at the bar downtown together except she invited, like, all of her friends? Didn't you guys break up right after that?"

"We did." I nod. "Which is exactly why I need people there that I really know. I'm awkward around people. You know that."

"That's true. I do know that. Remember how awkward you were when we first met?" Val laughs.

I laugh too and bring my hands up to my face. "God, no. Don't even talk about it. That was horrible."

"You spilled your coffee all fucking over me. Then you asked me to buy you a new one. Who does that?"

"Um, *you* ran into me." I smile.

"Pretty sure you're the one that ran into me."

I roll my eyes. "Whatever." We keep talking until I finally decide that it's four in the morning, and that's way too late for us to be out, especially since we both have class tomorrow. Val agrees, and we head back to his car.

"This was fun," he says.

"Yeah. We haven't been doing this a lot lately."

We don't really talk to each other on the way back to the apartment. It doesn't bother me since I've been doing a lot of talking today. I've probably done more today than I have in the past week and a half. When we get back inside, Val claims the bathroom, and I lock myself in my room. It's the first time I've been alone all day, and for once, I'm happy to be by myself. This only lasts for about an hour.

I have a dream that Val is badly injured. I'm at some restaurant with my mom, and I keep trying to tell her that we need to go help him, but she won't listen to me. I try to figure out where Val is, but everyone is ignoring me. Val keeps texting me, saying that he knew this was going to happen. He knew he was going to get hurt. Once I finally find him, he's at home in his room. He tells me that I can't help him and that I'd be better off just forgetting about him. I tell him that I can't do that, but he isn't listening to me. He says he knows he's going to die. He also knows that there's nothing that I can do for him. Then things get a hell of a lot crazier. I tell him that if he's going to die, then so am I. The kitchen knife that I've seen Val hold before is now in my hand. Val tells me that he'll die if it means we can do it together. He tells me to kill him. So I do. But when I try to do the same to myself, it doesn't work. I'm stuck here. Without him. And then I wake up screaming.

I don't have to knock on the wall to get Val's attention. I can hear him trying to open my door then looking around for a key. Once he gets my door open, he kneels beside my bed and holds on to my arm, because I won't take my hands away from my face. I'm sobbing, and I can't stop. He can't see me like this. He heard me screaming; I can only imagine that he was thinking about what had happened with Quinn.

"I'm okay," I whisper once I've calmed down a little.

"It really doesn't seem like you are," Val says.

I choke back a sob and shake my head.

"You're right." I put my hands in my lap. "I'm really not."

I start to cry again, and Val walks over to the other side of my bed. He sits beside me, and for some reason, I put my arms around him. Val is surprised at first, but he reciprocates. I cry onto his shoulder for who knows how long. After I've finally quieted myself down, Val asks me what it was about.

"You," I say.

"Me? What about me?"

"I killed you. You were dying, and you told me to help you. So I killed you. I don't know what's wrong with me. I don't know why I would even—"

I'm starting to get worked up again, and Val can tell. He tightens his grip on me and sighs. I don't know why this dream is getting to me. I know it wasn't real. I know it didn't actually happen. I know it could never happen. So why am I acting this way? I try to focus on something else. Anything else. But all there is to listen to are my cries and Val's unsteady breathing. I pull my head off his shoulder and look up at him.

"Jesus, don't tell me I made you cry."

Val laughs and wipes underneath his eyes. "No. You didn't. It's alright."

"So you mean to tell me you're not crying? You didn't just wipe away your tears?"

"Shut up." Val smiles and looks down at his hands. "You've just got me worried. That's all."

I sigh. "I didn't mean for that to happen."

"Seriously. It's alright."

"I'm sorry."

"Mckeyon," Val says seriously. "You don't need to apologize for this. It's not something you can help."

I nod once. "You're right." We sit there for a little while longer until I pick up my phone off my nightstand.

"It's six," I say. Val yawns.

"Seriously?"

"Seriously. You've got class in a few hours."

Val swallows and rubs his hands together a few times. "I don't care how much sleep I'm going to get. I'm staying with you until I know you're alright."

I smile a little. "Thank you," I say quietly. "But you really don't have to do that. I'm fine. It was just a dream."

"I'm glad you know that." Val nods. "You're not worried about me, are you?"

"What?"

"You had a dream that I was dying and that you killed me. Are you worried that something's going to happen to me?"

I shrug. "A little. I mean, I guess it's just with everything that's been going on, I kind of have to worry."

"I'm not going anywhere," Val says sincerely.

I nod. "I know that."

It's Saturday night, and I'm trying to figure out how on Earth I'm supposed to get my hair to look nice. I finally just give up and decide that my hair's going to do what it's going to do, and I walk out into the hall to see Val.

"Wow," I say. "You look nice."

Val smiles at me and finishes buttoning his shirt. "Thank you. So do you. Your hair looks good."

I roll my eyes and walk over to the closet by the front door. I take out the best pair of shoes that I own and put them on. I roll up the sleeves of my shirt a little and take a deep breath.

"Okay," I say to Val. "I'm officially ready. Thoughts?" I turn around in circle and raise my eyebrows. Val nods approvingly. "Nice," he says. "And me?"

"Flawless as always." I smile. Val smiles back and grabs his coat off the chair in our living room. As soon as he does, there's a knock at the door. Even though I'm closest to the door, Val says, "Got it." I hold up my hands and move out of the way. Val opens the door, and I see Jared standing outside. He smiles as soon as he sees Val.

"You look amazing," he says.

"So do you." Val smiles back at him. Jared pulls Val closer to him before they kiss. I gag a little bit and turn my head. Doesn't matter who it is, PDA just isn't for me.

Jared steps inside and gives me a little wave. "Hey, Keyon." He smiles. I smile back and put my hands in my pockets. "You two ready to go?"

"As ready as I'll ever be." Val rolls his eyes as we walk out the door. Jared smacks his arm before holding his hand.

We're the first ones to Grace's party since Grace told us to get there early. I kiss her before we get inside, and I see Val make a gagging motion to Jared. We are one and the same.

"Tasha and Alexis have been helping me cook for almost four hours," Grace says as she leads us into the house. She turns around to look at us. "Did you know cooking for fourteen people is expensive?"

"I would assume so." I smile at her, then I face-palm. "Oh, Grace. I completely forgot." I turn to the side and hold out my hand. "This is Jared."

Jared does that incredible thing where he smiles so brightly it could probably blind all of us. He holds out his hand, and Grace takes it. "I've heard a lot of good things." Jared keeps smiling.

Grace smiles back and shakes his hand. "So have I," she says. She lets go of Jared's hand and looks at Val. "Always nice to see you." She smiles again.

"You too," Val says.

I see Tasha in the kitchen carrying a plate of cookies over Alexis's head, while Alexis takes something out of the oven.

"Keyon?" Tasha puts the cookies down and walks over to where we're standing. "Wow." She laughs. "I feel like I haven't seen you in forever."

"That's because you haven't." I smile. She hugs me, and I awkwardly hug her back. As soon as we let each other go, the doorbell rings. Grace sighs and looks at her phone.

"I guess someone else thought it'd be a great idea to show up a half an hour early," she says. I smile at her sympathetically, and she gives me a small smile back before walking to the door. I hear her greet whomever is at the door before Jared says something about how he loves meeting new people. I shake my head, while Val says he completely understands.

Grace walks back over to us a minute later, two people trailing behind her.

"These are the people I was telling you about." Grace smiles as she walks up to us.

"Keyon, Val, Jared, Tasha, this is Tyler." She gestures to a guy who looks extremely happy to be here. "And Ailene." She then gestures to a girl who looks equally excited. We say hello and have a few minutes of small talk, AKA my least favorite thing in the world. Only because I'm so horrible at it. Thankfully, we have Jared here to do all the socializing for us.

After an hour, I'm pretty sure that everyone is here. We meet Danielle and Eva, which scares me a little since they both blatantly flirt with me for a good fifteen minutes before I finally remind them that I'm dating Grace. Macey and Bud are here, and we say our hellos. It's actually somewhat pleasant for a little while. And then *he* shows up. The doorbell rings again, and Grace hurries to welcome whomever is outside.

"Jesus fucking Christ," Val says.

"What?" I turn around to face the door, only to find that Nathan is standing there.

"God." Val puts a hand to his forehead. "Where's Jared? I need to show this fucker I found someone better than him."

"I think he's with Alexis, getting some things from the garage," I say as I stand up to walk over to Grace.

"Oh, Keyon, this is Nathan." She smiles.

"I know," I say dryly. "We've met."

Nathan gives me a cold smile. Grace looks back and forth between the two of us until she realizes that we aren't exactly the best of friends. She nods and grabs on to Nathan's arm.

"Why don't I introduce you to everyone else?" she asks him. Nathan nods but never looks away from me. They walk off, and I head back over to Val.

"I can't believe she knows him," I whisper.

"I can't believe anyone would *want* to know him." Val rolls his eyes. The door to the garage swings open, and Alexis and Jared walk in carrying two packages of water bottles. They set them down, and Jared walks over to where Val and I are standing.

"Everything good?" He raises an eyebrow.

"No," Val says. "My ex is here."

"Oh no." Jared sighs. "Which one?"

"The last one. The one I told you about."

Jared nods in understanding and looks around the room. "Right. I'll make sure he stays away—" He stops midsentence with his mouth still partly open. Val looks at me and raises an eyebrow. I shrug and look back at Jared. Then I see that Nathan and Jared have made eye contact.

"No way," Nathan says as he starts to smile. "Jared?"

"Nathan?" Jared walks over to where Nathan is standing. "Oh my god, I can't believe it." They look each other up and down before hugging tightly. Val leans his head toward me and whispers, "What. The. Actual. Fuck."

It isn't until then that I remember Jared's story about his old best friend, Nathan. There's no way that could be the same guy he was talking about.

"Where the hell have you been?" Jared asks Nathan, smiling.

"I got back about a month ago." Nathan smiles even wider. "I wanted to call or something, I swear. I guess I just thought it'd be too weird after all these years."

They laugh together before hugging again. I look down at Val and see that he doesn't look angry; he just looks hurt.

"Didn't know they were friends," he says.

I nod. I don't tell him that I might have known about this for a while. After a few minutes of Val and I complaining quietly to each other, it seems that Jared has finally remembered he has a boyfriend. He walks Nathan over to us and introduces him.

"We know each other," Val says plainly.

"Oh," Jared says. Then I see his eyes widen. He knows who Nathan is to Val. Thankfully, the guy Tyler, from earlier, walks over to Nathan and tells him to come talk to him and his girlfriend. Nathan says he will and follows Tyler through the kitchen. Jared gives Val a nervous look.

"Val, I had no idea he was even going to be here."

Val holds up a hand. "It's alright. I just didn't know you guys were friends." Jared gives me the same nervous look before glancing back down at Val. "Yeah," he says. "I haven't seen him in years, though."

Val nods.

"You know what?" Jared looks back at Nathan then turns around to face Val again. "If you don't want me to talk to him, then

I won't. I know what he did to you. He hurt you. That's enough for me to stay away from him."

Val sighs. "You don't have to do that. If you guys were close, then I'd understand—"

"We *were* close. We aren't anymore. I don't have to talk to him."

I put my hand on Val's shoulder as he looks up at me. "I'll give you guys a minute," I tell him before walking over to where Grace is.

Grace and I talk to Danielle and Eva for a while before Alexis says that dinner is served. I sit next to Val and Grace, with Nathan right in front of me. I guess that Val and Jared have decided that it's okay for Jared to talk to Nathan, since they're the ones making up most of the conversation at the table. Val looks a little annoyed, but I see him smile and laugh at what everyone's saying. Something that bothers me all night, though, is that I can't make myself dislike Nathan. He's just as charismatic as Jared is. I can see why they were close for so long.

Val notices that my laughs and smiles are real, and I can tell that he's actually getting upset. Especially when he says he needs a minute and goes outside through the front door. Grace holds my hand under the table and leans closer to me.

"Is he alright?"

I shrug. "No idea. He used to date Nathan. I think that's the problem." Grace's eyes widen, and she nods. She looks over to where Nathan and Jared are laughing about something together. The girl from earlier, Danielle, laughs at it too and asks, "How long have you two known each other?"

Nathan smiles and looks at Jared. "Well, if you count the years we were apart, basically all our lives."

"How long has it been since you guys have seen each other?" Danielle looks amused.

"What, like, ten years?" Jared says.

"Wow." The other girl, Eva, laughs. "I'm surprised you can still remember what the other looks like."

Nathan laughs then looks back at Jared. "Yeah, well, he has a face I don't think I could ever forget." Jared smiles at him, and I take a deep breath before putting my hand on his arm.

"I'm going to go find Val," I say. Jared looks concerned as he looks at the empty seat next to him.

"Oh," he says. "I didn't even notice he was gone. Do you want me to come with you?"

"No." I shake my head. "I'll get him back." Jared smiles at me, and I stand up. Grace tells me to be quick, and I nod at her.

I make it outside to find Val sitting on the steps outside the house. I sit down next to him and sigh. "You alright?"

Val sighs too. "No. I can't believe they're fucking friends. I get that they haven't seen each other in a long time or whatever, but I am so jealous it's not even fucking funny."

"Yeah." I nod. "I'd be jealous too."

Val scoffs. "I don't know about that. You seem to like him."

"I don't," I say. "I know how much you hate him. I know what he did. I'm not going to like him, okay?"

"Whatever." Val shakes his head. "You can have your own opinions. You know I do."

"You're right. But still. I can't like someone who hurt my best friend like that."

Val laughs. "Careful, Keyon. Getting a little emotional here."

"Sorry." I laugh too. "But it's true."

"I just can't believe Jared is acting like he knows nothing. Like he doesn't know what happened between us. Shouldn't that mean something to him? That Nathan really fucked me up?"

I shrug. "I think it should. But you've got to remember, they were best friends for a long time."

"Yeah," Val says. "Like Jared said earlier. They *were*. They aren't anymore. So I don't know why he's acting like they're still close."

"Maybe it's just because they haven't seen each other in so long."

"How long has it been?"

"Ten years."

"Jesus." Val puts his head in his hand. "They haven't seen each other in ten years and yet Nathan still seems closer to him than I am. What the hell am I supposed to do?"

"Maybe you should talk to him."

"Which one?"

I roll my eyes. "Why would I tell you to talk to Nathan? Go talk to Jared about it." I pull my phone out of my pocket and look at the time. "It's getting late. I'm sure Grace won't mind if you two leave."

"You're right." Val nods. A moment later, the front door opens, and Jared walks outside.

"Hey." He smiles at Val. Val looks at me and raises his eyebrows. I nod at him and stand up. I look at Jared before I go back inside. "Want me to tell Grace anything?"

"Tell her dinner was amazing and that we loved being here." Jared gives me a small smile. I give him one in return and head back inside. It looks like the party is about over, so I don't sit down. Grace walks over to me, and I put an arm around her waist.

"Everything okay?" she asks me.

I nod and smile. "Everything's great." We talk for a little while longer then say our good-byes. I stay with Grace until everyone is gone. I even politely shake Nathan's hand before he heads out. I stay at Grace's place for a little longer, but eventually, I get tired and tell her I should probably get back home. She kisses me and says we need to be alone more often. I tell her I was just thinking the same thing. She drives me home and tells me she'll see me soon.

When I get back inside, Val isn't here. I don't worry about it too much and assume that he's still with Jared. I'm so tired that the second I lie down on my bed, I fall asleep immediately. I don't hear Val get back home until the next morning. The door to the apartment creaks open, and I can tell that Val is trying not to wake me up. But he's too late; I'm already up. I walk out into the hall to see him fixing his hair in the mirror by our front door.

"Hey," I say as I walk over to him.

"Jesus, you scared me," he says. "I didn't know you were up."

I smile at him. "So where were you last night?" I can tell that he's holding back a smile, but he doesn't say anything. He walks right past me and says, "Shut the fuck up, Keyon. You know where I was." I laugh and shake my head as I follow him into the kitchen. Val takes two water bottles out of the fridge and hands one to me. I sit down at the kitchen table and crack it open. Val sits in front of me and does the same.

"Was it fun?" I ask before I take a drink. Val shakes his head and does that thing where he tries not to smile at me.

"We are not having this conversation," he says. I hold up a hand in defense.

"Trust me, I don't want to have this conversation."

"What'd you do after we left?"

"Nothing really. We talked for a little while, but that was about it. Nothing too exciting that you missed out on."

"Did you talk to Nathan?"

I raise an eyebrow. "Talk to him about what?"

"I don't know." Val shrugs. "Anything I guess."

"Well, I guess we did talk a little bit. As a group. Not one-on-one. I didn't want to talk to him like that."

"Yeah." Val leans back in his chair. "I know how that feels."

"Is Jared going to keep talking to him?"

Val sighs. "I have no idea. I said it was up to him, and I think that's what we agreed on. So I don't know. I hope he doesn't, but I wouldn't be bothered if he did. You know?"

"It wouldn't bother you?" I stand up and walk over to the counter.

"I don't think it would."

I plug in our Keurig and motion to it, asking Val if he wants anything. He shakes his head no, and I make myself something.

"Well, I don't know about that," I say, waiting for my coffee to be made. "You kind of seemed bothered last night."

"That's just because I'm a jealous little bitch. Besides, Jared understood when we talked about it. He told me Nathan really doesn't mean anything to him anymore."

I pick up my coffee and nod my head. "That's good. I'm glad he put your feelings first." Val nods. "We talked about something else too."

"What?"

"Quinn and Erica. We think we may have found a way they were connected."

I set down my coffee and sigh. "What'd you come up with?" I don't want to talk about this, but it seems like Val does, especially if he talked about it with Jared. I feel like Val's breaking his own rule. Don't talk about the murders.

"Jared knew Quinn."

"He did?"

"Yeah. They were friends. He said that when he found out she was dead, he thought she had killed herself."

I'm confused. "Why would he think that?"

"He told me she was suicidal. That she'd done something like that before. Remind you of anyone?"

My heart almost stops beating. Val couldn't know what really happened with Erica, could he?

"No," I say.

"You don't have to lie, you know. Hadlee told me about Erica and what she said to you." He sighs. "It wasn't your fault. You know that, right?"

I walk over to the table and sit down. "Yeah. I know that."

"Doesn't seem like you do." Val takes a sip of his water.

"I do, alright? I get that it wasn't my fault. I just really didn't want us to ever have to talk about this."

"Why not?"

"Because I lied to you." I laugh a little. "I shouldn't be lying to you. About anything."

"No." Val shakes his head. "You shouldn't. But it's fine. It's not like I'm mad."

"Yeah."

We're silent for a minute.

"Why did you think that makes a connection with them?" I ask.

"They're both suicidal, then after something bad happens to them, which makes their thoughts even worse, they die? Doesn't that seem kind of coincidental?"

"What? What do you mean something bad happened to them?"

Val shrugs. "You know, Quinn with her fiancé. Erica with her university or whatever."

"I told you I haven't seen her since last year."

"Oh, yeah. Well, she applied somewhere out of state to transfer, but she didn't get in or something. I talked to her about it for a little while the last time I saw her." Val pauses. "I mean, second to last time I saw her, I guess."

"Oh," I say.

"But yeah. Jared and I both thought that was unusual."

"So you're saying that whoever did this was basically trying to put them out of their misery?"

"Who knows," Val says. "Sounds plausible."

"I guess it does." I nod. "Why were you guys talking about that?"

"I don't know." Val looks up at the ceiling. "It was a bad night for me. Thought I might as well talk to someone about what's been bothering me. You know?"

"Yeah. I know. But I thought you said not to talk about the murders?"

"I only said that to you. I know you don't like talking about them."

"So it wasn't for you, it was for me?"

Val nods. "Basically."

"You really do not have to do that. We can talk about whatever's on your mind," I say.

"Really, Keyon. It's alright. I've talked about it enough for now. I'm fine."

He stands up from the table and walks down the hall into his room without another word. He said he's fine. So why am I so worried?

— • —

I'm going on a walk by myself a few days later when I see Nathan on a bench at the park Val and I always go to. I don't even think about what I'm doing. I go over to where he's sitting and stand in front of him. At first, I don't think he knows who I am. And then I see a wave of sudden realization rush over him.

"Keyon," he says. "What are you doing out here?"

"Why are you talking to me like everything's okay?"

Nathan raises an eyebrow at me. "What do you mean? You came up to me. And after the other night. I thought—"

"You thought what? Thought that just because we were acting friendly towards you that we were alright with you being there?"

Nathan holds up his hands. "Whoa. Who's we?"

"Val and I?"

"Why would you have a problem with me? I could understand Valentine not wanting to see me, but not you. We hardly know each other."

"Because of what you did to Val. Then you just come in and start talking to Jared like you didn't completely screw over the person he's in love with."

Nathan laughs at this. "Jared isn't in love with Valentine." I glare at him.

"Like you would know."

"I do know." Nathan smiles. "He told me last night."

I stare at him. "What are you talking about?" Nathan leans back and tilts his head to the right, still smiling at me. "Jared came over last night. Told me all about him and Valentine."

"Alright, but what does that mean?"

Nathan laughs again and shakes his head. "You know what? I don't need to have this talk with you. How about this, you don't say anything to Val, and we wait for him to find out on his own what Jared's doing. Yeah?"

"No," I scoff as I walk away. Nathan calls out at me, but I can't hear what he says. I walk back to the apartment as quickly as I can and knock on Val's bedroom door. He opens the door and rubs his eyes sleepily.

"Dude, it's like ten in the fucking morning."

"Yeah. I know. Where was Jared last night?"

"His place. Why?"

"Are you sure about that?"

Val gives me a quizzical look. "What do you mean?"

"I ran into Nathan, like, ten minutes ago," I say.

"What the hell? What did he say?"

"He said Jared was over at *his* place last night."

Val blinks a couple of times. "He was at Nathan's?"

"That's what Nathan told me."

"Jared wouldn't lie to me," Val says as he shakes his head. "He told me he was home."

"Alright. Good. I just got a little worried. I don't know. It's whatever." I turn around to go to my room, but Val grabs on to my sleeve before I can get away. "Worried because Nathan told you a blatant lie?" He raises his eyebrows.

"It's not just that." I sigh. "He said something about Jared not being in love with you."

"He what?"

"I don't know. That's just what he told me. I wouldn't believe any of it, but he told me not to tell—"

"Fuck," Val says as he runs his fingers through his hair.

"What?"

"He's doing what he does best."

I raise an eyebrow. "And what's that?" Val sighs before he says, "Come on." He grabs my wrist and pulls me out into the living room. We sit down on the couch, and he sighs again.

"Before I was with Nathan, I was dating this guy Matt, right?"

I nod.

"Well," Val continues, "I met Nathan about two months into Matt and I's relationship, and Nathan and Matt hit it off pretty quick. They became, like, really close friends. And then Nathan started telling me all kinds of things about Matt and what he was saying about me. He basically just convinced me to break up with him. So I did. And then I was dating Nathan. Now he's doing the same fucking thing except he's telling you because he knows he can't tell me."

I sigh. "He wouldn't have even told me anything had I not walked up to him."

"You walked up to *him?* Why?"

"I don't know." I shake my head. "Kind of felt like I needed to go off on him."

Val smiles. "I think I would've paid to see you go off on him. Or anyone, really."

"It wasn't that amazing." I smile a little myself. "I didn't really go off on him at all."

"Still," Val says. "God, you know what? I don't care. I don't fucking care. Nathan can say whatever the hell he wants about Jared, but I'm not believing any of it." As soon as Val says this, his phone goes off. He picks it up, reads whatever is on the screen, then drops the phone on the floor dramatically.

"What was it?" I ask.

"Jared asked if I would be mad if he lied to me."

I press my lips together. "Well, maybe he isn't talking about what we think he's talking about."

"Yeah," Val says as he picks up his phone. "I really hope not. What do I say?"

"I don't know. Would you be mad?"

"A little."

"Then say that." I shrug.

Val types out the message and leans forward on the couch. We wait about thirty seconds until his phone buzzes again.

"He says I'm probably going to be pissed at him then."

"Well." I take a deep breath. "That doesn't sound good."

"No. It doesn't."

He types something else, and then we wait about a minute.

"I guess Nathan wasn't lying," Val says quietly. "They actually were together last night."

"That doesn't mean that anything else he said was true."

"Yeah," Val says. "Hang on. I think I need to actually call Jared."

He stands up and walks out of the room and down the hall. I stay on the couch and think about how idiotic I am. Why had I even tried to talk to Nathan? What was wrong with me? I guess Nathan was right when he said Val would find out eventually, but I didn't want any of what he said to be true. But now there was a chance that it might be.

I decide that I don't want to sit around by myself, so I text Hadlee. We make a plan to meet up at her place in an hour since her sister won't be there. I lean back on the couch and start to think about death. Again. Jesus, I have problems. Feeling like I'm about to cry, I pull on my shoes and head outside. I take a seat on the steps outside of the building and take a deep breath. I think for a second that I hear Quinn's voice, and I turn around. But of course, I don't see her. I feel like I'm going absolutely insane.

I stay out here for an hour, and then I remember I should be at Hadlee's by now. Maybe I could just call and cancel. I decide against it and stand up to make my way to Hadlee's. I get there in about ten minutes, apologize for being late, and walk into her tiny apartment. I always wonder how two people can live here and have parties when it's even smaller than where Val and I are living. Hadlee makes some kind of tea for us, and I'm reminded of my unemployment. Now I'm even more stressed out. Wonderful. We sit on her couch, and I tell her about everything that's happened the last two days. I talk about Grace's party, meeting Nathan and then confronting him, Jared and Val, and the murders.

"I seriously think you need a day off," she tells me.

"I don't know if I could ever get a day off from any of this." I laugh. "All this drama just kind of follows me around."

"It does seem that way," Hadlee says as she takes a sip of her tea. "You do seem very, very stressed."

"I think that's because I am. More or less about other people. Not so much myself. Does that make any sense?"

"I think it does. I know you always tend to put others before yourself. Especially people like Val and Grace."

"Two of the three people that really matter in my life."

Hadlee smiles. "I'm hoping I'm the third person?"

"Of course." I smile back at her. "You know, I've been kind of worried about you."

Hadlee raises an eyebrow. "About me?"

"Yeah. You don't seem like yourself lately."

"I don't?"

"No. You're usually much more energetic. You seem kind of low."

She shrugs. "I don't know. I guess it has been sort of hard lately with everything that's been going on with you. I think we're alike in that way. We care a lot more about others than we do about ourselves." She smiles.

"You don't have to worry so much about me," I shove her lightly. She shoves me back and laughs.

"Well, *you* don't have to worry so much about *me*."

I shrug. "I can't help it. I keep thinking about you two and getting all upset for no reason."

"By you two do you mean Val and I?"

"Of course."

"Both of us are fine, Keyon. You don't have to worry about Val and Jared's theory or whatever."

"Their theory?"

Hadlee nods. "You know, the suicide thing. With the murders. You don't have to worry that it's true. Or that either of us are feeling that way." She sets down her drink and takes my hand in hers. "I promise you we're both okay."

I can't help it; I start to laugh. "This is so weird. I'm not used to having touchy-feely conversations like this. Val never lets me do that with him."

"Have you met Val?" Hadlee laughs too. "He's not really 'touchy-feely,' as you put it."

"You're right. He really isn't. I'm glad at least one of my friends are."

"Yeah." Hadlee nods. "Me too."

We change subjects and talk about things that don't make me want to cry and scream. I try to relax, but I can't help but feel tense the whole time I'm at Hadlee's. I think that's what makes her so hard to talk to sometimes. She can make you feel so high-strung. Like if you say the wrong thing, something bad will happen. I'm not entirely sure how to explain it. I've talked to Hadlee about this before, and she says she understands.

"Are Jared and Val alright? Has Val said anything to you?" Hadlee asks after a while.

"He texted me a little bit ago to say that they're alright. Why?"

"I was thinking the four of us could do something again. I think it's nice when we all get together. Don't you?"

"Yeah." I nod. "I do. What did you have in mind?"

"Maybe just go out for dinner? Someplace nice?"

"Sounds good to me," I say.

"You know"—Hadlee sighs—"you can bring Grace if you want."

I shake my head. "I don't want to bother you guys."

"She's your girlfriend, Keyon. Why should it matter if she's with us? Val brings Jared."

"That's different. You all like Jared. I don't think you or Val ever really liked Grace."

"I've never said that." Hadlee gives me these big doe eyes that make me want to cry.

"Yeah." I look down at my hands. "But still. If you like hanging out with just the four of us, that's fine with me. I understand."

Hadlee nods, and we continue on with conversation. But for some reason, my mind keeps going back to Quinn and Erica. I thought I had succeeded in pushing them out of my thoughts, but I was wrong. God, was I wrong.

———————•••———————

We decide that we're going to meet at this little Italian restaurant downtown on Friday. Jared and I are the first ones to arrive, and he greets me with that same bright smile I've seen on him so many times.

"Val isn't with you?" he asks me.

I shake my head. "He's got work until six. He's going to be a little late. So is Hadlee. Looks like it's just the two of us for a little while." I smile. Jared laughs and says that he's already gotten us a table. I follow him to a round table in the back corner of the main space of the restaurant. We have a couple minutes of small talk until Jared decides to get deep with me.

"I was reading something this morning on euthanasia," he says. Surprised by the randomness of his comment, I raise my eyebrows.

"What?"

"Do you know what that is?" Jared looks up from his drink at me.

"Isn't it what they do to people who are dying? Or going to die? Like, mercy killing?"

Jared nods. "Exactly. Mercy killing. I don't know what made me think of this. I just remembered a bunch of people on the Internet were arguing over the morality of it all. What do you think?"

"Wow," I say. "You're asking some hard questions."

Jared laughs a little and shakes his head. "You don't have to answer."

"No, it's alright. I don't know, though. I don't think it's right to kill anyone. Definitely one of the worst things a person can do. Even if the other person asks for it."

Jared tilts his head to the side. "You think?"

I nod once.

"Hm," Jared says.

"Why?" I raise an eyebrow. "What do you think?"

"I think that it's a good thing to show mercy." He stares at me. "*Especially* if the other person asks for it." He looks at me in a way that makes me feel like he's analyzing me. I see something in his eyes that I can't explain. For the first time, I feel uncomfortable around him.

"If someone's in that much pain," he continues. "If they're in so much pain that they actually want to die, I think it's the right thing to end their suffering."

I'm silent for a moment until I say, "What?" But before Jared can say anything else, he looks away and over at Val and Hadlee, who are walking to our table.

"Hi." Val smiles as soon as he sees Jared. Jared smiles up at him, and they kiss. Hadlee looks at me and rolls her eyes, but she's smiling. I force a smile back at her.

The rest of the night I try to focus on our conversations, but what Jared said keeps coming back up in my thoughts. Why would he want to talk about something like that? And why did it sound so suspiciously like what Val and his theory for the murders was? I decide that I'm going to tell Val about what Jared said when we get back home. The end of this night couldn't come soon enough. I keep up with what everyone is talking about. I laugh, I make jokes, I smile at the right moments, but for some reason, it still doesn't feel right. I feel like I've just uncovered something crucial to solving this puzzle, but I can't understand why.

When we all finally decide that we're done, Val drives us home, and I can't even wait for him to take off his coat before I start talking.

"Jared honestly scared the fuck out of me tonight," I say.

Val takes a step back in surprise. "Whoa. What does that mean?"

"You know how we were talking about that whole thing about suicide and the murders or whatever?"

"Yeah?"

"Well, you know how I said it was basically like the killer was trying to put them out of their misery or something?"

Val raises his eyebrows. "Where are you going with this?"

"Jared was telling me about fucking euthanasia or something, and he said that he thought mercy was a good thing. Then he said if someone was in a lot of pain and they were suffering, then killing them would be the right thing to do. Doesn't that freak you the hell out?"

Val stares at me for a few seconds before he bursts out laughing. "It kind of sounds like you're accusing my boyfriend of being a murderer."

I hold my hands up in the air.

"You're fucking kidding me," Val says, keeping a smile. "Seriously. Tell me you're kidding. I can't tell if you're being serious or not."

I laugh a little. "Why on earth would I make something like that up?" Val gives me a look like he can't believe what I'm saying.

"You think Jared is a serial killer," he says flatly.

"Well." I scratch the back of my head. I'm beginning to realize how stupid I sound.

"Look, Keyon." Val gets a few steps closer to me and puts a hand on my shoulder. "I get that you're scared. And I want to know who did this just as much as you do. But I think you need to just take some time and think things through. Get your head straight."

I push his hand off me and walk past him. "You don't have to talk to me like I'm a child."

"Keyon," Val calls out after me, but I'm already in my room behind a locked door. I sit down on my bed and tell myself I'm not going to cry. Not anymore. Not over anything. I'm not sad. I'm angry. I'm angry at whoever did this. I'm angry that Val doesn't believe me. Which makes no sense because I don't even believe me. I take out my phone and call Grace. I tell her everything that's on my mind, and she tells me the exact same thing Val did. That I need to think things through. That I'm not even thinking clearly. That I'm grieving, and I need some more time to process things. That my mind is just trying to make any connections it can so that I have someone to blame. I tell her that she's right and that I love her. Of course, she loves me too, and we hang up. And then I do something stupid. I scream.

Val knocks on my door extremely violently, but I don't open it. A minute later, I assume Val has used a key because he's standing in front of me, asking me what's wrong. But I can't answer him. I don't know what's wrong. I tell him this, and I feel like I can see him hurting. I can't stand that I'm making him upset, so I tell him to leave me alone. He says no. I tell him I don't want him here, and he just shakes his head.

"Jesus Christ, Valentine," I say. I can't tell if I'm crying or screaming. Maybe both. "I already told you I don't know what's wrong. And I know I'm making you upset, so can you *please* leave before I make it worse for you?"

Val shakes his head again. "You're not making anything worse for me." I stare down at the ground and look at my feet. Val lowers his head so that he can almost look me in the eye.

"Seriously," he says. "You're not. And it's okay if you don't know what's wrong. Sometimes it's nothing. Sometimes it's everything. I understand."

I look up at him and sigh. "Yeah," I say as I wipe underneath my eyes with my sleeve. Val looks me up and down and takes a deep breath.

"You alright?" he asks me.

I nod. I can't bring myself to say anything to him. There's no way that I can be sure that I won't start crying again.

"Sorry," I finally say.

"For what?"

"I know you hate talking like this. You know, being serious and everything."

Val looks at me, but I can't figure out what he's thinking. "I can be serious when I know I need to be."

I laugh. "You'd do that for me?"

"Of course." Val smiles. "Now, can I sleep? You've kind of been keeping me up."

I shake my head and smile. "Yeah. Go for it. I think sleep would be a good thing."

Val gives me one last small smile before leaving my room and closing the door behind him. I stare at the closed door for a moment before collapsing onto my bed and drifting off into a place where I'm finally free from everything.

On Monday, I go to class. Grace comes over for a few hours. Val and I have a late lunch together. We grocery shop. I finish most of my assignments. I have a normal day. But none of that makes it normal. What makes it normal is that neither Quinn nor Erica cross my mind the entire day. I don't think about Jared either. Val doesn't even mention his name. Then I start to think of what happened Friday night. It concerns me a little that none of the other apartment dwellers have said anything about the screaming that seems to be happening constantly now because of me. Maybe they're just worried it'll be another incident like what happened with Quinn. Maybe they just don't want to be involved. Whatever the case, I'm just glad that they're leaving me alone. I can only imagine that if Quinn had been alright when we went to her apartment that she'd be uncomfortable with all these people asking if she was okay. I know I would be.

I'm going on a walk by myself at around eight that night when I run into someone I've run into out here before. But this time, he comes up to me first.

"Hey, I need to talk to you," Nathan says as he jogs over to me.

"You need to talk to me?" I laugh a little and quicken my pace. "Did you know I'd be here or something?"

"Lucky guess." Nathan shrugs. "But for real. I need to talk to you about Valentine."

I roll my eyes. "Yeah, okay. Because I care about what you have to say."

"Keyon, come on." Nathan struggles to keep up with me. "This is serious. I talked to him on Sunday, and he told me something I think you should be worried about."

I stop walking. "You saw him on Sunday?"

"Yeah. And he said—"

"You know what? I don't really care." I start walking again, and Nathan sighs loudly.

"Dude, seriously. I wouldn't be out here waiting for you if I didn't have something important to say to you."

"So you knew I was going to be here then?"

Nathan shakes his head. "I didn't know, alright? I just need to tell you what he told me."

"Val and I are closer than you might think. Whatever you're about to tell me, I probably already know."

"Then let me say it. No harm done if you already know."

I slow down and then stop moving. "Fine. What?"

"Can we sit?" Nathan gestures to a bench to the left of us. I shake my head no. He holds up his hands and says, "Okay. Fine. Yeah. We'll stand."

I roll my eyes and wait for him to start talking.

"I told him I wanted to see him so that I could try and fix things, you know?" I cringe at him using a phrase that I associate with Val. I nod.

"Well," Nathan continues, "he said he'd give me a chance to talk to him nicely. But I guess things didn't go as well as he thought they did, because he said that lately I'm making him feel the way he used to feel."

"And what does that mean?"

"Do you remember when he was really depressed?"

I raise an eyebrow. "No?"

"He took medication and everything. He didn't tell you about that?" I can see Nathan's stupid mouth curling up at the corners. He's happy that he knows something I don't. I don't want him to think he's better than me, so I play along.

"Oh," I say. "That. Yeah. I remember that. What about it?"

Nathan's subtle smile fades as he continues. "Well, that's what he meant when he said he was feeling the way he used to. Wanting to kill himself or whatever."

This shocks me, but I don't let myself show my surprise. "He's already told me about that," I lie. "But thanks for trying to help him out." I turn around and start to walk back to the edge of the park. I half-expect Nathan to follow me, but he doesn't. I'm still a little unnerved that it really seemed like he knew where I was going to be and when I was going to be there. Then I start to panic. Finally understanding what Nathan has just told me, I start to walk a little faster.

Hadlee had told me that neither she nor Val were feeling this way. Had she known Val had been thinking things like that? She must not have known. Otherwise, she would've told me. She wouldn't keep something that important from me even if it wasn't her secret to tell. Unless she assumed that Val had already told me about it. There was always that possibility. I can't help but freak the hell out now that I know that Nathan is actually telling the truth about something. I can't wait until I get back to the apartment. I take out my phone and call Val.

"Hey," he says cheerfully when he answers.

"Are you okay?"

"Am I what?"

"Okay. Are you okay?"

I hear Val's hesitation. "Yeah? Why? Are you?"

"Yeah, everything's fine. We just need to talk when I get back."

"Well, this doesn't sound good." Val laughs.

"It's not," I say.

"Oh," Val sounds surprised.

"Yeah. Just stay home, alright? I'll be right there."

I don't give Val a chance to say anything else; I just hang up and walk even faster. I make it to the apartment in about ten minutes, and Val is sitting on the floor with his laptop when I walk in. He turns around and raises an eyebrow at me. "You good?"

"Yeah," I nod. "Yeah. Um, I saw Nathan."

Val rolls his eyes and groans. "Jesus, again? Is he stalking you or something?"

I laugh and sit down in front of him. "Seems like it. But he told me something kind of interesting, and I'm not exactly sure how to talk to you about it."

Val shuts his laptop and looks at me questioningly. "Just say it, I guess."

"You've been taking antidepressants?"

If Val feels any kind of emotion, he doesn't show it. "Yeah," he says.

"And you told Nathan about it. How long have you known him?"

Val keeps a straight face. "Two months."

"And you didn't tell me."

"No." Val sighs. "I didn't. I didn't want you to freak out. Which is exactly what you're doing."

I open my mouth but can't think of anything to say. "What? No I'm not." Val raises his eyebrows.

"Alright, whatever." I shake my head and look down at my hands. "Yes. I'm freaking out a little bit. But only because Nathan told me that you told him on Sunday you felt like you wanted to kill yourself."

Val shakes his head. "I never said that."

"Well, you told him that you felt the way you used to feel."

Val presses his lips together and looks away from me. "I really never wanted to talk about this with you. Didn't want to make you upset."

"Little late for that." I shrug.

"I just really didn't want you to know, alright? Not after what I told you about what Jared said."

"What?"

"His theory about the murders?"

"So you think he's right?" I lean forward a little.

"Like I said before, it seems plausible. It could happen. But I guess we can't know for sure until someone else is killed."

I can't believe what I'm hearing. "So you're basically just waiting for someone else to die? Just to see if Jared's right?"

"I mean." Val looks down at his closed laptop. "Don't you want to know if he's right?"

"Of course I want to know. But I'm not just going to let another person die for the sake of some stupid theory Jared has."

Val shrugs. And then I think of something.

"Are you trying to get yourself killed?"

Val looks at me seriously. "What?"

"If you believe in Jared's theory, that if someone really wants to die, then they're going to get killed, is that what you're trying to test? You tell someone you're suicidal and hopefully word gets around about it? So that way you'll be able to face whoever's doing this?"

Val laughs, but there's no warmth in it. "I can't believe you think I'm actually pretending to be suicidal to catch a killer. I honestly thought you might want to help me."

I sigh, realizing that I'm being a complete idiot right now. "Val, that's not what I—"

"Really? You didn't mean that?" Val looks at me with dark eyes. His usual energy is gone. "I spend so much of my damn time with you, Keyon. And every time you have a stupid fucking problem, who's there for you? I am. Now I understand it isn't exactly easy to help someone who doesn't seem like they need help, but now that you know I've got a lot of shit going on, you think I'm fucking lying about it." Val stands up and looks down at me. "I really, truly believed that if you found out about this, the first thing you'd want to do is help me."

I try to tell him that that is what I want to do, but he cuts me off.

"Instead, you just ask if I'm fucking making it all up just so we can catch someone based on a theory that may not even be right. You know what I think? I think you're just flat-out obsessed. You're obsessed with these murders. You're not worried about me, you're just worried about who killed fucking Erica. That's it, isn't it?"

"Val—"

"You know, I don't care anymore. We've done this too many times, and I think I'm done."

I'm silent for a few seconds. "What are you saying?"

"I mean, I think I need to stay somewhere else for a little while. This"—he gestures to the both of us—"just isn't working out right now."

He says nothing else. He goes to the closet, puts on his shoes and coat, and then leaves. I don't go after him. I just kind of sit on the floor in silence for a few hours. By the time I check my phone, it's almost two in the morning. I'm not really sure what to do. I don't want to talk to anyone. I don't even want to be myself right now. And then I do something *really* stupid.

I get up and walk down the hall into Val's room. I look around the room and head over to his dresser. There really isn't a point in me doing this. There might not even be a chance that I'll find what I'm looking for. I look around a little while longer, rifling through drawers, looking under stacks of books, and then I find it. It's a piece of yellow paper with a phone number and the name Nathan written across it. I take my phone out of my pocket and make the call. I don't expect him to answer an unknown number, but he does.

"Yeah?" He answers the phone, and I can't describe the feeling I get when I hear his voice. Hatred? Nervousness? I have no idea.

"Nathan, it's Keyon."

"What?"

"I got your number from Val." This isn't a complete lie. Technically, I did get his number from Val.

"Alright? Why are you calling me at two in the morning?"

"I don't really know," I admit.

Nathan doesn't speak for a minute. "Is Valentine alright?"

"Yeah. He's fine. I just need to ask you something about him."

"Well, since this is already weird enough, why don't we just talk about this somewhere else? In person?"

Nathan's words remind me of some of Quinn's first words to Val and me. And I guess some of her last as well.

"Now?" I ask.

"No, not now. Maybe tomorrow? Are you free?"

"I don't know." I shake my head even though I know that Nathan can't see me. "I think this is something I need to talk about right now. Can't we just do this over the phone?"

Another moment of silence from Nathan. "Is Val with you?"

"No," I tell him.

"Well then, would you mind if I came over?"

I want to tell him I would mind, but I don't say that. Instead, I throw all pride out the window and tell him that he's welcome. I give him the address, then we hang up. I mentally slap myself for making such a poor choice, but I decide that it's too late now. Whatever is going to happen is going to happen whether I like it or not. I sit on the couch and wait in silence for about twenty minutes until I hear a knock at the door. I hesitate to get up, but I convince myself that I need to do this. I can't just leave him hanging. I open the door slowly, and the first thing Nathan does when he sees me is smile.

"Hey," he says.

I'm a little uncomfortable given our short history together, but I give him a small smile back and motion for him to come inside. He looks around the room. "Nice place."

"Thanks," I say. I sit back down on the couch and nod my head toward the chair beside me. "Want to sit?" I look toward the chair because I'm not really sure if I want him sitting directly next to me.

"Sure." Nathan nods. He takes a seat, and we stare at each other for a minute until he says, "So what was it you needed to ask me?"

"It's about Val."

Nathan nods. "I know that. What's the question?"

"First, let me tell you something."

Nathan raises an eyebrow but says nothing. I explain to him Jared's theory about taking out people who are suicidal and have attempted before. Nathan listens closely and doesn't say a word through my entire speech. I'm worried he'll think I'm crazy, but it's not like I care what he thinks. I tell him that I made Val angry with me when I basically accused him of faking his depression. I also tell him that I don't know why I even said something like that. Val wouldn't make anything up like that just because of something Jared said.

"I'm still confused." Nathan shakes his head. "What was the question you wanted to ask?"

I sigh. "Has Val ever tried to, you know."

"Kill himself?"

I nod. Nathan leans back and looks up at the ceiling, pressing his lips together. "Yeah," he says. "Wasn't in a very good place when I met him. But I don't think he tried around that time. I think it was way before that." He looks back at me. "Before he met you, I think."

I'm not sure what to say. "He told you this?"

"Yes."

I lean forward and put my elbows on my knees.

"Go on," Nathan says. "Tell me what you're thinking. You're wondering why he never told you."

"No, I know why he never told me. He said it was because he wouldn't want me to worry."

"I don't know." Nathan shrugs. "Seems a little weird that he'd tell me but not you. You know?" I cringe. "I mean, really, Keyon. Why would he tell someone he'd been dating for three days that he's attempted suicide but not tell his best friend of two years?"

I glare at him. "What are you getting at?"

"What I'm saying is maybe there's another reason that Valentine didn't want you to know."

"And what might that reason be?"

Nathan shrugs. "Hell if I know. I'm just saying that I think there should be a little more trust and less secret keeping in your relationship. Don't you think?"

I ponder what I should say next. "Yeah," I say. "I do think so." I stand up from the couch and pace around the living room slowly for a few seconds. "Why would he keep that from me but not you? Why would he make up such a stupid excuse for why he didn't tell me? Didn't want me to worry? Bullshit. He told you. Why would he want to make you worry about him? It doesn't make any sense. Doesn't make any fucking sense." I run my fingers through my hair and look back down at Nathan, who seems incredibly amused.

"Sorry," I say. "Didn't mean to get all worked up like that."

"Fine with me," Nathan says coolly. "I'd be worked up too. He says he's your best friend, but it doesn't seem like he tells you anything."

"He didn't even tell me he was gay until last month." I don't know why I'm still upset about this, but I am.

"He didn't tell you?" Nathan looks genuinely surprised.

"No." I shake my head. "He wouldn't even tell me your name when I asked who he was going out with."

"Kind of a dick move if you ask me," Nathan says.

"I don't know," I say as I sit back down. "It's not like he's morally obligated to tell me everything, right?"

"Well." Nathan yawns. "Do you tell him everything?"

I nod. Nathan yawns again. "Then why shouldn't he tell you some of the stuff going on with him? Doesn't seem like a fair trade. Being friends with someone is a two-way street."

"I never thought I'd be saying this, but you're right. I completely agree with you. What is wrong with me?"

Nathan sighs and gets up out of the chair. He sits down next to me and puts a hand on my shoulder. I flinch, but I don't move away from him. "Nothing's wrong with you, alright? Nothing. I think we've just established that you didn't do anything wrong. Val did. Don't you think?"

I nod. "Yeah."

"Maybe it's a good thing he's not here." Nathan pulls his hand away from me. "God works in mysterious ways. Maybe this is the universe trying to tell you something. He must've left for a reason."

"Maybe it was because I called him a liar."

"In a way, he is."

"I guess you could be right." I sigh. "About it being a good thing that he's not here. I was beginning to think his boyfriend was a murderer anyway."

Nathan laughs. "You're talking about Jared?"

"Yeah." I look at him seriously.

Nathan stops laughing. "I've known Jared a long time, Keyon. Sorry if I say I don't believe you."

"I don't even think I believe me." I run my fingers through my hair again and take a deep breath. "You're probably right. No way that's true," I say.

Nathan looks away from me and pulls his phone out of his pocket. "It's about four."

I almost laugh. "Is it really? In the short time that I've known you, I never pictured us talking for this long. About anything."

"Like I said"—Nathan looks back over at me—"God works in mysterious ways."

"What does God have to do with this?"

"Ever heard the phrase about how he has a plan for us all? Maybe this was his plan."

I do laugh this time. "God's plan is for us to talk about suicide and how awful my best friend is at four in the morning?"

Nathan laughs with me. "Yes. Exactly. That's exactly what I meant."

"Don't take this the wrong way." I stand up again. "But I think it's probably a good time for you to leave."

"Need to be alone for a little while?"

I smile. "Yeah. That, and get some sleep."

"Probably a good idea for me too." Nathan smiles back at me before walking to the door. He turns around for a split second and says, "Surprisingly, it was good seeing you." And then he leaves. I stand in my hallway for a few minutes, just staring at the front door. I'm secretly hoping that Val will walk in, but I know he's not going to. He probably won't for a while. I feel like I just betrayed him completely. I was with Nathan. In our apartment. But I don't care, because Nathan is absolutely right. Val is being a horrible friend to me. Why haven't I noticed? I know that Val told me I really needed to start blaming myself, but how could I for this? This is his fault. It's his fault we got in this fight. He decided not to tell me things. He decided to leave. I didn't. I haven't done anything wrong.

So why do I feel so guilty?

A week passes, and Val doesn't come home. I don't have Jared's number, so I can't ask if he knows where Val is, but I'm going to assume that they're together. Hadlee tells me that she hasn't heard from either of them. The last time she talked to Val was the day before he and I got in our fight. She has no information for me. I'm not really sure how much longer I can stay here by myself. Normally I'd be out doing things with Grace, but since she got promoted the other day, she's been spending most of her time at work. And I don't think I've ever felt so alone in my life. So I do the only thing I can think of doing. Even when I completely mess everything up, I know that there's at least one person who will still want to see me. I take my phone out of my pocket while sitting on my bed, and I make the call.

"Mckeyon?"

"Um, hey, Dad." I stand up and walk slowly around my room. "How is everything?"

"I think I should be the one asking that question." He laughs.

"Yeah." I laugh a little too. "I guess you should be. I think you already know that everything isn't that great right now."

"That's why you called?"

"Actually"—I sigh—"I called to ask for a favor. It's kind of big, so you don't have to do it. But I just—"

"What do you need, Keyon? You know I'm here if you need me."

I sigh again. "Can you come out here?"

"Say again?"

"I—"

I'm not really sure what to tell him. I haven't seen him in almost two years, yet here I am. Asking him to come see me. He really has no reason to visit. He only lives an hour away, but it's not like I went out of my way to see him. He shouldn't have to come and see me. But I need him. And I'm not sure who else I can talk to. He deserves to know what's going on in my life.

"I think I just need to see you," I finally say.

Dad laughs. "I don't have a problem with that. How soon do you want me there? Or do you want to come here?"

"Well." I scratch the back of my head. "I would go to you, but I don't exactly have a car."

I was dreading explaining this one to him. He bought me that car.

"You don't?" I can hear the concern in his voice. "What does that mean?"

"It's a long story. I'll tell you when I see you. Do you think you could come up tomorrow? Or maybe even today? If you want to."

He laughs again. "Let me just get some of my things together, and I'll see you in a few hours, yeah?"

I smile. "Yeah. Okay. See you." We hang up, and I already feel better. It's not a big improvement, but it's a start.

I wait around for about two hours until I decide that I should probably clean up the apartment because I haven't since Val left. I clean dishes, do some laundry, clean up the bathroom, all that good stuff. Then I start to stress myself out even more. I haven't seen my dad in two years, but now we're going to be in the same small apartment together for who knows how long. What if I'm not how he remembers me? What if he's not how I remember him? I did make several phone calls to him over the years, but that didn't mean we were as close as we used to be. Was he going to stay here? Would he stay in my room or Val's? Would it be wrong for him to use Val's room? Would it be wrong for *me* to use Val's room? I have no idea. There's a knock at the door. Well, now I have no more time to think about this. I take a deep breath and walk over to the door. I take yet another deep breath and pull it open. That's when I see Jared.

"You look awful," I say. And I mean it. It looks like he hasn't slept in a few days.

"Yeah," he says. "I know. It's been kind of a rough couple of days. I'll explain later." He looks behind me. "Is Val here?"

I almost laugh. Not because I find this funny, I'm just not sure what to do now that I have absolutely no idea where Val is. "No." I shake my head a little. "I honestly thought he was with you."

"He was. Then we got in a fight last night. I don't know where he is now." Jared looks heartbroken. "I really thought he might be here."

I can almost feel my own heart breaking for him. "I'm sorry, I don't know where he is. Do you want to come in? My dad's going to be here soon, but even if you're here, it won't cause problems or anything. I'm sure he wouldn't mind."

Jared sighs, and I see him force a smile. "Yeah," he says weakly. I give him a small smile and step to the side to let him in. I lead him into the kitchen and immediately make us some coffee. Jared takes the mug I hand him with a smile. "Thank you," he says as he sits down at the table. I follow his lead and sit in front of him.

"You seem worried," I tell him.

"Are you not?"

I sigh. "Val and I really aren't on the best of terms right now. Like, at all. But I'd be lying if I said I wasn't worried now."

"Now?"

"I mean, yeah. I wasn't worried when I thought he was with you. But now that I know he's not, I'm really not sure how to feel."

"Val told me you guys got in a fight, but that's about it. What happened to make him so mad?"

I don't know how to get into this conversation. I can't tell Jared about our fight without telling Val's secret. But I suppose if Nathan knew about what Val was going through, Jared must know by now. Although, I still don't know how to go about this.

"Has Val mentioned anything about medication that he might be taking?" I figured that this was probably the best way to see what all Jared knows.

"The antidepressants. I know. What about them?"

Once again, I get incredibly offended that someone else knew about Val and I didn't. But I don't say anything to Jared.

"Alright, you know what? I have no idea how to talk about this without straight up asking you. Do you know about Val's suicide attempt? Or that he's suicidal?"

Jared's eyes widen, and I can see his extreme concern. "No. I had no idea. Did he tell you that?"

"Well, Nathan actually told me. But Val confirmed it. But I had no idea either until last week."

"So you think that maybe he—"

Jared doesn't finish his sentence, but I know what he's thinking.

"Don't worry," I say quickly. "He'll be alright. I'm assuming you've tried calling him?"

"Twenty-three times." Jared sighs. "Have you tried calling him?"

I'm about to answer, but I hear a knock at the door.

"It's probably my dad," I say quietly as I stand up. Jared nods, and I open the door.

Neither of us say anything at first, and then we hug. Awkwardly.

"Um." I put my hand to the back of my head and turn around toward the kitchen. "I know I told you to come, but I kind of have someone over right now. There's a little bit of an emergency."

Dad walks inside and sets his duffel bag near the couch. Then he gazes into the kitchen and notices Jared at the kitchen table. Jared instantly changes his expression. He smiles and stands up, walking over to us. He holds out a hand, and Dad takes ahold of it.

"Pleasure to meet you, Mr. Ambrose." Jared keeps on smiling. "I'm Jared."

"Jared." Dad nods. "Pleasure to meet you too. Although, I don't think I've heard the name before."

Jared looks at me, and I'm assuming he's trying to telepathically ask me if my dad would be alright if he knew about his and Val's relationship. I nod.

"I'm Valentine's boyfriend," Jared says. "Keyon and I became friends a little while ago."

"I see." Dad nods and looks over at me. He picks his bag back up and raises his eyebrows.

"Yeah, um, you can put it in my room. First door on the right down the hall."

Dad smiles at me then politely at Jared. He heads down the hallway, and I see him go into my room.

"Jesus, I feel awkward," Jared says to me.

"You do?" I raise an eyebrow. "Wow. That never happens."

"I know. Should I leave?"

I shrug. "We are kind of having an emergency." Jared silently agrees, and Dad walks back down the hall. I take a couple steps to get into the living room and take a seat on the couch. Jared follows, and Dad sits in the chair next to us.

"So," he says, suddenly all business. "What's this emergency?"

"We don't know where Val is," I say.

"I don't understand." Dad shakes his head. "I thought you said you two lived together?"

"We do. That's the problem."

I tell him everything. Literally everything. I start with the murders then Grace. Then Jared tells him how he came into play. We tell him about Nathan and what he told me at the park. I tell him about the fight Val and I had and how he left. Jared explains that he was staying with him until they got in a fight as well. I then express my concerns about Val and what he might've done. Dad thinks about all this for a moment.

"Mckeyon," he says. "Can you try calling Val? Just once?"

I nod and take out my phone. "Wait." I stop. "What if he answers?"

"What do you mean?"

"What am I supposed to say to him?"

Dad looks at me seriously. "You ask him where he is and how you can help him." I look to Jared for affirmation, and he nods. I look back down at my phone and take a deep breath before calling. It rings five times. I don't get an answer.

"Nothing?" Jared asks.

I shake my head no. "Nothing. What do we do now?"

"When is the last time you saw him?" Dad looks to Jared. Jared sighs.

"I don't know. Last night, I guess."

"So it hasn't been a full day?"

"No."

Dad turns to look at me. "Mckeyon, what do you think we should do?"

"I guess we can wait it out." I sigh. "But I'm worried. What if that's the wrong decision?"

"Maybe we should just go to the police," Jared says.

Dad sighs. "I think it might be too early for that. He's not a child. He can leave whenever he wants to. He could've left to go see family, for all we know. I don't think they would even treat this like a missing persons case. I think we'll just have to wait until we can get ahold of him."

I'm about to say something about how maybe we *should* call the police, just in case, but my thoughts are interrupted when Jared's phone goes off. Mine goes off less than a second later. Jared looks at his phone immediately, and I see him let out a sigh of relief. I don't check my messages just yet.

"He apologized," Jared says. "But he says he might need some more time." Jared looks up at me. "What should I say? What does yours say?"

I take a deep breath and look at my phone. Val says that pride can go to hell and that he's sorry. I smile. I tell Dad and Jared what the message says and tell Jared he should ask where Val is. I send Val a message asking if I can call him. He doesn't text back, because he tells me he's coming up the stairs right now. I tell Jared this, and he looks confused.

"I thought he said he needed more time?"

I shrug. The door to the apartment opens. Val drops a bag on the floor and shuts the door behind him.

"Hey," he says.

I'm not sure what I'm feeling right now. I want to jump up and kiss him I'm so happy, but at the same time, I want to strangle him. Jared gets up before I do and hugs Val tightly.

"I'm so sorry," Jared whispers. Val tells him it's alright and looks at me over Jared's shoulder. I give him a small smile and then turn to my dad. "I bet you didn't think today was going to turn out like this." Dad laughs. "No, not really," he says.

Val pulls away from Jared and walks over to me. He looks at Dad first and gives him an awkward smile before turning back to me. "Um, can I talk to you for a second?"

"Yeah." I nod as I stand up. "Um." I look at Dad and then Jared. "We'll be right back." I pull Val outside of our apartment and shut the door. Then I totally lose it.

"What the hell?" I ask as I hit Val on the arm.

"Jesus," he says. "Not really expecting that to be the first thing you say to me. Why the fuck did you hit me?" he asks, rubbing his arm.

I can feel tears threatening to spill out, but I ignore it. "Do you know how worried I was?"

"Probably not very."

"Are you kidding me? Val, I know we fought, but do you think that means I'm just going to stop worrying about you?"

Val shrugs. "You thought I was lying about being fucking suicidal," he says. He doesn't sound angry. Just hurt.

"I know. And I'm not going to lie and say I wasn't thinking that at first, because I was. But then I realized I was being a complete idiot. I should've believed you, alright? And yes, I want to help you. So does Jared. I told him about it. We just want to help you. And when you left his place, he came over to ours, and when he told me he didn't know where you were, I thought—"

Val sighs. "You thought I'd done something really stupid, huh? No, Keyon. I'm fine, okay? I'm fine. I didn't do anything."

"Well, I know that now," I say, barely a whisper. "But I didn't before, and I had to lie to Jared and tell him that you'd be alright even though I had no idea if you would be." I take a deep breath and get my voice back. "And I'm sorry. I shouldn't have said any of that to you. I'm sorry."

Val almost smiles. "I'm sorry too," he says. "For walking out. We both did things we shouldn't have."

I nod at him. "Okay. Yeah. You're right. Are we good?"

"We're good," Val says after a moment.

"I feel like we should hug or something."

Val laughs. "I don't know if I'd go that far. Want to go back in?"

I nod. Val stops me before I open the door, though. "I almost forgot," he says. "Who the hell is that guy in there?"

"Oh." I laugh a little. "That's my dad. I kind of panicked and called him."

Val nods once, and I open the door for us. Jared is talking to Dad, and Dad looks like he's having a pretty good time. He laughs at whatever Jared says when we walk in and then turns to face Val and me. I expect the mood to drop, but it doesn't. Dad stands up and walks over to us. He holds out a hand for Val, and Val takes it.

"Valentine, I assume?" He smiles.

"Mr. Ambrose." Val smiles back. "Never thought I'd actually meet you."

"Never thought I'd meet you either," Dad says as he pulls his hand away. "Glad you're back. Seems like you've got the whole world and then some worried about you."

Val laughs, a real laugh, and nods. "Seems like it, doesn't it?" We all sit down, and Val assures us several times that he's alright. Eventually, Val says he needs to talk to Jared for a little while, and they leave. That's when Dad decides to get serious with me.

"Mckeyon, I think you need to find someone to talk to."

I raise an eyebrow. "What?"

"You heard me. Have you ever thought about therapy?"

I almost laugh. "Are you being serious right now? I don't think I'm the one who should be getting therapy in this place."

"Well." Dad sighs. "I do think Val needs it too, based on what I know, but I think you could use it as well."

"Why?"

Dad looks at me seriously. "When's the last time you've had a nightmare?"

"Dad—"

"Come on, Mckeyon. I know they've been going on since you were younger. Have they stopped? Or are they still there?"

I can't lie. If I do, I know he'll see right through me. "I still get them. Not often, but they do happen."

"Don't you think you need to talk to someone about that?" Dad leans toward me. "And murders? Don't you think you need to talk to someone about *that*? Why didn't you tell me that had happened? And to your girlfriend too?"

"Erica and I aren't exactly together anymore, Dad."

He sighs. "I know that. I just think that having that happen is something very traumatic that you might want to talk to someone about."

"Even if I did want a therapist, how am I supposed to pay for one?"

"I'd pay for it," Dad says this without hesitation.

"Dad, come on."

"I'm being serious, Mckeyon. I really think you could use this. That roommate of yours too. Too much has happened with you both. I think it'd be a good thing for you, or both of you, to go and get some help."

"Help? How is that going to help? Is therapy going to bring Erica back? What about the girl from our building? Is therapy going to stop me from having nightmares? Is it going to just suddenly make everything okay?"

Dad shakes his head. "I never said it was going to do those things. I just think that you could use it. You could use someone to talk to who might know how to help you better express your feelings."

"How would you know if I need to 'better express my feelings'? In case you've forgotten, we haven't been around each other in years."

"Mckeyon." Dad sighs. "I don't want to get into this with you. Can you please just tell me that you'll look into seeing someone? Just to give me some peace of mind? I'm only suggesting this because I want what's best for you."

I sigh. I'm being terrible to my dad for no reason. "Fine," I say. "Yeah. I'll do it. I'll go see someone."

So I do. Dad is staying at a hotel, which means he's close enough to me to make sure I'm actually going places and doing what he says. Val drives me to some behavioral health clinic and parks the car outside of the building.

"Do you want to do this alone?" he asks me.

I nod. "For the first time, yeah. I can do this."

"Alright." Val sighs. "Pick you up in an hour then?"

"Yeah," I say as I open the car door. I step outside and walk into the building. They're playing old music in the waiting room, and there's only two other people here. I walk up to the receptionist and smile politely at her. She smiles back and says, "Name?"

"Um, Mckeyon Ambrose? I'm here to see—"

"Nancy?" The woman looks down at some papers on her desk.

"Yeah," I say. "Her."

"Why don't you take this." She hands me a blue folder with a single sheet of paper inside. "And go sit out here in the waiting room. Nancy will call for you when she's ready."

I nod and walk over to an empty seat. I take out the piece of paper from inside the folder. It says my name on the top, with an empty space next to the word *diagnosis*. I look farther down the page and see that this is where the therapist checks off a box next to whatever you have. I see several columns with different disorders or problems. Severe depression. Recurring severe depression. Schizophrenia. Psychosis. Trichotillomania. What even is that? I'm still scanning over the paper and the unchecked boxes when I hear my name being called.

"Mckeyon?"

I look up to see a woman probably in her early forties calling my name. We make eye contact, and I smile at her as I stand up. I walk over to her, and she smiles back sweetly. "How are you today?" she asks me. I nod my head and say, "Alright." She keeps smiling at me, and then I follow her down a short hallway. We go into the last room on the left, and I see her desk, followed by two empty chairs. Weird. I thought you were supposed to lie down or something during these things.

"Well," she says as I sit down. "My name is Nancy. Is this your first time seeing someone like me?"

I like that she says *someone like me* instead of using the word *therapist* or *psychiatrist* or whatever. I can tell that she's trying to make me feel a little more comfortable being here.

"Yes," I say.

"Alright." She smiles again. "Why don't we start off by having you tell me why you're here today?"

"My dad thought I should talk to someone."

"And why would he think that?"

"Because I have nightmares." I sigh. "And my friend and ex-girlfriend were murdered."

Nancy looks surprised. I can tell that she's faking, though. She's had to have heard worse.

"Murdered?" she says, still faking surprise. "Tell me about that."

I take a deep breath. I guess I kind of have to tell her. If I don't tell her exactly what's bothering me, how is she supposed to help me? I start off by telling her about Erica and our history together. Then I tell her about meeting Quinn and her dying the next day. Then I explain what happened on the night that Val told me about Erica. She asks if my nightmares had anything to do with the murders. I tell her that only a few of them did. They had all been about Val lately. I tell her about what Val and I do when I have nightmares.

"So he's been helping you?" Nancy asks. "He wakes up to come and talk to you?"

"Not the past week. We got in a fight over something really stupid. Well, I guess it was over something stupid I said. Then he left for a little while. He stayed with his boyfriend until *they* got in a fight. Then I called my dad to come see me because I was so worried. But Val came back that day. So I guess things are okay now. But I don't know for sure. I think I kind of really hurt Val this time. We don't fight that often, but lately it seems like we've been fighting all the time." I sigh. "Sorry," I say. "I'm rambling." Then I realize that that's probably the stupidest thing I could've said. You're pretty much supposed to ramble on about your problems to your therapist.

Nancy looks at me sadly. "Why are you apologizing?"

"I don't know." I shake my head. "Just felt like the right thing to do."

"Do you apologize for a lot of things?"

"What?"

Nancy leans forward in her seat. "I'm just trying to get a feel for what kind of person you are."

"Well, I don't know." I shrug. "I guess I do kind of say sorry a lot. It's just what I do."

"Is there a reason that you would do that?"

I think about this. I suppose it could go along with me starting to blame myself for basically everything now. Now that I feel like things are actually my fault, I have to apologize for everything that happens or everything that I do. I decide that telling Nancy more about Erica and feeling guilty for what happened to her could be helpful. So I start off with how we first met. How she started flirting with me first. Then I tell her about how amazing our relationship was, except for how attached I became. Then I work up the courage to tell her about Erica's crashing my car and that she blamed me for it. I tell her that I just blamed Erica for being crazy; I couldn't blame myself for what happened to her.

"You know that isn't your fault, Mckeyon," Nancy says. "Sometimes we don't know what's going on with someone we're close with, but it's their choice not to tell us what's going on. It isn't your fault if you couldn't stop someone from having depression or doing something like Erica did."

How did she know that that was exactly what I needed to hear?

"It's just that I just found out, like, two weeks ago that Val feels the same way Erica does. Or did. Then when I tried to ask him about it, he said he didn't want to tell me because he didn't want me to worry. That's when I got mad at him. You know, for not telling me something really important like that."

"I think it's very respectable that he cares about you so much."

"I don't know. It didn't really feel like he did at the time."

"I do think he should've told you if you two are as close as you're telling me, but like I said before, it's not your fault that you couldn't help out with what he's going through. You didn't even *know* what he was going through. So you can't blame yourself for this."

I let out an exasperated sigh. "But I *do*. How couldn't I blame myself? I've known him for almost two and a half years, and yet for some reason, he didn't think it was important to tell me he was depressed. Or suicidal or whatever. It just makes me so mad."

I suddenly feel embarrassed for letting out all my feelings like this. I know that that's what I'm supposed to do in here, but I can't help but feel like I need to apologize again.

"Do you get angry often?" Nancy looks at me with something in her eyes that I can't quite explain.

"Not usually." I shake my head. "I mean, kind of. I think it's kind of a normal amount of angry. If that makes sense."

Nancy laughs a little. "It does make sense. I think that there is a normal amount of angry. I'm glad you can understand that."

I shrug. Nancy laughs again. "All I get is a shoulder shrug? Tell me something else. How do you feel about doing this?"

"About talking to you?"

Nancy nods once.

"Well, I don't know. You seem nice. And I guess the part where I just get to rant for an hour is nice too. It's alright. It's not like it's bad."

"That's good. Can I ask you another question?"

"Mhm."

"Going back to the nightmares." Nancy sighs. "Do you think you can give me a time frame about when they started? Was it recently?"

"No, not recently. My mom died when I was around eight. I think they started around then." I look down at my hands. "They used to all be about her."

"Tell me about that."

I shrug. "I don't really know what to say. I guess they were just dreams where she would get hurt. Or I would hurt her." I take a deep breath. "Wow, I just realized that probably made me sound like a crazy person. I would never hurt anyone. That's the worst thing you could do to someone."

"Hurting them?"

"Well, yeah. I mean, I guess you could hurt them mentally too, but I'm talking about physically. Like, whoever killed Erica and Quinn. Why would they do that? Why would you want to completely destroy someone's life like that? I've heard a theory from Val, but that's all I've got."

"What was Val's theory?" Nancy tilts her head to the left.

I sigh. "You know how I said we got in that fight over him being suicidal? Well, I guess that kind of started when he told me about his boyfriend, Jared, and what he thought the reason for the murders was. Quinn and Erica were both really depressed, I guess, and they'd both attempted suicide before. So Jared thought that maybe the killer did what he did to put them out of their misery or something. That's why I thought that Val wasn't being serious about what was wrong with him. I honestly thought for a moment that he was just making it up so that there might be a way for the killer to find out and try to kill Val."

"But Val is alright now?"

I shrug. "I honestly don't know."

"It seems like you worry about him a lot."

"Because I do."

"It actually sounds like you worry about a lot of things."

"Yeah," I say. "I guess I just have a lot on my plate right now. Or all the time. But I guess even more so now."

"Mckeyon, I think you made the right choice coming here. I'd like to see you again in about two weeks. Is that alright with you?"

I look at the clock behind her and see that an hour has already passed. I look back down at Nancy and sigh. "Yeah, that's fine."

She smiles at me for about a minute straight, and I get a little awkward.

"It was nice meeting you," she says. "Hopefully we can figure this out together."

I nod and smile at her before she stands up to lead me out of the room, picking up my blue folder before we go. We get back to the receptionist, and I see Nancy write something on the paper in the folder. I notice she doesn't check any boxes; she just writes the payment and hands it to the receptionist. That was a little disappointing. I want to know what's wrong with me. I give the receptionist some information, and then it's over. Not as bad as I thought it would be.

Val isn't waiting for me when I get outside; my dad is. I walk over to his car and jump inside to the passenger's seat.

"How was it?" he asks.

"Not that bad," I answer him honestly. "It's kind of nice just going off about your problems."

"Do you think this is going to help you?"

I shrug. "I don't know. Maybe." I hear my phone go off and tell my dad to hang on for a second. It's Grace. She's sent me a message that she just got done talking to the police. She doesn't say anything else. I tell Dad this, and he says he'll take me to go see her. I'm absolutely terrified. The only thing going through my head is that someone else is dead. And honestly, that's probably true.

Dad brings me to Grace's house once I tell him where it is. I get out quickly and tell him I'll find a way back to the apartment later. I knock on Grace's door, and Tasha answers.

"Keyon," she says sadly.

"Hey," I say. "Where's Grace?"

Tasha sighs. "In her room. You can just go ahead and see her."

"Is Alexis here?"

Tasha says nothing. She steps out of the way as I walk inside and then closes the door. I see her walk down the hall to the right and into her room. Now I'm really panicking. I head down the other hallway and find Grace's room. I knock twice before opening the door. I see Grace sitting on her bed, knees to her chest. I can tell she's been crying.

"Grace?" I walk over to her cautiously and kneel beside her bed. "You alright?"

"It happened yesterday," she almost whispers. She doesn't look at me.

"What happened yesterday?"

"Alexis went out alone to her friend's house because she was having problems." Grace sounds like she's about to cry again. I wait for her to keep talking. "Then Tasha and I got a call from her friend saying that—"

Grace actually does start crying now. I don't have to ask her what exactly happened. I think it's pretty obvious. I sit down on the bed next to Grace and pull her to me.

"I thought she had killed herself," Grace cries. "But this"—she coughs—"being murdered. She didn't deserve that."

I barely heard the last part of what she said.

"Did you say you thought she'd killed herself?"

Grace looks up at me. "What? Keyon—"

"I know. I'm sorry she's gone. I really am. I'm so sorry. But what do you mean you thought she killed herself?"

"Keyon, you're being really insensitive right now."

I sigh. "Can you please just tell me what you mean?"

"She was suicidal," Grace says. "What else could I have meant?"

She starts crying again, but I can't focus on her. Alexis had been suicidal. This is what Val had been waiting for. Someone else to die to confirm Jared's theory. I have to tell him, unless he already knows.

"Grace, I—"

I let go of her and stand up from her bed. "I'm so sorry. I have to go."

"What? Mckeyon, where are you—"

"This is important," I say.

"One of my best friends was murdered yesterday and you're—"

"I'm sorry," I say again. "This is just *really* important."

And then I leave. Grace calls out for me, but she doesn't follow me. I leave the house and call Val. I tell him where I am and that I have something he's going to want to hear. He picks me up less than ten minutes later, and I start talking.

"Alexis was murdered yesterday," I tell him.

"Holy fuck, what? Where? Is Grace alright?"

I shake my head. "I'm not sure. I kind of left her as soon as I found out that Alexis was suicidal."

Val takes his eyes off the road for a second to look at me. "What?"

"Grace told me that when she found out Alexis was dead, she thought she had killed herself. She told me Alexis had been feeling that way. But she didn't kill herself because, like I said, she was murdered. This is the third case where this has happened." I pause for a moment. "I think Jared's theory might be right."

"I never thought it would get any worse than two people," Jared says as he paces around our apartment. "But a third murder? And one that matches my theory? It doesn't make any sense."

I look up at Jared from where I'm sitting on our couch. "Wait, what do you mean it doesn't make any sense? I thought you were sure about your theory or whatever."

"That's all it is, Keyon. A theory. How are any of us supposed to know if it's actually true?"

"Well, you've been right so far," Val says as he leans forward next to me. "This is the third victim to be suicidal. I mean, technically all of them have been. That has to mean something."

I think back to what Jared said to me about euthanasia. Mercy killing. I can't help myself; I ask about it.

"Are you on their side?" I look away from Jared.

"What?" he asks.

"You told me that you agreed with mercy killing. If someone's in enough pain, then it's a good thing for someone to end their suffering."

"Keyon, come on." Val looks at me.

"In some situations, I think it's the right thing to do," Jared says when we make eye contact again.

"Wait." Val holds up a hand. "What? Jared, you actually agree with that stuff?"

"You don't?"

Val stares at him for a minute.

"Guys," I say. "Really. I'm sorry for bringing it up. Can we just talk about what we all really want to know?"

"And what's that?" Jared looks down at me.

"Who did this. Who's been killing these people."

"Now that"—Jared points at me—"is something I'd love to know. Because frankly, I think we need to be watching out for Val."

"What?" Val raises an eyebrow. "Why would you have to watch out for me?"

Jared and I stare at him.

"Seriously." Val rolls his eyes. "I know I wasn't exactly alright a few weeks ago, but I swear to God I'm fine now.'"

"How do we know that, Val?" Jared kneels down in front of him. "You didn't tell either of us you were feeling—"

"Jared." Val grabs on to his hand. "Please. Believe me." He looks over to me for help. I sigh.

"I believe him," I say. "We need to trust him. We need to trust each other. We have to actually work well together if we're going to figure this out."

"We?" Val continues to stare at me. "Why can't we let the police handle this?"

"We haven't told them what we think," Jared says as he stands back up. "If we do eventually go to the police, they're not going to take us seriously if we tell them that the person doing this is some kind of psycho who's killing suicidal people."

I look up at him. "Why wouldn't they take us seriously? We have proof. It's a solid theory. I think they'd appreciate any information we could give them."

"I don't know about this." Jared shakes his head. "What if they think we're connected to it in some way?"

Now Val is asking questions. "Why would they think that? We just want to help solve whatever's going on. Why would that make us suspects?"

Jared looks surprised. "All three of us knew at least two of the people murdered. You both knew all three. Plus, we now have a theory that's probably right. Wouldn't that make us seem suspicious?"

I narrow my eyes at him. Yes, that would make us seem suspicious. Just like how I've been suspicious about Jared lately. "You know, you seem awfully worried about that."

"What?" Jared looks at me.

"You seem pretty worried that they're going to accuse you of something. We all know we're innocent. So why get worked up about getting caught for something we didn't do?" I stand up.

Jared laughs a little. "It almost sounds like you're calling me the murderer."

"Maybe I am."

Val stands up and grabs on to my arm. Tightly. "Mckeyon, really. We're not doing this again."

"Again?" Jared raises his eyebrows at me. "So you've talked about this before? About how you think I'm a killer?"

I shake my head but never break eye contact. "I never called you a killer. I *never* said that."

"Is that not what you're saying right now? You seem to think I'm worried about becoming a suspect."

"Are you not?"

"Of course I am," Jared almost yells. "We all should be. With the way this looks, if we all go to the police, they're just going to think we're trying to cover our asses. It looks too much like we're involved."

"Maybe that's because we are involved, Jared. We've been involved since day one," Val says.

I didn't expect Val to be on my side. I'm surprised.

"But we don't have to be," Jared says. "If we avoid talking to the police, then it's almost like none of this happened."

I laugh. "Almost like none of this happened? You're joking. You've got to be fucking kidding me."

Jared takes a step back. "What?"

"You think I can just forget about the fact that a girl I was in love with for a long time was murdered? What about Quinn? The girl I'd barely known for two days? Or Alexis? Do you think Grace is going to be able to just forget about her?"

"I never said—"

"That's pretty much what you said," Val whispers. "You said that it'd be like nothing happened."

Jared reaches out to take Val's hand. "Val, that isn't what I—"

"Don't touch me right now," Val says as he backs away. "You're scaring me."

Jared looks hurt. "Fine," he says. "Go to the police. Do whatever. But when they start to pin this on you, don't say I didn't tell you so."

And then he leaves. He doesn't look at me, and he doesn't look at Val. He just leaves the apartment. Val and I stay standing. I look at him, but he doesn't look back.

"I'm starting to believe you," Val says quietly.

"What?"

"Jared. Something"—he takes a deep breath—"something isn't right. I understand what you meant when you said he was scaring you. He's scaring me now too."

"Val—"

Val turns his head to look at me. He's crying. I've never seen Val really cry before. I almost don't know what to do. "I don't want you to be right," he says. "I want it to be someone else. It can't be Jared. I don't want you to be right. Because that means we would've fought for nothing."

Now I *really* don't know what to do. Val's crying. He's getting emotional on me. I've always been the one to get emotional on *him*. But now that it's reversed, I'm kind of stuck between a rock and a hard place. I sit him down on the couch and do what Jared did earlier. I kneel in front of him and sigh.

"I doubt that Jared is the one doing any of this," I say. "I think he's just scared."

"But you said before—"

"I didn't mean what I said before. I mean what I'm saying now. He's just scared. He's as scared as you and I are. There's nothing we can do about it right now."

Val takes a deep breath and leans his head back before looking back down at me. "Do you think we should go to the police?"

"You talked to the police about Quinn, didn't you? And Grace talked to them about Alexis."

Val nods. "You're right. I don't think we need to." Val stands up, and so do I.

"You alright?" I ask before he can run off.

"Yeah." Val smiles at me. He pulls his phone out of his pocket and looks at the time. "You should probably get your dad over here to say good-bye," he tells me.

I nod at him, and then he's gone. He's locked himself in his room. I text my dad and tell him what's going on. I also mention that he can come over if he wants to before he heads back home. He says he'll be here in a couple minutes, and I lie down on the couch with my face pressed into a pillow. I think I'm about to fall asleep when I hear a knock at the door. I groan and stand up to answer it.

"Hey," I say to my dad, rubbing my eyes.

"Did I wake you?" he asks as he comes inside. "I called you just a few minutes ago."

"I know," I say. "I'm just tired, I guess. Lots going on."

"I know. You texted me about Grace's roommate."

"Yeah. That, and Val and I think that Jared could possibly be the killer."

Dad stares at me for a moment. "What?"

"Never mind." I wave my hand at him. "When did you plan on leaving?"

Dad motions to the door with his thumb and says, "I left the car running. I don't think it's really going to take us that long to say good-bye."

"Probably not." I shrug.

"See you when I see you, yeah?" Dad smiles.

"Yeah." I wrap my arms around him, and we hug for about five seconds. He puts his hand on my shoulder after we pull away.

"Take care of yourself. Alright, Mckeyon?"

"I will."

"If you need anything, you know you can call me."

"I know."

We look at each other for a few seconds before he gives me another hug. Then he walks out the door, shutting it gently behind him. I sigh. I need to call Grace. I need to apologize. I walk down the hall and into my room, taking my phone out of my pocket. I hesitate to call, but I eventually build up the courage to talk to her. But I guess it doesn't really matter since she doesn't pick up. She doesn't answer the second time either. Or the third. I give up and lie down on my bed. I don't really want to talk to anyone right now anyway.

———•◦•———

I go to Hadlee's on Saturday. Her front door is unlocked, and I walk right in. Although, I don't see her. I see Jared, sitting on Hadlee's couch. We stare at each other for a few moments. Neither of us say anything until I start to open the door to Hadlee's apartment again.

"Keyon, wait," Jared says.

Before I can leave the place, I hear Jared stand up.

"Where's Hadlee?" I ask as I turn around.

"Bathroom."

"And why are you here?"

Jared sighs. "I thought that she might agree with me. That we shouldn't go to the police."

"And what did she say?"

"I said that we needed to talk to them." Hadlee walks out of the bathroom and crosses her arms once she sees us. I look at Jared.

"Did you tell them anything?" I ask.

"Yes," Hadlee answers for Jared.

Jared sighs again and looks down at me. "I didn't mention your name if that's what you're thinking."

"Did you mention Val's?"

Jared shakes his head. "No. I didn't. I said that it was my idea and mine alone."

"Tell him what they said," Hadlee says quietly.

"Well, most of them thought I was crazy. At least I think they did. But there were some people there that actually believed me. I saw that Emmett guy."

I sit down. "Erica's brother? That Emmett?"

"Yeah. He believed me. Said it made perfect sense."

"Are they going to do anything about what you told them?"

"What are they supposed to do?" Jared and Hadlee sit down at the same time. "Are they just going to keep an eye on every single suicidal person in the state? There's nothing they really *can* do. I told you already. Going to the police would be pointless. And it was."

"I thought you were scared about becoming a suspect?"

"I was," Jared says. "But I needed to prove to you all that I'm completely innocent. In case you were wondering, it doesn't feel nice having any of you thinking that I'm a murderer."

I look at Hadlee. "You thought he had something to do with this too?"

"For a little while, yes." Hadlee nods.

"I'm sitting right here, you know." Jared sighs.

"Jared, it's fine. We know you didn't do anything."

"Doesn't seem like you thought that way a few days ago. Especially when Val told me he was scared of me."

"You know he didn't mean that," Hadlee says.

Jared nods. "I know. But he still said it. Which is why I needed to go to the police."

"You still had to ask for another opinion about it," I tell him. "You went to Hadlee before going to the police."

"I'm glad he did." Hadlee looks at me. "It feels a little like you guys have been keeping me out of the loop. I'd like to know what's going on if you think you have a way to find a serial killer."

"That's where the problem is," Jared says. "We *don't* know how to find the killer. All we know is who they've killed and why they're doing it. And that second part might not even be right."

"I have an idea." I look at Hadlee then over to Jared. "Why don't we just forget about this?"

Hadlee raises an eyebrow. "Forget about it? What are you talking about?"

"Grace told me a little while ago that if this was really bothering me, then I should forget about it. Maybe we could all try that."

"Somehow I don't think Grace still feels that way. You really think she's going to forget about Alexis that fast? Because I don't think she will."

I shrug. "You never know. I think I've pretty much gotten over Erica. Why couldn't Grace get over Alexis?"

Jared laughs. "You're insane," he says. For some reason, this comment really bothers me. Maybe it's because it's the first thing I've ever heard Jared say that wasn't supposed to be nice.

"Really?" I look at him. "How do you figure that?"

"Based on what I know, you hadn't seen Erica in over a year. You didn't even really love her anymore. You'd completely moved on. And Grace? You think she's going to just 'forget' about a girl she's been living with since she first started college? You really think that's possible?"

"Jared." Hadlee holds out a hand. "That's enough."

I'm starting to get a little pissed off. What was going on with Jared? I can understand that he's scared, but honestly, what the hell was he even talking about? Didn't he suggest before that we should forget about all this?

"You know what?" I say as I stand up. "I think I need to leave. I didn't know he was going to be here."

"I didn't either," Hadlee says.

Jared sighs from where he's sitting on the couch. "I think it might be better if *I* left. Seems a little bit like I'm unwanted here."

"Jared." Hadlee puts a hand to her forehead. "That's not what—"

"No, really." Jared stands up. "It's alright. I'll go. I wouldn't want to make either of you more upset." I can see Jared relax a little more. He seems more like himself now. "I'm sorry. For everything that I've said." He looks down at his hands.

God, now I feel like the worst person alive. He's scared. Just like the rest of us. None of us had any right to accuse him of something so horrible. I'm about to apologize, but Jared's out faster than I can blink, leaving Hadlee and me alone.

"I'm sorry," she says. "I really didn't know he was going to show up. I would've texted you about it, but I didn't want you to not want to be here. I know you two aren't exactly friends right now."

"I don't know," I sit back down. "Now I just feel bad for him. Which is stupid, because I've been the one making him feel bad."

"It wasn't just you. It was Val and I as well. You can't put all the blame on yourself."

"I feel like I *should* be blaming myself for this, though. I think it's pretty much my fault that him and Val are fighting."

"They're fighting?"

I sigh. "Yeah. Val told me about it last night."

"Why would their fighting be your fault?"

"I'm the one who basically convinced Val that Jared's a murderer. I think that's probably the reason that they're fighting."

"There's no way Val would actually believe that."

"He might." I shrug.

Hadlee takes a deep breath. "I hear you went to go see a psychiatrist."

"Yeah?"

"Do you talk about this kind of stuff there?"

"Well, I've only gone once, but I guess we did talk about this a little. Not Jared being a murderer, just the murders in general. Kind of."

Hadlee starts going off about how I might need to see this person more often, and if I can convince Val to go, then he should see someone too. I only half listen to her speech. I do start to tune in when she begins talking about Grace. I tell her that I left Grace in a bad spot, and Hadlee says that if I'm going to apologize, then I need to do it in person. But I don't want to. I don't want to see Grace right now. I can't stand talking about any more dead people. And I know that's what Grace is going to want to do. I tell Hadlee I'll apologize, we talk for a little while longer, and then I leave.

I make it back to my place and lie on my bed for about four hours straight until I hear Val come home. I stand up and get out of my room to greet him, but I'm surprised by who he's with.

"Hey," Nathan says from where he's standing at the front door. I notice he has an arm around Val.

"Hey," I say slowly. "What are you—"

"He called me on accident. He said he meant to call you but—"

Nathan is cut off by Val's laughter. "I forgot you didn't have a car," Val says. "How were you supposed to come and rescue me if you don't even have a car?"

I look at Val and sigh. There's no way he's sober right now.

"Yeah," Nathan says, looking away from Val and back to me. "I drove him back here."

"Wait a second." Val pushes Nathan away from him. "You drove? In my car?"

"How else was I supposed to get you home? You were basically passed out in the front seat, Valentine."

Val looks at me in disbelief. "He drove my car. All the way down to our apartment. Can you believe that?"

"No," I say. "I can't believe that. Val, I think you should go to bed."

Val nods a couple of times and walks away from Nathan and over to me. He puts a hand on my shoulder and sighs. "You're a good guy, Keyon. You really are. I'll tell you everything tomorrow, alright? No secrets."

I nod even though I don't really know what he's talking about. He takes off down the hall, and I hear the lock click as soon as he shuts the door to his bedroom. I look at Nathan, and he gives me a sympathetic smile.

"Sorry I keep randomly showing up in your life. I'll get out of here."

"No, really," I say. "It's fine. Thanks for taking him home. Even if he didn't mean to call you."

Nathan shrugs. "Yeah, okay. I'm just glad we made it back alright. And I'm glad he wanted to go here, not to his boyfriend's."

I raise my eyebrows.

"No, no." Nathan shakes his head. "It's not like I'm jealous of Jared or anything. It's just that I'm a little freaked out because of what Val said to me on the way over here."

I take a seat on the couch, and Nathan does the same. "What did he say to you?" I ask.

"That he believed you."

"Believed me? What does that mean? Believed me about what?"

Nathan sighs. "Jared being the killer. I still don't believe a word of it, but now that Val seems to think it's true, I don't know."

I put my head in my hands. "God, I'm so done with this. Jared didn't do anything wrong. He went to the police to talk to them about some ideas he had about the murders. I know for a fact he did nothing wrong. I think Val's just looking for someone to blame. Just like I was."

"Sorry for bringing it up." Nathan holds up his hands. "I guess I shouldn't have. You seem a little upset about this."

I laugh. "A little? It's kind of destroying my life right now."

"You think it's just you?" Nathan raises his eyebrows.

"What?"

"I came back out here a month ago. I was just trying to see if I could find my best friend again. That's all I fucking wanted. And then I just had to meet Valentine. So now I'm wrapped up in all of this whether I like it or not because he won't leave me alone about it. He won't even leave me alone about *you*."

"I don't get it." I shake my head. "What does Val talking to you have to do with murders destroying *my* life?"

"I didn't say it had anything to do with you. I said it wasn't just you. I wanted to come back here and pick up where I left off, but ever since I met you and all these other people, things really haven't been normal for me. At all."

I still don't completely understand what it is that he's going off about, so I say the first thing that comes to my mind. "Then go home," I say seriously. "If you don't like it here, then leave. It's not like anyone's forcing you to stay."

Nathan stares at me for a moment. "I can't leave now. I don't want to."

"Why not?"

"I just don't, alright?" Nathan takes a deep breath. "I'm gonna get out of here. Wouldn't want to bother either one of you more than I already do."

I watch as he stands up from the couch and walks out of the apartment, slamming the door behind him. Val wanders back out into the living room a second later and looks at me carefully.

"You alright?" I ask him.

"Yeah. You'll never believe what he told me on the drive back here."

"I thought he said you were basically passed out the whole time?"

Val rolls his eyes. "You think I'd actually trust him to pick me up when I'm not sober? No way in hell. I wouldn't let him near me like that."

"I don't understand."

"I just wanted to get his opinion on the murders." Val sighs and sits down next to me. "I actually didn't drink a thing."

I raise an eyebrow. "Really? And what kind of information did this lying get you?"

"He doesn't trust Jared."

"He doesn't?"

Val shakes his head. "No. He doesn't. He has a reason not to, though."

"What is it?" I lean forward, suddenly very interested.

"When did Jared first meet Grace?"

"I don't know. Her dinner party, I guess."

"Exactly. And do you know what Hadlee texted me today?"

I shake my head.

"She told me that Jared said something he shouldn't have known."

"What does that mean?"

"She said he knew about how long Alexis and Grace had been roommates."

I take a deep breath. "I was over at Hadlee's today, and I did hear him say that. But I don't see how that would make him untrustworthy."

"Well, I don't think that proves anything, but Nathan said it wasn't the first time he's said something about someone he hadn't known for very long."

I don't understand. Val isn't making any sense. "I still don't know what you're talking about," I say. "I thought that you trusted Jared?"

"I do," Val says quietly. "I do," he says again. "I just don't know what to think."

"So let me get this straight." I hold up a hand. "Nathan told you all of this while you were supposedly passed out in your front seat?"

"Supposedly *passing* out in the front seat. I was still talking to him. But I guess he figured I was so fucking wasted I wouldn't remember anything he said to me, you know?"

"Well, what else did he say?"

"I don't know. I guess it was just things about you, Grace, and Hadlee that he shouldn't know."

"Alright," I say slowly. "What do you mean by 'shouldn't know'?"

"Nathan was just going off and ranting about how Jared won't shut up about me and you and whoever else. Did Jared know you were going to marry Erica?"

"No. Not unless you told him."

Val shakes his head. "I didn't tell him. But apparently, he knew. He was talking to Nathan about her death, and he was saying how awful he felt for you because of how serious you two used to be."

I take a deep breath. "That's a little unusual."

"That's what I said. What do you think we should do?"

"I don't know." I shrug. "I still don't know where you stand on this."

"What?"

"There's not really an easy way to ask this, but do you think Jared did all of this?"

Val looks offended. "Of course not. I just think that something really weird is going on."

"Weird? That's the best way you can describe what's happening?"

"Well, do you have anything better?"

"Yeah," I say. "It's fucking devastating."

Val sighs. "Yeah. You're right." Neither of us say anything until Val changes the subject.

"Have you apologized to Grace?"

I shake my head. "No. She still won't call me back."

"You should apologize in person if you actually want her to forgive you."

"You're probably right. I just don't know what to even say to her. It's been almost three days. What if she doesn't want to forgive me?"

Val rolls his eyes. "Keyon, you'll be fine. You two always make up, you know?" I want to believe Val, but I'm having a lot of doubts right now. About everything. I can't stand talking about these murders anymore. I always tell myself that if someone brings it up, I'm going to ignore it, but I just can't help talking about it. And Grace is no exception. I know that if I go to apologize, she's going to want to talk about Alexis. Which is completely understandable. I just don't want to talk about her dead friend with her. I decide to change the subject again.

"Are you worried that they're still hanging out?"

"Who, Jared and Nathan?"

I nod.

"I don't know. He can spend his time with whoever he wants. Doesn't bother me."

I raise my eyebrows at him.

"What? I'm being serious. And it's not like they're going to be friends much longer."

"What is that supposed to mean?"

"Would you want to hang around someone you thought was a murderer?"

I sigh. "Nathan really thinks that?"

"He seems to." Val shrugs. "You know what? I'm so fucking done talking about any of this."

"Me too," I say.

"I'm going to talk to Jared and get our normal relationship back if it kills me. No pun intended. You need to go talk to Grace."

I nod. "You're right. Good idea."

Val drops me off at Grace's house fifteen minutes later then heads down to Jared's. I stare at Grace's door for a few moments, debating whether or not I should actually do this. Before I get a chance to run away, the door opens, and I see Grace standing in front of me.

"Hi," I say.

She stares at me.

"How did you know I was out here?"

"Saw you get out of Val's car through the window."

"Right." I nod. "I came to apologize."

Grace crosses her arms. "Really?"

"Yeah," I say. I don't say anything else. I realize too late that I'm an idiot for not apologizing straight away, because she slams the door in my face. The harder I try, the worse it seems to get for me.

"Mckeyon?"

I hear Nancy say my name, and I stand up. I pick up my blue folder off the chair next to me and walk over to the woman who's about to get her ear talked off.

"How are you today?" She smiles at me.

"I'm good," I say and smile back.

We walk down the same short hallway we went down two weeks ago and head into her office. I sit in the empty chair on the right side of the room and hand Nancy my paper as she sits down in front of me. She looks it over and then glances up at me. I must seem distracted or something because she says, "You alright?"

"Oh." I cough. "Yeah. Totally fine. Are you?"

I mentally slap myself. Why would you ask your therapist if they're alright? God, I'm an idiot. Thankfully, Nancy just laughs.

"I am alright. Thank you for asking," she says.

"You're welcome." I look down at my hands awkwardly.

"So." Nancy leans forward. "What's going on in that head of yours?"

"So much." I cover my face with my hands in frustration, slowly trying to wipe away this overwhelming feeling.

Nancy leans back in her seat and relaxes. "Tell me what's going on."

I do. I tell her everything else that's happened. I explain to her who Alexis was and what happened to her. I tell her how I left Grace and how she hasn't talked to me in almost two weeks. The thing that I talk the most about is Jared and how we all have a low-lying mutual agreement that he's the one who killed Quinn, Erica, and Alexis. Nancy doesn't even seem surprised. I tell her about Nathan, and that's when she starts asking questions.

"Are you friends with Nathan?"

I shake my head. "I wouldn't say so. I mean, he's not bad, but at the same time, he's pretty bad. Does that make sense?"

Nancy laughs a little. "It does to me. Do you think Val is worried that Jared is spending all this time with Nathan? Or with any of you?"

"I don't know." I shrug with one shoulder. "I asked him about Jared and Nathan, and he said it didn't bother him, but I don't know about the rest of us."

"Are you bothered by Jared talking to you and your friends?"

"Well, no. I mean, no. He just, yeah."

Nancy raises an eyebrow at me. "He just, yeah?"

"Yeah," I say. "I don't know. Val says that he trusts him. And I think I'm starting to gain a little bit of my trust for him back, but like I said, I don't know. I just don't want to say to Val that I don't trust him or don't want him over, because I know he does. I can't do that to him."

"Is Val someone who's very important to you?"

"Well, yeah. He is."

"Do you want him spending his time with people that aren't good for him?"

I blink a few times. "You're saying that the people around him are bad for him? Like Jared?"

"I'm only saying that because that's what you said."

I think about this. Is that what I was saying? It must've been. I tell her no; I don't want Val being with people who are bad for him. She asks me what I'm going to do about that, and I tell her that I have no idea. I leave the place half an hour later feeling even more stressed out than when I first arrived.

Val is waiting for me in his car when I walk outside, and he looks just as bad as I feel.

"Jesus," I say. "You alright? You look terrible."

Val rolls his eyes. "Thanks. I know. Can we leave? And not go back home? Ever?"

"What?" I laugh a little as I get into his car. "Why would we do that?"

"Because I went to a goddamn jewelry store today, Keyon."

I raise my eyebrows as he starts to drive. "A jewelry store? For what?"

"I'm going to sound like a total hypocrite. You know how I said when you were dating Erica that no one should get married in their twenties?"

I snap my head sideways to look at him. "Valentine, you are *kidding me*. You're going to propose to Jared? Now?"

"No. Jesus Christ, no. I thought about it. I'm not actually going to do it."

"Good," I say. We stop at a red light, and Val turns to look back at me.

"Good?" he asks. "You don't want us to get married?"

"Do *you* even want you two to get married?"

Val sighs and averts his eyes back over to the road. "No. Not now at least. Especially not now. Not with everything that's going on. Just in case."

"Just in case he's a murderer?"

Val smacks my arm hard then puts his hand back on the wheel. "Shut the fuck up. You know that's not what I was going to say."

"Then what were you going to say?"

Val lets out an exasperated sigh but doesn't say anything else for a few minutes. "I'm serious, though. I do not want to go back home right now."

I shrug. "Then let's not. Where do you want to go?"

"You're not even going to ask why I don't want to stay home?"

"You said you were thinking about to proposing to Jared, even though you've only been together for two months. I know you didn't bring up the length of the relationship, but I felt like *I* had to bring it up just to make sure you knew how stupid you sounded. But anyway, I'm going to assume that Jared wants to see you or something, because you're freaking out about him and what you were thinking about doing. Am I right?"

"Spot on," Val says. "Let's get the hell out of here. Where are we headed?"

I shrug. "How adventurous do you want to be?"

"I don't know." Val stops at another red light, then he looks at me seriously. "Call Hadlee real quick."

I don't question him; I just whip out my phone and dial Hadlee's number. She answers on the second ring.

"Hey," she says. I tell Val I'm putting the phone on speaker and press the button.

"Hey," I respond. "Val said I needed to call you. He's in the car with me right now."

"Okay? What's up?"

"You travel a lot," Val says loudly.

"I do," Hadlee agrees.

"If you were having a horrible time and just wanted to get away from literally fucking everything, where would you go?"

Hadlee is silent for a moment. "Last summer I went up somewhere really nice in Michigan. I don't know what exactly you mean by traveling, though. Do you want to stay in Wisconsin?"

"Sure," I say.

"No," Val says at the same time. We stare at each other before the light turns green.

"Okay," Hadlee says slowly. "Like I was saying, I went to a place called Copper Harbor in Michigan, and it was absolutely gorgeous. I'd love to go again."

"Then come with us." Val smiles.

"Are you crazy?" I cover the phone with my hand. "We can't just up and leave the state."

"Why not?"

"Hadlee." I take my hand off the phone. "Val's an idiot. We're not leaving the state."

"Yes, we are!" Val yells. "I need to get the fuck out of here, and you're coming with me whether you like it or not."

"Are you talking to me or Keyon?" Hadlee asks.

"Both of you."

"Sounds fun," Hadlee says. "I'm in. When are we leaving?"

I throw one hand up in the air and take a deep breath. "Well, fuck it, I guess. We can leave today."

Val laughs. "Yes! That's the spirit!" he says rather cheerfully. "Okay, Hadlee, meet us at our apartment in, like, an hour."

Hadlee tells us she'll see us then, and I hang up. Val and I say nothing to each other the rest of the way home, but I can tell he's happier than he was when I first got in the car. We spend about ten minutes packing a bag for the both of us before Val's phone goes off. He picks it up off his nightstand, and I hold out a shirt for him.

"Do you like this one?" I ask. "I've never seen you wear it."

"Don't pack it," Val says as he looks at his phone. "Fuck, it's Jared."

"What did he say?"

"He said Hadlee told him we were going out of town. Literally what the hell. You can't trust that girl with anything." Val types something furiously on his phone.

"What did you say to him?"

Val presses another button on the screen and looks up at me. "I invited him."

"You invited him," I repeat him.

"Yes."

I throw the shirt that I'm holding at Val. "Why? You know everything's all confusing right now."

"Maybe for you." Val shrugs. "But I'm in love with him, and I like spending time with him, so if that bothers you—"

"It doesn't," I say quickly. I remember how angry I was at Val for him not wanting me to be with Grace. I couldn't do the same thing to him. "Bring him along." I shrug. "I don't mind."

Val raises an eyebrow. "You don't?"

"No. Of course not. You do you."

Val gives me a weird look but nods anyway. Hadlee shows up half an hour later. Jared shows up ten minutes after that. And then we leave.

The drive takes about three hours. It would've taken longer, but Hadlee insists that we don't make any stops to "keep us on schedule." I don't know what schedule she's talking about, but we all listen to her. The car ride isn't as awkward as I thought it would be. I find myself laughing and talking with the three others the whole time. Normally. Just like we used to. There isn't even a little tension between us.

As soon as we get there, we immediately start arguing about the cost of hotels and things to do. Jared and Hadlee want to pay for all of it. I almost accept their offers, but Val gives me a look that says I am being extremely inconsiderate, and then we offer to split it up evenly. After figuring out the cost, we end up at a pretty decent hotel. Hadlee suggests taking one room to save money, but with me being my awkward self, I tell her I can't sleep in the same bed as her. Hadlee says it's alright, and Val says something about me being a pussy, but I ignore him.

We settle into our rooms, and I lie facedown on my bed. Hadlee laughs and flops backward on hers.

"I'm so glad we're doing this," she says. "I love being an adult with money."

"I would love to be an adult with money." I laugh with her.

"Come on." Hadlee flips onto her side at the same time I do so that we're both facing each other. "Aren't you excited?" she asks me.

"Well, we're already here, so I kind of have to be."

Hadlee rolls her eyes. "Don't be so negative. It's nice getting away from everything that's going on. You have to agree with that."

"I don't know if having Jared here means that I can get away from everything that's going on."

"Oh, shut up. Jared's fine. I thought we'd moved on from this?"

"Maybe you have. I know I haven't."

"Don't you want things to be normal again?"

I sit up in my bed. "I've had three people I know get killed. And we literally accused Val's boyfriend of being a murderer. I don't know if things can ever be normal again."

Hadlee sighs and puts her face in a pillow. "Keyon, it's fine." She mumbles. "I'm sure he's over it by now."

"Over the fact that he's killed people?"

Hadlee sits up and throws her pillow at me. "Not funny," she says. I can see her smiling, though. There's a knock at the door, and Hadlee jumps up to answer it. Jared and Val walk in a second later, and Hadlee sits down next to me on my bed. Jared sits down calmly on Hadlee's bed, and Val lands on his back dramatically next to him.

"So," Val says. "What are we supposed to do? What'd you do last time, Hadlee?"

Hadlee shrugs. "Looked at some of the cool nature stuff they have. Took a lot of good pictures. Went out to eat a lot. Nothing too fancy."

"Sounds wonderful." Val sighs.

A couple minutes later, we decide that we need to wait until the sun sets to go do something cool. Hadlee tells us about how beautiful the sunsets are, and Jared agrees that he thinks it'd be amazing to see. We go out to eat at some restaurant that sounded appealing to us and spend about an hour and half talking about whatever. Once we leave, Hadlee tells us about a viewing deck that people go to to watch the sunsets. We all agree that it sounds like a good idea and head over to where the rest of the tourists seem to be gathering.

We sit on the edge of the deck (Hadlee on my left, Val on my right, leaning his head on Jared's shoulder), and I take a minute to actually breathe. Hadlee was right; the sunsets here must always be absolutely amazing, because this one is amazing. I stare at the red-and-orange light, slowly swirling into darker purples and blues. I think I could stay here the rest of my life it's so perfect. Val and Jared are laughing quietly about something before Val turns to face me.

"What do you think?" he asks.

"I think I'm in love," I say.

Hadlee laughs. "Don't tell Grace that."

"God," I bring my hands up to my face. "Grace. Do you think she'll be pissed I did this without her?"

"I think she's just pissed at you in general right now." Val nods.

"You're right. Man, let's just not talk about this. At least not while we're here. I don't want to think about anything that's going to make any of us upset."

Everyone nods, and we look back up. Jared sighs, and I hear Val ask what he's thinking about. I turn my head and listen to their conversation.

"Do you have any regrets?" Jared says, half to me and half to Val.

"What do you mean?" Val asks.

Jared sighs again. "Just, anything that you regret. Something you wish you didn't do." I look back up at the dark sky and laugh a little. "I think we all have regrets. I know I do."

"That makes two of us." Hadlee nudges me playfully.

"Three," Jared says.

"Four," Val almost whispers.

"Good thing we're all on the same page," I say just as quietly.

I don't exactly know what we're talking about, but whatever it is, I'm okay with it. I guess I could say that there's a chance we're all thinking about something depressing, but I don't think that's true for me. I'm not thinking about much of anything. Absolutely nothing. It's almost heaven. We all stay this way for a while until we start shivering. Hadlee stands up first and suggests we all head back to the hotel. Everyone agrees, and we eventually make it back to our rooms. Hadlee takes over the bathroom first, and I sit down on my bed quietly.

After a few minutes, I decide that Hadlee is going to take forever, and I go outside. Not just in the hallway but actually outside. I can see half of a bench around the corner at the front of the hotel, and I walk around to take a seat. I almost sit on someone until I realize that it's Val.

"Oh," I say. "Hey. What are you doing out here?"

Val looks up at where I'm standing. "I could ask you the same thing." He motions for me to sit down next to him. "Jared already fell asleep," he says. "Figured I could use even more fresh air. You know?"

I nod as I sit down. "I know. What did you think Jared was talking about earlier?"

"What do you mean?"

"About having regrets. What do you think made him say that?"

"I don't know." Val shrugs. "Maybe it was just the fact that we were sitting in silence. Nothing to bother us. When that happens, your mind tends to just go everywhere. I'm sure he wasn't thinking about anything too serious."

"Yeah," I say. "Probably not. What were you thinking about? I was going to ask, but I didn't want to, like, you know, put all of the attention on you."

"You should've. I love attention." Val smiles, and I laugh. "But seriously." He sighs. "I don't know what I was thinking. I guess I was a little more worried about you guys. What were you thinking about?"

I sigh. "I know I said I didn't want to talk about things that would make any of us upset, but if you really want to know—"

"I do."

"Alright." I sigh again. "I was thinking about that night at Quinn's place. When I said I wanted you to look around. I should've gone in myself."

Val brings his hands to his face and rubs his temples. "Keyon, come on. You can't get upset over that."

"Why can't I?"

"It's alright. I'd rather have myself be a little freaked out than you have nightmares over it or something."

"Already have those," I mumble.

"I thought you had nightmares about me?"

"I do. Or I did. But I did have another one about Quinn the other night."

Val looks at me seriously. "Why didn't you tell me?"

"Didn't want you to worry."

"You're such an asshole."

"Why?"

"You've got to fucking tell me when this happens. I freak the hell out if I don't know what's going on with you."

I laugh a little. "You also freak the hell out if you *do* know what's going on with me. What am I supposed to do? Do I tell you or not?"

"You tell me," Val says. "You always tell me. Got it?"

"Yeah." I nod. "I got it."

Val pulls his phone out of his pocket and looks at the screen. "Jared woke up and wants to know where I am. Better head back upstairs," he says as he stands up. "You coming?"

"Yeah, I'm coming."

We walk back inside and take the elevator up to our floor. Val stands outside my door before I walk in.

"Do you think I'm crazy for wanting to marry someone I hardly know?"

I raise an eyebrow. "You think you hardly know him?"

"No, I mean, I'm pretty sure I know everything about him. I meant to say someone I haven't known for that long."

I shrug. "If you're in love, then you're in love. You can't help how you feel. I don't think you're crazy."

Val nods. "Wise words. I'll remember that." He smiles at me before walking across the hall and into his and Jared's room. I stare at their door for a few seconds before walking back into my room with

Hadlee. She's sitting on her bed, drying her hair with a towel, when she says, "Where were you?"

"Talking to Val outside." I lie back on my bed and sigh. "I probably shouldn't tell you this, but did you know Val was seriously considering proposing to Jared?"

Hadlee snaps her head toward me. "No."

"Yes. Crazy how fast people can fall in love."

"It is crazy," Hadlee says. "I think it's nice, though. It's nice to see Val happy like that."

"Yeah. It is." I pause. "Do you think he's okay?"

"What do you mean?"

"I don't know. He told me a little while ago that he wasn't feeling, like, you know. But I don't know. I guess I just don't believe that everything's okay. Especially not with everything that's been going on. Wouldn't that just stress someone out more? Not make them feel better?"

Hadlee shrugs then throws her towel on the floor as she lies back on her bed, getting under the covers. "I think he's okay. Even if he wasn't, don't you think he'd tell you that something was wrong?"

I sigh and kick off my shoes. "Maybe. It just feels like he keeps so many things from me. It seems likely that there's a lot that I don't know."

"Well, it's not like he has to tell you everything."

"I know that." I get under the covers, not bothering to change clothes. "I don't know. It's whatever."

I see Hadlee roll her eyes. "Whatever," she says. "Okay. Yeah. I'm going to bed. See you in the morning?"

I nod before closing my eyes. "See you in the morning."

I'm asleep for maybe an hour before I sit up in bed, completely out of breath. I don't even remember what the nightmare was about. I just know that I'm terrified. I look next to me to see Hadlee sleeping soundly. I'm almost jealous. I pick up my phone off the nightstand in between the two beds and see that it's about three. I'm not exactly sure what to do. Waking up Hadlee doesn't seem like an option and neither does waking up Val. So I basically just sit there for an hour, trying to calm myself down. It doesn't really work, and I think that

I'm having a panic attack or something. What are you supposed to do when that happens?

At seven, Hadlee is still asleep, and I grab the key to our room off the nightstand, heading downstairs to the dining area. I pour myself a cup of coffee and take a seat at one of the tables. There's maybe six other people down here, but I wouldn't expect anyone to be up this early. Since I only got about four hours of sleep, I rest my head on my hand for a few moments and fall asleep almost instantly. It isn't until eight that I hear someone saying my name. I open my eyes and see Jared standing in front of me.

"Morning." He smiles as he sits down across from me.

"Morning," I respond groggily. "God, how did I fall asleep at a table?"

Jared takes a sip of whatever he's holding in his hand. "You get a lot of sleep last night?"

"Not really."

"Nightmares?"

I raise an eyebrow. "Yeah. How did you know?" Jared ignores the question and leans back in his seat, taking another sip of whatever he has.

"Val isn't up yet," he says. "Thought I'd just come down here and see if you or Hadlee were awake."

"She's still asleep," I tell him. "It's just you and I for now."

Jared smiles as he finishes off his drink. "What do you think we all should do today? Got any ideas?"

I shrug. "Not really. I think what Hadlee said at dinner last night about hiking or whatever sounded nice. What do you think?"

"I think that sounds great. I'm kind of sick and tired of being inside all the time." He looks to the left and out the window beside us. "Went out there earlier, though. Cold as hell." He looks back toward me. "You alright?"

I hadn't even realized I'd started to fall asleep again. "What? Yeah. Just tired is all."

"I understand." Jared sighs. He's about to say something else, but my phone rings.

"Hang on," I say, taking my phone out of my pocket. "It's Grace."

"Better answer it," Jared says.

I nod and press accept on the screen. "Hello?"

"Where are you?"

I cover the phone with my free hand and look to Jared. "She wants to know where I am. What do I say?"

"Just tell her where you are. Be honest."

I silently agree and put the phone back up to my ear. "Home," I say. I close my eyes and call myself an idiot about a thousand times. Jared puts a hand to his forehead. "Why do you ask?" I say cautiously.

"Just wondering. Since I saw this really interesting picture of you, Val, Hadlee, and Jared on Val's Snapchat this morning."

Jesus Christ, I'm going to kill him. "Oh," I say.

"You didn't have to lie to me," Grace says. "I'm okay with you leaving or whatever it is that you're doing. A heads-up would've been nice, though."

"I'm sorry," I tell her. "It's just that I didn't think you really wanted to talk to me."

Grace sighs. "I do. I wanted to say that I'm sorry for giving you the silent treatment for so long. It was immature."

Great. Now she's the one apologizing when she knows as well as I do that *I* should be apologizing. "It's okay. I'm sorry too. I was being an idiot. I shouldn't have acted like that."

Jared looks at me questioningly. I wave my hand at him, trying to say that I'll tell him later.

"It's alright," Grace says. "I forgive you. When are you coming home?"

"I don't know. We shouldn't be out here too long."

"I hope not." Grace pauses for a moment. "I miss you."

I smile. "I miss you too. How about I call you later tonight?"

"I'd like that. I'll let you go."

"Alright," I say. Neither of us say anything for a minute until I say, "I love you."

Grace hesitates, and I think I'm about to have another panic attack. "Love you too," she finally says. We hang up, and I set my phone on the table, putting my head in my hands.

"Everything good?" Jared asks.

"Yeah. I kind of left Grace crying alone in her room a few weeks ago after what happened with Alexis, and I hadn't really apologized until just now. We didn't talk for about two weeks. But I guess everything's okay now. Maybe."

"Maybe," Jared repeats me. "May I ask why you left her crying alone?"

"I'm just stupid. Really, really stupid."

Jared laughs a little, and then I hear Val's voice.

"Thanks for telling me where you were going to be, guys. Real considerate," he says.

"You're welcome." I smile at him. Val rolls his eyes and sits down in the middle of Jared and me.

"Where's Hadlee?" I ask, looking behind him.

"I don't know." Val shrugs. "Why are you wearing the same clothes you had on yesterday?"

I lean back in my chair and bring my hands to my face. "I'm a mess."

"Don't worry about it." Val waves his hand. "No one's judging. We're on vacation, no one gives a fuck what you do."

"Well said, Valentine," Hadlee says as she walks up to the table. I didn't even see her coming over here. She sits down in the last empty chair across from Val and sighs. "What's the plan for today?"

"I was thinking"—Val pulls out his phone and sets it in the middle of the table, showing us pictures of trails and flowers—"we could do this. I know you love this kind of stuff," he says, looking at Hadlee. I see Hadlee's eyes light up.

"You're right," she says. "I think this looks amazing."

I agree with her. Anything I can do to get my mind off everything, I'm going to do it. We all eat a little then head back up to our rooms to get changed. We drive out to some of the more famous trails in the area and get out of the car. Val says something about how he's excited to get out and smell the roses. We all laugh and follow Hadlee into the trees to our left. There's still some snow on the ground, but it's pretty obvious why people would want to come out here. Flowers of every color, shape, and size litter the ground. I think that Hadlee might cry. I look up at the sky and breathe it all in. Just what I needed. We walk and talk for another hour and a half or so until we come across a waterfall. Jared and I freak out then bond a little over our mutual love for waterfalls. Val calls us nerds, but we stop to sit by it anyway. Hadlee takes out a camera that makes her look like she means business. She takes a couple pictures and shows them to us, making me wish I had talent.

"God, this is incredible," Val says as he leans backward on the grassy area we're all sitting on.

"You can say that again." Jared smiles.

"I could probably stay here forever." I look over at Hadlee. "You picked a good spot. Totally worth the drive."

"Totally." Hadlee laughs. "I'm glad you all like it."

"I think that when I die, this is going to be my heaven," Val says.

Jared and I give each other nervous looks. "Don't say stuff like that," I tell Val.

"Dude, I was kidding," he says defensively. "And honestly, I think that my type of heaven is more of an endless concert kind of scene."

Jared and Hadlee laugh, but I stay silent. I don't like hearing Val talk about death. Not even if he's joking. I know that's probably just me being a buzzkill or being overprotective of him or something, but I don't care. It's not my fault if I worry easily. We talk for a little while longer before Hadlee suggests that we head back to the hotel. We all agree and start walking. I try to focus on what everyone is saying on the way back, but I can't focus. I can't focus when we go out to eat. I can't focus when we sit in Hadlee and my hotel room and watch movies. I can't even focus when Hadlee asks me what's wrong. In the middle of *Saw 4*, I stand up and walk out of the room. I run down the stairs, not bothering to take the elevator, and go outside. I sit on the same bench I sat on last night and take my phone out of my pocket to call Grace. She picks up on the third ring and greets me cheerfully. I don't even remember if I tell her hello or not.

I tell her what's been going on. I tell her about what happened during the two weeks where we weren't speaking. I tell her about Val leaving, my dad visiting, how I went to therapy twice already, and then I tell her about Jared's theory. The theory that all of us believe in. I don't care if she's not ready to talk about the murders; I need to talk about it before I go insane. I tell her that I'm worried about Val. She asks me why, and I explain everything from what Nathan told me about pills, to Val saying he was feeling suicidal. Grace can tell that this upsets me the most, and we talk about it for a little while. After an hour or so, I feel better. I tell her that I'm alright and that I love her, then I thank her for listening to all my problems. She says that she loves me too and that she's happy to help. Then we hang up. I sigh. Just when I thought I was going to forget about everything that's been going on. A second later, I hear the doors to the hotel slide open, and I turn around to see Jared walking over to me, hands shoved in his pockets.

"Val and Hadlee were worried, but surprisingly, both of them fell asleep," he says. "Figured I'd get out here and see what was bothering you." He sits down next to me and looks my way.

"Val," I tell him. "I don't even know why. I guess I just don't believe that he's okay. I hate to think that he's only pretending that everything's good. I called Grace, and we talked about it. So—"

"What?" Jared interrupts me. "You told Grace?"

"Yeah? Why is that a problem? It's not like she's going to tell anyone."

"I know that," Jared says quietly. "It's just that, don't you think we should keep this between us? You, Hadlee, and I?"

I shrug. "I guess. I mean, I just figured that maybe—"

"Keyon, you can't just go around telling other people's secrets."

"Alright." I hold my hands up in defense. "I got it. Sorry."

Jared sighs and looks down at his hands. "I didn't mean to get angry. I'm just worried."

"Yeah," I say. "So am I."

We sit in silence for about five minutes before Jared looks back at me. "Are we alright?"

"Yeah." I nod. "Why wouldn't we be?"

"We haven't exactly talked in a while. I didn't know how you felt about how we left things."

"Bad, I guess. I didn't mean to just completely put all of the blame on you."

"It's okay." Jared looks away from me and stares at something I can't see. "I get why you'd think it was me. I'll admit, I've been a little weird lately."

I laugh. "A little. But it's alright. There's a lot going on with all of us. I can see why you would be on edge. I think we all are."

Jared nods but doesn't say anything else.

"Anyway," I say, "we should probably go back in. See what everyone's doing. Or if they're even awake."

Jared laughs. "Good idea. If they sleep now, there's no way we're going to get them to sleep later."

"Good point." We stand up from the bench and walk back inside. We wait around in silence in the elevator, but it isn't uncomfortable. I feel normal around him again.

Our trip lasts two more days. Two perfect, normal days. Then everything falls apart again. Once we make it back home, Val gets fired. I've been missing too much school. And that's when the worst thing of all happens.

It's almost two in the morning on Saturday night when I finally get back to the apartment from Grace's house. I'm on a little bit of a high from what Grace and I were doing, so I don't notice that I have sixteen missed calls from Val. I don't notice that Jared runs into the building before I do. I don't even notice that his car is in the parking lot. I do, however, hear him yelling Val's name while I'm walking up the stairs to the third floor. This, obviously, makes me walk a lot faster. I get to the top of the steps and see Jared banging relentlessly on our door, calling out for Val.

"Jared, hey, what the hell is going on?" I ask rather loudly.

"Keyon." Jared grabs my shoulders. "Please just open the door."

I don't ask any questions. I take out my key and unlock the door as quickly as possible. Jared rushes in before I do and runs down the hall to Val's bedroom. I see him pause outside of the open door for a moment before he puts a hand up to his mouth. This is all too familiar. Images of Val standing outside of Quinn's bedroom flash through my mind. I run after Jared and tell myself that I can handle whatever I'm about to see. Jared still moves faster than I do and goes into Val's bedroom. I follow closely behind him and kneel down on the ground as soon as I see Val. Jared's saying something, but I can't comprehend anything that's happening. Why do I always shut down in situations like this? Val's barely keeping his eyes open. He's lying on the ground with his back against the edge of his bed, eyes darting back and forth between Jared and me. I still don't know what Jared's saying; I'm too focused on Val's arms. I don't know what he used, but he has two deep-looking horizontal cuts across each of his arms. I shouldn't have believed that he was okay. I never should've been that stupid.

Jared is saying Val's name over and over, asking him if he can hear him, and Val is barely responding. The first intelligible thing to come out of my mouth is "We need to get him to the hospital. There's too much blood."

Jared is silent for a moment. "No," he says.

"No?" I look up from Val and over to Jared. "What do you mean 'no'? Do you see him? If we don't get him some help soon, then—"

"I said no." Jared snaps his head to the side to look at me. "We're not bringing him anywhere."

"Jared." I look back down at Val. "We need to take him to the hospital. Now. I'm calling 911."

I stand up, but Jared grabs on to my arm tightly. "Mckeyon," he says. His tone makes me stop moving altogether. "If you call *anyone*, I will never forgive you."

I stare at him for a moment. "I don't understand what you're saying. Why can't we—"

"Because we just *can't*, Keyon. Alright?" Jared yells. "You have to trust me on this. We have to just do whatever we can here. We can't let anyone know what's happening."

"I don't—"

"Mckeyon, stay with him for a minute."

Before I can object, Jared rushes out of the room. I kneel down to get closer to Val and touch his arms gently. I take a deep breath and nod my head a few times, trying to tell myself that I can do this.

"Hey," I tell Val. "You're going to be fine, alright? You're going to be fine. Everything's okay. You don't have to worry. It's alright."

Val tries to take a deep breath. "I don't want—"

"Val, please don't say anything. Jared's getting something right now. It's alright. Just calm down." I say that last part to myself. I can do this. I need to be here for Val. Jared comes into the room a second later holding towels and duct tape.

"Is this the best you could do?" I ask him.

"What, do you have any better ideas?"

"Yeah," I say. "Call a fucking ambulance."

Jared drops what he's holding and leans forward, grabbing a fistful of my shirt in the process. "I swear to God if you suggest that one more time, I—"

"Alright," I barely whisper. "I get it. Do what you want."

Jared loosens his grip on my shirt and looks down at Val.

"Valentine, I need you stay really still," he says.

I almost laugh at this. Val is so close to passing out there's probably no way he could move at all. Jared takes one of the towels and wraps it tightly around Val's right arm. It immediately turns a dark shade of red. He holds the towel down with one hand and picks up the duct tape with the other, tearing off a long strip with his teeth. He wraps the duct tape around Val's arm even tighter than he wrapped the towel. He repeats the process for Val's left arm then takes a deep breath. He looks down at his hands, and I notice they're completely covered in Val's blood. I also notice that he's shaking. A lot.

"This wasn't supposed to happen," Jared whispers. "This was never supposed to happen. I told him I would help him. I told him I would—"

Jared starts to cry. Val holds up an arm and offers Jared a hand. Jared takes Val's bloodied hand in his and starts to cry even harder. I'm not sure what to do now, although I know exactly how Jared feels. I told Val that all we wanted to do was help him. And I meant that.

I never wanted this to happen. This is what I've been so goddamn worried about. But I'm not going to cry. I'll let Jared do that. Val needs to know that at least one of us can stay strong for him through all this. I don't know exactly how long we sit here. Val fades in and out of consciousness, and eventually, I think he falls asleep. Jared is still holding his hand, and I still have no idea what to do. So I ask.

"What now?"

"I don't know," Jared shakes his head and wipes underneath his eyes with one of his hands. "God, I don't know." He keeps on shaking his head. "Do you think this will be enough?"

"I honestly can't say. I hope it will be." I look up at Jared. "He's going to be okay."

Jared looks back at me with watery eyes. "I hope to God you're right." He looks back down at Val. "I don't think I could live with myself if he—"

"Don't say that," I tell him. "Don't say anything like that. This isn't your fault."

"There are so many things I wish I could tell you, Keyon."

I pause. "What?" Jared doesn't answer me, because Val opens his eyes. Jared and I both lean forward a little, looking Val up and down.

"Fuck," Val says.

I laugh. "Are you okay?" I know I sound like I'm panicking, but I can't help it. I don't know how much longer I can pretend like everything is fine. Val doesn't respond with words; he just shakes his head. I turn to look at Jared.

"He may be awake now, but he still lost a lot of blood. We really might have to—"

"What did I say about saying something like that again?" Jared whispers, not taking his eyes off Val.

"Sorry," I say. "I just don't know what else we can do for him."

"He'll be fine. What we've done now is enough."

———————◆•◆———————

Two months pass without a problem. I'm careful with what I say around Val. I don't want to upset him, not even a little. He notices that I'm being cautious, and we have a serious talk about how it's pissing him off that I'm treating him like he's fragile. I drop the argument and let him have his way. Whatever keeps him happy. I see Jared more often. He's over a lot, our group of four goes out together a lot, and most nights Val isn't even home. It doesn't bother me since I've been spending more and more time with Grace. I spend the night with her, she spends it with me, and to be honest, Val doesn't seem to notice. I can feel us drifting apart, but I don't think that there's anything I can do about it. Hadlee says that I need to talk to him, but I don't know how to bring it up, seeing as how we never talk. I want to talk to him because I know he needs me. He needs someone. Yes, he does hang out with all of us, but that's not what he needs. I can tell that he feels worse than ever. He needs someone he can *really* talk to.

I tell Nancy this a week later, and she agrees with Hadlee. She thinks I need to talk it out with him. Find a time when neither of us are busy and have a real conversation.

"But what if he doesn't want to talk to me about serious stuff like that?" I hold out my hand.

"I'm sure he will," Nancy says. "I'm sure he misses you just as much as you miss him."

"Yeah." I lean back in my seat. "I doubt that."

"How do you know he doesn't feel the same way you do?"

"Because I know Val. He's really not emotional about these kind of things."

Nancy shrugs. "You never know. What do you think you should do?"

"Talk to him, I guess."

So I try. Val comes home from wherever he was and sits down on the couch. I walk out of my room and stand in front of him.

"We need to talk," I say.

Val raises his eyebrows. "We do?"

"Yeah. We do." I throw my hands up in the air. "I don't feel like we're friends anymore."

"What are you talking about? You're kind of my best friend."

"Am I? Am I really?"

Val rolls his eyes. "You sound like a teenage girl. Seriously."

"Val, I mean it. What's going on?" I sit down on the couch next to him. "Is everything—"

"Everything's fine, Keyon. You don't have to worry about me. I tell you this all the time."

"And I never believe you. You know that. You said you were fine before, and then you—"

"Can we not talk about that?" Val raises his voice. "Please," he says a little more softly.

"I'm sorry. I didn't mean to bring that up. I'm just scared, that's all."

Val sighs. "I don't want you to be. That wasn't supposed to happen. You weren't ever supposed to be scared for me."

This reminds me of what Jared said the night we found Val on the floor of his room. This wasn't supposed to happen. I want to ask questions, but I don't want to make this conversation any worse than it already is. But I'm an idiot, and I can't help myself.

"Do you remember anything about that night?"

Val looks over at me. "What?"

"Anything that Jared said? Do you remember anything?"

"Kind of. I remember him saying that he didn't want me to do it or something."

"That it wasn't supposed to happen?"

Val sighs. "Yeah. That was it. Why?"

"What do you think he meant by that?"

"What? What do you think he meant?"

"Well, I know he probably meant he didn't want for that to happen, but I can't help but think—"

"You can't accuse him of anything again, Keyon. I won't let you. And if you do blame him for something, I'm not going to listen to you. I'm sorry, but that's just how it is."

I nod. "I understand. If I were you, I wouldn't listen to me either."

"Then why even say something like that?"

I sigh. "I don't know. I'm sorry."

"God, no. Stop. Don't apologize. I hate when you apologize even when you don't need to."

"I just thought—"

"It's fine. Alright? Really."

Val changes the subject, and we talk for another hour and a half or so. It's nice, talking to him. I still feel tense, but I can tell that Val is unbothered. Once Val decides he's going to do some schoolwork, I make the choice to head out to Grace and my favorite coffee shop, minus Grace. I order once I get there and sit down at a small table with my drink. I play on my phone for a while to calm myself down until I hear someone say my name.

"Hey," I say as I turn around to see Emmett. I motion to the chair in front of me. He smiles at me and takes a seat.

"Haven't seen you in a while," he says.

"I feel like you say that every time you see me."

Emmett laughs. "Maybe that's because it's true every time I see you. How's everything been?"

I shrug. "Same as always, I guess."

"Really?"

"Yeah." I pause. "Why do you ask?"

Emmett shifts uncomfortably in his seat. "I heard about your girlfriend's roommate a little while back. I thought you might have known her or something."

"Not really. I mean, we've talked before, but it's not like we were close. Grace was definitely closer to her."

"Yeah." Emmett nods. "Can I ask you something about that? It feels a little like no one else is willing to talk to me about what happened. To any of them."

So Emmett wants to talk about the murders too. I'm glad I ran into him. It's all I've been thinking about the past five months, and I think that I've basically talked all of my friends' ears off about it already.

"We can talk about it." I shrug.

"Why do you think any of it happened?"

I look at him closely. "What do you mean?"

"I mean, what do you think the motive was for whoever did this?"

I furrow my brow. "Well, I kind of agree with Jared's theory. I thought you did too."

"Who's Jared again?"

"You met him that day we were all out to eat."

"Right." Emmett nods. "Right. But I don't know what theory you're talking about."

I lean back in my seat. "Jared said he ran into you at the police station. He said that you agreed with him."

Emmett shakes his head slowly. "I stop in at the station a lot, but I've never seen him there. I still don't know what you're talking about."

"Jesus Christ," I say.

"What?"

I lean forward. "I'm going to tell you a few things."

"Okay?"

"Jared has this theory that all of us pretty much believe in. He thinks that whoever is doing this is basically doing it because they think they're doing something good. Like, mercy killing. He thinks, well, we all think that whoever is doing this has some complex that if someone is suicidal and attempts to kill themselves, then actually killing them would be the right thing to do. Does that make sense?"

"Killing people because they want to kill themselves. I understand."

"Good." I nod. "Well, for a while, Hadlee and I, maybe even Val, thought that Jared could possibly be the one behind this. Yes, he did tell us about his theory, but he also told me he agreed with those kind of views. The mercy killing views or whatever. Still with me?"

Emmett nods.

"Okay," I continue. "We all suspected him, and of course, he didn't like that. So he told us he went to the police and told them about his theory to see if they would actually listen to him. He told us they all thought he was crazy, except for you. He said you were there and that you listened to what he said. He said that you told him it made perfect sense."

"But the thing is, I didn't say that. I never saw him."

"I know that now," I say. "Which is why I'm kind of freaking out. Why would he lie about going to the police?"

Emmett sighs. "You really think you have a reason to suspect this guy?"

"Yes."

"Well, he probably lied because if he did go to the police, then that would basically be turning himself in, right?"

"Maybe. I don't know. They can't arrest someone for homicide if they think that the person is trying to solve the case, can they?"

"You're right." Emmett nods. "But still. He shouldn't have had to lie about going to the police. Unless he was scared you or someone else would go to the police first."

"He told me he was scared of becoming a suspect. He thought we should all be scared."

"And what was his reasoning behind that?"

"He said it would seem suspicious that we knew all of the victims. I didn't agree with him on that. I was more focused on how concerned for himself he seemed to be."

Emmett rests his chin on top of his hands and takes a deep breath. "What do you think we should do?"

"I can't tell Val." I shake my head. "Either he won't believe me, or he just won't listen to me. I think I need to tell Hadlee."

"The blond girl?"

"Yeah. Her."

"You think she'll be able to help?"

"I think that she'll believe me."

Emmett stares at me for a minute. "I believe you."

"Thank you," I say. "I just need to figure this out. I have to."

I call Hadlee and tell her that Emmett and I are coming over and that it's important. I don't explain what's going on, but she doesn't object. Emmett drives us over to her place in about five minutes. We run up a flight of steps to get to her front door, and I knock loudly. She opens the door in a matter of seconds and ushers us inside.

"What's going on?" she asks as we all sit down in her living room.

"Jared lied to us," I tell her.

"What?"

"Remember when he told us he went to the police and told them about what he thought was going on?"

"He didn't," Emmett says.

Hadlee looks back and forth between us. "How do you know he didn't?"

"He said he saw Emmett, remember?" I hold out a hand.

Hadlee's eyes widen as she looks at Emmett. "You didn't see him?"

"Only ever saw the guy once in my life. And it sure as hell wasn't at the police station. He straight up lied to you both. I never saw him, and I definitely never agreed with anything that he said."

"What do we do?" I look at Hadlee.

"I—" She stands up and turns to the side, covering her mouth with one hand. "I don't know. Maybe this doesn't mean anything. Maybe we're wrong."

"Hadlee, come on." I stand up to face her. "He had no reason to lie to us if he wasn't guilty. This *has* to mean something."

Emmett stands up with us. "Maybe we can talk to him about it."

Hadlee and I look at him like he just suggested we kill the president. "Are you crazy?" I ask him. "We can't talk to Jared. We have no idea what he'll do."

Hadlee puts a hand on my arm. "Have you told Val?"

"Val isn't going to believe me. You know that."

"He might believe all three of us."

I'm about to say something, but my phone rings. I take it out of my pocket and look at the screen. "It's Val. What do I do?"

"Answer it," Hadlee tells me.

"Tell him what's going on," Emmett says.

I let out an exasperated sigh and answer the call, putting it on speakerphone. I motion for everyone else to stay quiet. "Yeah?"

"Where are you?"

Hadlee mouths the words "Tell him."

"I'm at Hadlee's," I say. "Why?"

Val sighs. "I've been thinking about what you said earlier and you're right. I do think we need to start talking—"

"Val, this is very important to me, and it means a lot that you want to talk about this, but something really, really important is going on right now, and I think you need to know about it."

Val doesn't say anything for a minute. "Okay."

"You're going to hate me when I say this, but—"

"Jared lied to us," Hadlee interrupts me.

"What?" Val asks.

"He told us he went to the police to tell them about his theory to see if he could help, but he didn't."

"Okay."

No one says anything. "Okay?" I repeat him.

"What do you want me to say to that?"

"Val, I'm sorry, but we all think Jared has something to do with what's been happening."

"You know nothing's happened in months, right?"

"Yes, but—"

I hear my phone beep, and I look at the screen. He hung up.

"Well, that's great," I say.

"I still think we should just talk to Jared," Emmett says calmly.

"What would we even say to him?"

"I don't know. Maybe just let him defend himself. There's still a chance he hasn't done anything. We can't make assumptions just because of one lie."

I want to argue with him, but I really can't. He's right. If we're going to blame Jared for anything, we have to give him a chance to explain himself if he can.

"Should we call him then?" Hadlee looks at Emmett and me.

"We should probably talk to him in person," I say. "That way, he can't just hang up like Val did."

"So what? We just tell him we want to hang out? Won't that seem a little weird because Val won't be with us?"

"We're friends with him. It won't be weird. It'll be fine. And we could always tell him that it's serious or something. We just won't tell him that it's about him."

We call Jared to tell him that he needs to come over to Hadlee's. I tell him that it's an emergency, and he says he'll be right over. We wait about twenty minutes until there's a knock at the door. We all look at each other.

"Should I even be here for this?" Emmett asks.

"Yes," Hadlee says as she stands up. She walks toward the door and takes a deep breath before opening it. She smiles at Jared, and he smiles back before she steps to the side to let him in. He notices Emmett and freezes.

"What's the emergency?" Jared looks at me.

Hadlee closes the door behind Jared. The look on his face tells me he knows he's in trouble. I almost want to laugh.

"We know you lied about going to the police," Emmett says. I'm surprised. I didn't think that Emmett would say anything. I don't know what I expect Jared to do, but I definitely don't expect him to get angry.

"So that's what this is about," he says. And then he laughs. "I can't believe I actually came over here."

"We just wanted to hear what you had to say." Hadlee sighs.

"Why do you care? It seems like you three have already talked about this. What I have to say doesn't matter."

"Jared." Hadlee brings her hands up to her face. "I want you to tell us that you're innocent. I don't want our stupid assumption to be right."

Jared laughs again. "Let me guess, Keyon told you I was a murderer? Is that what happened?"

I can't really help how I feel now; I don't like that he's singling me out like this.

"We know you are," I almost yell as I stand up. "So just fucking admit to it already."

"I can't admit to something that isn't true."

We all look at him. "Jared," Emmett says. "You and I both know that you didn't go to the police. We never saw each other. I never agreed with your theory. You just wanted to make Keyon and Hadlee trust you again."

Jared stares him down. "You don't know anything about me."

"We know that we can't trust you," I say.

Jared looks at me for a moment before he says, "I'm not the one you should be worried about."

"What is that supposed to mean?" Hadlee gets a step closer to him.

Jared continues to stare at me. "Why don't you ask Keyon that?" He turns around and opens the door to Hadlee's apartment, then he leaves. He closes the door quietly behind him, and Emmett and Hadlee look at me.

"Keyon?" Hadlee questions.

I hold up my hands. "I have no idea what he's talking about. I swear."

"I want to trust you." Emmett shakes his head. "I don't trust Jared, but if he says you're involved in all of this, then that scares me."

"I'm not involved in any of this," I say. I'm starting to panic. I can't have Jared turning people against me. "Other than knowing the victims, I'm not involved. I don't know anything."

"Keyon, I'm sorry." Hadlee looks at me with what looks like tears in her eyes. "But I don't think I want to talk about this anymore. I think you two need to leave."

I look at Emmett, and he nods. I nod back at him and look down at Hadlee. "You're right. That's probably a good idea. I'm sorry."

"It's fine," Hadlee whispers. She opens the door for us, and Emmett and I leave.

Emmett tells me he can drive me back to my apartment, but he needs to go home. I tell him that sounds like a good idea, and he takes me back to Val and my place. Once I get there, I unlock the door and walk inside only to see Grace sitting on the couch.

"Grace," I say, clearly surprised. "What are you doing here?"

She smiles at me and stands up. "Val let me in," she says. She walks closer to me and wraps her arms around my neck. Then she frowns. "You okay?"

"Yeah." I smile. "I'm okay. How are you?"

"Better now," Grace says as she kisses me.

"Is Val still here?" I look down the hallway.

"No, he left as soon as I got here." She gives me a playful smile. "Why? What did you want to do?"

I really don't want to turn down whatever Grace is about to offer, but I'm so completely terrified that I don't think I could focus on anything like that right now.

"I actually want to talk to you about something," I say seriously.

Grace looks disappointed but nods anyway. "Sure. What is it?" She sits me down on the couch, and I take a deep breath. "I'm really sorry if you don't want to talk about this, but I think I know who's behind these murders."

Grace's eyes fill with an emotion that I can't quite explain. "What?"

"I think it's Jared. I know that sounds crazy, but we've been talking about it a lot over the past couple of months, and when Val had his incident two months ago, Jared said some things that really made me think. And I think we all need to stay the hell away from him."

Grace ignores every comment I made about Jared. "What do you mean by Val and his incident?"

"I don't know if I should even be telling you this." I sigh.

"You can say whatever it is you want me to know." Grace takes my hand in hers. "I'm listening."

"You know how I told you a little while ago that I found out about Val being suicidal?"

"I remember."

"I'm sorry," I say quietly. "I'm just really scared because of what I'm about to say. Jared said that we couldn't let anyone know about what happened."

Grace looks like she's about to kill someone. "Keyon, you can't let someone else scare you like that. That isn't okay. It's alright. You know that you can tell me anything."

I nod. "I know." I mentally prepare myself to tell her, and I take a deep breath. "Two months ago, Val tried to kill himself. He—"

"Wait." Grace holds up a hand. "What?"

"He attempted suicide."

Grace stands up from the couch and looks down at me. "Why didn't you tell me?"

"Why are you so angry? I was legitimately scared Jared was going to kill me or something if I ever brought this up around anyone. He wouldn't even let me call an ambulance."

"That's just like him." Grace laughs.

I don't say anything for a minute. "What? What's just like him?" Before Grace can answer my question, the door to the apartment swings open. and Val and Jared walk in.

"Whoa," Val says. "Sorry to interrupt whatever's—"

"No, no." I wave my hand at him as I stand up. "It's cool."

"Okay." Val claps his hands together. I'm assuming that he's going to forget the accusations we made against his boyfriend earlier and attempt to talk to Grace and me normally because he says, "Why don't we all go out and do something? We're all here. Sound like a good idea?"

I notice that Jared and Grace are looking at each other, Grace clenching her jaw tightly. I'm standing here, trying to piece together every bit of information that I have. How would Grace know that something is "just like Jared?" Haven't they only met once before? I think back to what Jared said earlier. He wasn't the one we needed to worry about. And apparently, I would know what he meant. And then I think about something else.

I think about Jared's theory. About the killer taking out people who've attempted suicide. When I had told Grace that Val was suicidal, Jared freaked out. Then when Val actually did try to kill himself, Jared didn't want anyone to know. Now Grace was upset that I didn't tell her about Val sooner. It doesn't make any sense.

"Jared," Grace says. "Can I talk to you out in the hall for a second?"

Jared looks nervous. "Um, yeah. Sure." He kisses Val quickly and follows Grace out into the hall. Val raises an eyebrow at me. "What was that about?"

I shrug. "No idea. We were actually talking about him, and then she got all mad."

"Mad at Jared?"

"Yeah."

"Don't they hardly know each other?"

I shrug again. "That's what I thought. Who knows. Maybe they hang out."

"Weird," Val says. We stand in uncomfortable silence for about three minutes until Grace and Jared walk back into the room.

"You guys ready to go?" Jared smiles at Val and me. I give him a look, but he just keeps on smiling. I notice how forced it seems.

"I know this really great restaurant downtown," Grace says. She grabs my hand and nods toward the door. "Come on, I'll drive all of us."

I look down at our hands and see that she's tracing circles over my thumb with hers. I look to my left and see that Jared's gripping tightly onto Val. I frown. When I look up at Jared, he's staring down at the ground, obviously upset about something.

Val smiles up at Jared, and Jared gives him barely half a smile in return. I reluctantly follow everyone out into the hall, and Val locks the door behind us. We head down the stairs and outside over to where Grace's car is parked.

"Hey," I whisper to Val before we get any closer to the car.

"Yeah?" Val whispers back.

"Let me sit by you on the way there."

"You don't want to sit by Grace?"

"Please?"

Val stares at me for a moment before nodding. Before either Jared or Grace can object, Val and I are sitting next to each other in the backseat. Grace's music is loud, and her and Jared are talking, so I doubt they'll be able to hear what I'm about to say to Val.

"Did you tell Jared that Erica tried to kill herself?"

Val gives me a weird look. "What?"

"Can you just answer the question?" I whisper rather loudly.

"Well, yeah."

"Yeah what?"

"Yeah, I told him. It was a crazy fucking story. I had to tell someone."

I sigh. "You told me before that Jared and Quinn were friends, right?"

"Yes. What's with all the weird questions?"

"Grace was friends with Alexis. She probably knew a lot about her," I say, half to myself and half to Val.

"Keyon, you're kind of freaking me out."

I zone out completely, and Jared asks Val a question. Soon, everyone but me is having a nice conversation about who knows what. A minute later, we stop outside of Grace's house.

"What are we doing here?" I ask her.

"I just need to grab something real quick." She turns around to smile at me before stepping out of the car. Jared and Val are talking about something, but I honestly can't tell you what it is. I feel sick. I try to reason with myself. My mind is playing tricks on me. I don't even know what I'm thinking. I'm not thinking. Val turns his head to look at me.

"Hey," he says. "Are you alright?"

I don't look at Val; I look at Jared. He looks back at me and swallows hard. That's when I know that something is very, very wrong.

"Why are we doing this?" I ask, my voice quiet.

Val tilts his head to the side. "What?"

"I don't trust—"

I cut myself off. I can't ruin this for Val. I can't ruin anything for him. But he needs to know that whatever's going on, Jared is in on it. I don't say anything else to either of them. I open my door and run into Grace's house. She's standing in her kitchen, putting something in her purse when she looks up at me. She frowns. "Are you okay?"

"What do you know?"

"I'm sorry?"

I walk quickly over to where she's standing, the counter separating us. "What do you know about Jared? You shouldn't know anything about him. Something's going on."

Grace sighs. "Keyon—"

"I don't want you to lie to me."

"I won't," Grace says seriously. She lifts her chin and crosses her arms. "I've known him for a while. About half a year."

I stare at her. "What? Why didn't I know that? And why would both of you lie—"

"There's a lot of things I wish I could tell you," Grace says.

Her words remind me so much of Jared's that I take a step back, completely terrified. "I don't know what you're talking about."

Grace walks around the counter and holds a hand out for me. "Come on." She smiles. "Let's just go back out there. Okay?"

I take another step back. "Not until you really tell me what's going on."

"Fine." Grace puts her hand up. She takes a deep breath and runs her fingers through her hair. "I wanted to help him."

"What do you mean?"

"He—"

Grace is cut off by the sound of her front door opening. Val walks in first, Jared trailing behind him, nervously rubbing his hands together. "I tried to stop him," Jared says.

"And I don't understand why." Val turns his head to give Jared a dirty look. "Keyon." He turns back to face me. "You okay? You kind of just freaked the hell out and ran off. Jared didn't want me to come after you."

I look at Jared. He avoids making any eye contact with me. "I'm fine," I tell Val, even though I have no idea what's going on. I decide to be an idiot and tell him what Grace just told me. "Did you know that Grace and Jared have known each other for almost six months?"

I hear Grace make a noise. "Mckeyon, this really isn't important."

"What?" Val looks at Jared then back at me. "I don't think I understand."

"I don't think I do either." I spin around to face Grace, but she isn't looking at me. She's looking at Jared.

"What do you want me to do?" She holds out a hand toward him.

"I don't know," Jared says, looking back and forth between her and Val, still completely ignoring me. "There's not much we really *can* do at this point. I keep telling you I wasn't meant to do this."

Grace laughs. "You haven't done anything."

"Okay," Val says. "This is fucking creeping me out. What are you two talking about?"

"Nothing." Jared shakes his head. He looks at Grace. "Can this wait?"

Grace glares at him before sighing and turning to look at me. "I need to talk to Jared outside for a minute. Can you and Val wait here for us?"

I nod, and Grace drags Jared out through the front door. I look at Val, and we both panic.

"What is happening right now?" I ask as we both get a few steps closer to each other.

"I have no idea," Val says. "But it's obvious there's something that they're not telling us."

"Yeah. Obviously." I pause. "Do you really still not believe me?"

Val is about to answer me, but a familiar song plays on my phone, and I know that Hadlee is calling me.

"Yeah?" I answer her.

"I just figured out everything," Hadlee says.

"What?"

"Do you have any time to talk?"

"Not really. Val and I are with Jared and Grace right now. Well, Jared and Grace are actually outside talking, but—"

Hadlee cuts me off quickly. "Listen to me for a minute. Make sure Val hears this too. You need to get the fuck out of wherever you are."

I put the call on speakerphone. "What?"

"Do you remember the party I had about six months ago?"

"Yes."

"Jared and Grace were both there. There's no way I could've had a party without the two of them talking. You know how small my place is."

"That makes sense," I say. "Grace literally just told me she's known Jared since around the time you had that party."

"Good. So we're on the same page. Now, think about this. That girl from your building and Jared used to be friends. Jared told you that, right?"

"Val did."

"Whatever. The point is, they were friends. And Jared knew about Erica through you, right?"

"Once again, that was Val. Val told him about her."

Hadlee sighs. "And Grace and Alexis had been friends for who knows how long, yes?"

"Yes."

"So Jared and Grace both knew that the girl in your building, Erica, and Alexis were suicidal."

"Hold on," I say. "Where are you going with this? And why do you keep bringing up Grace?"

"Grace? I think she's in on this, Keyon. Jared said that you would know who we had to worry about. Who's the only other person that—"

"Stop."

"Stop what?"

"I don't want you accusing my girlfriend of being a killer, Hadlee. I'm not going to listen to this."

So I don't. I hang up on her. Val looks at me seriously. "Mckeyon, I think she could be right."

"There's no evidence that Grace is a part of any of this." I shake my head. "We have way more on Jared."

Val nods once. "Can I just put something out there?"

"Yeah."

"You asked me earlier about what I thought Jared meant when he said my suicide attempt wasn't supposed to happen. What do *you* think he meant by that?"

"I don't know. When I first told him you felt like killing yourself, he was worried, but when you actually tried to do it, he wouldn't let me call anyone."

"Wait, what?" Val takes a step away from me. "I thought you just said it wasn't that bad."

"Jared told me to say that. He said if I called anyone, then he'd never forgive me."

This is when I have possibly the most important thought I've ever had in my entire life.

"He'd never forgive me," I repeat myself. "He would be the one to know about the victims being suicidal. He knew Quinn, you told him about Erica, and Alexis—"

I stop myself. If I'm going to continue with this thought, I have to accept the fact that Grace is involved. She knew that Alexis was suicidal. I tell myself that I need to just throw the idea out there.

"And Grace knew about Alexis," I say. "Together, Grace and Jared knew three people who were suicidal. And every one of them were killed. Then—"

"Stop, stop." Val shakes his head at me and holds out his hand. "Are you saying that they might be working together?"

I take a deep breath. "I think we can both agree they've been acting really weird tonight."

"Yeah. That's true. But I don't think—"

"Grace was mad earlier that I didn't tell her about your suicide attempt," I blurt out.

"What? I thought you said she was mad at Jared?"

"She was. I told her he didn't want me to call anyone or tell anyone about it, and she got angry."

Val lets out a short laugh. "Oh my god," he says. "Your girl-friend was pissed because she wanted to know that I'd tried to kill myself so she could kill me."

"No, Val. Th-that's not true," I stammer. "We don't know—"

The front door of the house swings open, and Jared walks in in front of Grace.

"Alright." Grace smiles at me. "I think we're ready to go."

If she feels the tension in the room, she doesn't show it. I give her a tight-lipped smile and nod. I look at Val, and he's giving me a look that tells me he doesn't want to go anywhere with Grace. Honestly? I don't either.

"Maybe we could just stay here," Val says nonchalantly. "I'm kind of tired of going out. What do you think?" He turns to Jared, who looks like an absolute nervous wreck.

"Yeah." Jared smiles. "I think that'd be fine. But this is Grace's place. I mean—"

"Don't worry about it." Grace gives him a small smile. "I don't mind."

If I felt like I could object, I would. But I don't. Instead, I play pretend. I act normal. I don't act like Val and I just had a conversation about the people we're with being killers. We all help make dinner, then we sit at the table and eat together. Halfway through the night, I swear I almost forget that I can't trust these people. It's not until Val says we should probably leave that I come back to reality.

"Keyon." Grace smiles at me. "Do you think you could stay here tonight?"

I don't even hesitate. "Sure. Yeah." I look at Val, and I know he's silently wishing I had said no. Grace smiles wider at me then relaxes. She looks to Val and Jared. "How about I drive you two home? That okay?"

Val looks at me for help. And for the millionth time tonight, I don't know what to do. I give him a look that hopefully he reads as *Say no,* but I don't think he gets the hint because he says, "Yeah, okay." That's when I know I need to step in.

"Actually." I stand up at the same time Grace does. "I think I'm going to go home with Val. I'll ride with you guys."

Grace frowns at me. "You don't want to stay here?"

"I'm not feeling too well," I say.

"You should probably come back with us then." Val looks at me nervously. "Rest up and all that."

"I can't do this anymore." Jared holds up his hands and stands up from the table. "Grace, what should we do?"

Grace sighs then looks at me with an expression I can only describe as pained. "I don't know."

"What are you talking about?" I ask, slowly stepping back from the table.

Val stands up as well and looks at me, same nervous expression on his face.

"We can't just sit here with them any longer," Jared says quietly, turning his head toward Grace.

I can't believe that he's talking about Val and me like we aren't in the room.

"I know that," Grace says. "But maybe they don't think—"

"Are you fucking kidding me?" Jared slams a hand on the table and turns his whole body to face Grace. "We both heard their conversation. They know."

"I'm sorry," Val says carefully. "What do we know?"

Grace laughs nervously. "I don't know what Jared's talking about."

"Jesus Christ, Grace. Can't we just end this now?" Jared holds up a hand. "This has gone way too far."

Now Grace is getting angry. She looks at Jared with fire in her eyes. "We aren't finished yet. You know that. There's still so much we can do."

"You mean so much *you* can do? You know I can't do this one. We've been over this."

I have no idea what's going on. All I know is that this can't be good. I walk a few steps closer to Val and grab on to his wrist. "I think Val and I are going to leave," I say.

"You can't." Grace shakes her head. "Not together. It's not going to work out like that."

I glare at Grace then pull Val away from the table, heading toward the front door.

"Jared," Grace says calmly. Jared rushes in front of me and knocks me backward with one hand.

"She said that you aren't leaving with him," he says, running his fingers through his hair.

"What the hell is wrong with you?" Val shakes my hand off him and walks up to Jared. He pushes him backward and balls his hands into fists. "Why are you acting like this?"

Jared takes a deep breath. "It was never supposed to come to this, Valentine. I didn't think you'd end up like them."

"Like who? What are you talking about?"

Jared looks back at Grace and sighs. "What do I say?"

"It's pointless to hide anything now." Grace shrugs. "Just tell them."

Jared finally makes eye contact with me. "You're smarter than I thought you were. Either that or I'm just not very good at pretending."

Val speaks for me. "Jared, seriously. What are you talking about?"

"When we were having our conversation earlier," Grace says. "We heard you two talking in here. We know you already have us all figured out."

I stop breathing. This can't be happening. Val is in just as much denial as I am.

"No, no," he says. "We didn't know what we were talking about. It's a stupid theory Hadlee has. And Jared"—Val turns to face his boyfriend—"you went to the police, you told them about your idea. You tried to help."

"I told you he didn't go to the police," I say.

"Keyon—" Val's voice breaks.

Grace walks over to her kitchen counter and opens up her purse, pulling out a small serrated knife. Jesus fucking Christ. "Val, it really isn't that hard to understand," she says. "I mean, did you really not believe in Jared's so-called theory?"

"No." Val takes a step back. "Jared, you wouldn't tell us your motives if you were actually the one killing people. That wouldn't make sense."

Jared sighs. "It made it look like I was on your side." He takes a step toward Val, but Val just takes another step back. "But you're wrong. I've never killed anyone." He looks my way now. "You were wrong too. I said I couldn't admit to something that wasn't true, and I can't. I've never hurt anyone. I had help."

I turn to look at Grace. She's giving Jared a smile that makes my blood run cold. Every part of me is telling me I need to get the hell out of here, but I can't. Val still believes that Jared is innocent. He won't leave with me. There's no way he will.

"Really." Grace gets a few steps closer to me. "I didn't do anything wrong. Jared had told me about that girl, Quinn, in your building, and I'd been watching her for a while. I thought that when Val heard me in the apartment building, he'd figure me out, but he didn't. So I kept watching the girl. She tried to kill herself the afternoon after you met her. I'd always wondered why people didn't show more sympathy towards people with depression or suicidal thoughts.

All they really need is help. And what better way to help them than by giving them what they want?"

I laugh and then realize that I must sound insane for laughing in a situation like this. "You're fucking crazy," I tell Grace. "Killing suicidal people isn't helping anyone."

"It's helping them," Jared says. "If someone is hurting, why would we let them live in a world where all they're really doing is suffering?"

"So all this time, you just wanted to kill me? So you could help me or whatever? That was it?" Val is crying now, but of course, no one says anything about it.

"I didn't know you were suicidal," Jared says with a look of sincerity on his face. "And when I found out, I did everything I could think of not to let Grace find out." He laughs softly and turns his head in my direction. "But your friend here decided that she needed to know all about it." He takes a deep breath and looks at Grace. "Give me that." He holds out his hand. Grace doesn't even hesitate. She hands Jared the knife she's holding and takes a step back. I hold up my hands and back away slowly toward Val. There's only one thing I can think to do.

"We won't tell," I say. "We won't tell anyone. It makes sense what you're doing. I can understand."

Jared laughs and takes a step forward. "Oh, really? Can you? Because I don't think you can. Do you know how hard it is to find out the person you're in love with has to die? Do you understand the kind of pain I'm going through?"

"Please don't do this," Val whispers. "You don't have to do this. Like Keyon said, we won't tell anyone. We never will. We can still have a life together just like we wanted. Isn't that what you said we could do?" Val pauses. "Or is that not what you want anymore?"

Jared relaxes a little. "I can't just let you suffer, Val. Grace is right. There's only one thing we can do to help you."

I think that by now, I've heard everything that I needed to hear. I grab Val's arm and pull him as fast I can over to the front door. This was probably the stupidest thing I could've done. Jared's at the door before we even get close, and he punches me square in the jaw with his free hand. I didn't expect him to hit me, and the force of it was so intense I pretty much just fall to the ground. Val kneels down next to me and pulls me farther away from Jared.

"I *really* didn't want to do this," Jared says. He looks over at Grace. Grace just sighs.

"You didn't want to do anything." She shakes her head disapprovingly. "You made me do everything for you."

Once she says this, I, stupidly, ask the question we all already know the answer to. "You were the one that killed them? All three of them?"

Grace sighs again and walks over to me, a sad look on her face. She gets down on the ground next to me and uses her hands to brush my hair away from my face. "You weren't supposed to find out. You were never meant to be involved in this." She looks at Val. "You weren't either."

"Then why do anything to us?" Val asks. "Why not just let us go?"

"We can't exactly let the only people who know our secret go," Grace says as she stands up.

"Jared." Grace steps back to look at both Val and me. "I think it's time for you to actually do something."

Jared is visibly shaking. "I can't," he says, looking at Val. "You know I can't. I can't hurt him."

"And I can't hurt Mckeyon!" Grace yells at him.

I'm tuning out everything that they're saying. The only thing I'm thinking about right now is how I'm supposed to get Val out of here. If we have to fight our way out, I know we could both take on Grace, but neither of us are any match for Jared.

"We don't have any reason to hurt them." Jared points his knife toward us while looking at Grace.

Grace crosses her arms. "You said yourself that Val was suicidal."

"Yeah." Jared nods. "Was. I'm pretty sure neither of them want to die right now."

I don't know why Jared's trying to help us, but I think I could use this.

"We don't," I say. "And you don't want to hurt either of us."

Jared laughs at me. "You're the one that got Val into this mess. I wouldn't mind hurting you."

Well, there goes my entire plan. I look at Val and see that he's not crying anymore. He just looks angry now. Before I can stop him, he stands up and walks right over to where Jared is standing. "You're not going to hurt me," he says.

Jared sighs. "Val—" Jared doesn't get to finish whatever he's about to say. Val hits him hard across the face. Grace laughs. I almost laugh with her.

"We're leaving," Val states.

I don't expect this to work, but Jared nods, a shocked expression on his face. Val grabs my arm and walks toward the front door slowly, never taking his eyes off the knife in Jared's hand.

"Jared, what the hell?" Grace gets closer to us, as Val unlocks and opens the door. I'm ready to run outside, but I'm caught off guard by the look Jared is giving me.

"I knew I shouldn't have trusted you," Grace says to him.

Jared sighs then slams the door shut again with his free hand. "Goddammit, Grace, I can do this!" he yells right before shoving me down hard and grabbing on to Val's shoulder. I don't have any time to protest; Jared thrusts his knife right into Val's stomach. As soon as I stand up, Val goes down. Jared pulls the knife out quickly and turns toward me. For some reason, all I'm thinking about is what might happen if I scream. Would someone hear me and come to help? Or would screaming just get me killed? I don't have much time to think about this, since Jared looks like he's about ready to do to me what he just did to Val. I'm surprised he isn't fazed by what he's done. He swings his arm forward, aiming for my throat, but I move to the side quickly and avoid him completely. I almost forget that Grace is in the room until I fall backward onto her. I stand up immediately after I fall and run past her through the kitchen.

Jared is asking Grace if she's alright and what they should do. I hear Grace yell at Jared to go after me, and I rush out of the kitchen and down the flight of stairs to my left. I make it to the basement and run toward the back door of the house. I fumble with the lock for a minute, and I can see Jared at the bottom of the stairs out of the corner of my eye. I push the door open and step outside just before Jared comes up behind me. I slam the door closed as hard as I can, hitting Jared in the head and knocking him down. It's just now that I can feel tears streaming down my cheeks. I don't have any time to try to process what's happening. I know I need to keep moving, but I can't leave Val. I have to go back for him. I think about how I left him alone with Grace. I run through Grace's backyard and say a prayer in my head, asking God to make sure Grace hasn't done anything to my best friend.

I make it through the backyard and run along the side of the house. Finally arriving at the front door, I take a few deep breaths before I decide I can't go inside. Grace is probably still in there. She and Jared wouldn't both go the same direction to follow me. Or maybe they aren't following me at all. Maybe they're sitting inside right now, waiting for me to come right to them. I put my ear against the door and hear the familiar sound of Jared sobbing.

"Can you just help me?" I hear Grace yell. Jared says something I can't quite make out, and I hear the sound of flesh against flesh. I'm not sure who hit who, but it shut both Grace and Jared up. I wait until I think that they're away from the door, and I open it slowly. I stick my head inside and look at the ground. There's blood pretty much everywhere, but Val is gone. I don't bother to shut the door behind me; I figure that'll make too much noise. I walk in carefully and look to the door on my right. It's wide open, and I can hear Jared and Grace talking about something. Then I realize there's something really smart I could do.

I dash through the kitchen and down the hall to Grace's room. I lock the door and sit down on her bed, taking out my phone. I call 911. They ask me what my emergency is, and I tell them everything. I stay on the phone with them until I see that I have another call coming through. Since I'm an idiot, I put the operator on hold and answer the other call.

"Hadlee, you were right," I say.

"What?" Hadlee asks me. "What's going on? What's happening?"

I start crying again, words pouring out of my mouth faster than I can think about what I'm saying. "Jared killed Val," I say. "He killed him, Hadlee. He stabbed him right in front of me. I'm still inside, I don't know what's going on. I can't—"

I don't really know what I'm talking about. I don't even know if what I'm saying is true. Val could very well be alive; I just wouldn't know. Hadlee is telling me over and over that it'll be okay. I tell her I called for help, and then I remember I still have someone on the other line. I put Hadlee on hold and go back to the operator I was talking to. They're still there, and I tell them what happened. They tell me that someone should be there soon. I don't have time for this. They're not going to get here fast enough. I need to get to Val now.

I end the call and put my phone back in my pocket. I leave Grace's room quickly and quietly, making my way back over to the room I know that Grace and Jared are in. Before I go in, I look at the coffee table in the living room and see the knife from earlier. I run over to grab it and get back to the room I assume Val is in. I take one deep breath before going inside. Grace is the first to notice me. She's kneeling next to Val on the ground, Jared doing the same thing in front of her.

"Jesus, not again," she says. Jared stands up quicker than I can blink and rushes over to me. I'm afraid he might hit me again, so I hit him first. He barely reacts before grabbing both of my arms and throwing me to the ground.

"Please don't kill him," Grace pleads. I notice that she's crying. This doesn't make sense. She wasn't having an emotional reaction to any of this a few minutes ago. Jared nods at her then looks down at me. He must not notice that I'm holding Grace's knife. I still have a chance. I have this thought right before Jared slams his foot against my face. I hear a crunching noise and feel a warm, steady stream of what I assume is blood coming from my nose. Jared turns away from me and goes back over to kneel next to Grace. I can't tell what they're doing since I can barely see anything. I think about when I first met Jared. I could never picture him doing anything like this. Then I hear something that sounds a lot like a garage door opening.

"I thought you said Tasha wouldn't be home tonight," Jared says quietly.

"I didn't think she would be," Grace says as she stands up. She runs out of the room and closes the door behind her. I'm left alone with Jared and Val, who may or may not be alive. I can hear Grace talking to Tasha for a few minutes, but I don't move. I'm still in too much pain. After another five minutes or so, I think about something. What if I waited too long? What if Val can't hang on any longer? What if he's been dead this whole time? I need to move. Now.

I spend about thirty seconds standing up. Jared has his back to me, and I'm being quiet enough that he doesn't know what's going on. I take a shaky step toward him and reposition the knife in my hand so that I'm gripping onto it just a little more tightly. Jared notices me a second too late. He turns his head to look at me and I completely panic. I raise my arm up and bring the knife down hard into the left side of Jared's back. Jared lets out a scream, and I hear footsteps coming toward the room we're in. I pull the knife out of Jared's back as he jerks his body toward me. He goes to grab my neck, but I'm faster than he is. I shove the knife into his chest, which is much easier said than done. He stares at me with wide eyes. I expect him to scream, but he doesn't. I do. The door to the room we're in swings open, and I hear Tasha screaming as well. I calm myself down and try to breathe. I want to turn around and tell Tasha she needs to get away from this, from Grace, but I'm frozen, staring back at Jared. Tears are running down the sides of his face, but he doesn't say anything. I hear Grace scream. She tells Tasha to run, and they do. I almost want to laugh. Even after all this, Grace is going to pretend like she's innocent and doesn't know what's happening.

Jared tries and fails to take the knife out of his chest then falls to the ground. I spend another minute looking at him, his blood seeping into the carpet. I can't comprehend what's going on. I don't know what I've done to him. I finally snap back to reality and look at Val. His eyes are still open, but he's not blinking. I get closer to him and put my ear to his chest, listening for a heartbeat. I hear the steady rhythm and let out a sigh of relief. I grab his shoulders and shake him a few times until he looks at me.

"Val," I manage to choke out. "We need to leave. Okay? Can you hear me?"

Val nods slowly, and I nod back at him. I gather up all my strength and put my arms underneath his to pick him up. He tells me quietly that he can walk on his own, but I don't believe him. I basically drag him out of the room and out of the house, getting his blood all over me. He's saying something about Jared, but I don't know what to tell him. Jared is dead. We sit outside for barely a minute before I hear sirens. I start to cry yet again. I look down at Val, who by this point is passed out in my arms. The sirens get closer, and I see an ambulance speeding down the street. I wave my hands to get the driver's attention, barely able to see what I'm doing since I'm crying so hard. Everything that happens next happens quickly. I'm asked a few questions, but I don't know how to reply to any of them. A blanket is wrapped around my shoulders as Val and I are pulled into one of a few ambulances.

The next couple of days are a blur. I talk to a lot of police officers and people whose professions I'm unsure of. Val is alright, but I don't see him for a few days while he recovers. Not because I'm not allowed to see him, but because I feel like if I take one look at him, I'm going to burst into tears. I call my dad, and he comes back out to stay with me. I have nightmares almost every night that week. My dad wakes up to talk to me about them, but it doesn't help as much as it probably should. They're mainly about Jared and what I did to him. I know I killed him. I know what happened. I also know that it was self-defense, but that doesn't make me feel any better about myself. Sometimes I'll wake up crying or calling out for Grace. I know that this is pointless. They found her at Tasha's boyfriend's house the night that everything went down. She was arrested, and I don't think I'll ever see her again. I'm more upset about this than I thought I'd be. I pictured myself being happy knowing that she could never hurt anyone again, but for some reason, I feel guilty about what happened to her. Everyone says I did the right thing, but I'm not so sure if I did.

I See Nancy twice a week for the next month. She thinks that I need a break from everything for a while. I couldn't agree more. Eventually, she suggests I get medication for my nightmares. So I do. I even stop having them after a while. That's when Val starts to get them. He'll knock on the wall between our rooms a couple of times a week, and I'll wake up to go see him. Sometimes we'll talk the rest of the night, and sometimes we won't say anything. Either way, I think it makes Val feel a little better. I know that Val thinks about that night a lot, but I don't. I don't want to. And honestly? I don't think I need to.

I'm sitting in Hadlee's apartment with her and Val when Hadlee asks the question that completely sets me off.

"Are you okay?"

I stand up from the couch and run my fingers through my hair. "No, not really. I know it was months ago now, but I kind of had to watch my best friend almost die."

Val throws his hands in the air. "Yeah. And I kind of had to almost die. Neither of us are okay, Keyon."

"Which is ridiculous," I say, spinning around to face him where he's sitting on the couch. "This shouldn't have happened."

"You're right." Hadlee leans back in her chair. "It really shouldn't have. But it did. You can sit down, you know."

I shake my head. "I don't think I'm calm enough to sit down right now."

"Hadlee," Val says as he stands up. "Thank you for having us over, but I think Keyon and I need to talk for a minute."

Hadlee sighs but stands up to give Val a hug. She whispers something to him, and Val nods, giving her a small smile. She gets a few steps closer to me and holds out her arms. I smile at her sadly and hug her. "I'm sorry," she says.

"I'm just glad we were okay."

We let go of each other, and Val raises his eyebrows at me. "You ready?" I'm not exactly sure what he means by this, but I nod anyway. We thank Hadlee again and head outside.

"Where are we going?" I ask Val as we walk along the sidewalk.

"Where do we always go when we need to talk?"

I roll my eyes. "Let me guess, the track at the park?"

"The one and only."

I smile. We walk a little while longer until we make it to the park. We step onto the track circling the pond and start to make our rounds.

"Can I ask you something?" Val puts his hands in his pockets.

I shrug. "Go for it."

"I understand if you don't want to talk about this."

"It's alright. If you don't mind, neither do I."

Val sighs. "I just don't understand why you did it."

"What?" My heart starts to beat faster. I don't want to talk to him about what I did to Jared. He doesn't deserve to have to think about that.

"You came back for me," Val says. "Why did you do that?"

"Oh." We aren't thinking about the same thing. I almost want to cry. I did come back for him. How could I leave him there?

"You didn't have to do that." Val sighs again. "You could've just escaped yourself. Called the police."

"I did call the police. You know that. I couldn't leave you with them. I didn't know what they might do."

Val looks down at the ground as we walk. "You could've been killed."

"So could you. You think I was going to let that happen?"

Val doesn't say anything after that. We walk in silence for a few minutes before he finally says, "I'm sorry I didn't believe you. I feel a little like this all happened because I didn't listen, you know?"

"You can't blame yourself for this. Do you not remember when Hadlee called me that night? She told me she thought Grace was in on it, and I didn't believe her. I reacted the same way you did. It's okay."

Another moment of silence.

"It feels weird talking about it with you. We haven't done that yet," Val says.

"Yeah. I think it's kind of important to talk about it. I haven't really said much to anyone about it yet."

"What about your therapist?"

I shake my head. "Not even her. I should probably do that."

"Yeah." Val laughs. "Probably."

We walk a little longer until we come across one of the benches on the side of the track. We both sit down, and I sigh.

"You know what sucks?" I look up at nothing.

"What?"

"Every time I come out here now, all I can think about is Nathan."

Val groans. "Gross. I still think he was stalking you or something. That's creepy as hell. How do you think he feels about all of this?"

"Does he even know about all of this?"

Val shrugs. "Everyone kind of knows about it."

"Well." I sigh. "I don't know. It probably doesn't feel too good knowing that your best friend of ten years tried to kill your ex-boyfriend."

Val actually laughs at this. I like that he still has a sense of humor. Nothing's changed in him. "True," he says. "God, that sounded so fucked up. Seriously, how did any of this happen? I wanted to live a relatively normal life."

"I'd say it's been relatively normal."

Val rolls his eyes at me, and I laugh. "I'm kidding," I tell him. "I think my life's been messed up ever since I met you."

I look at Val, and he seems a little hurt. "In a good way," I add quickly. "Well, mostly."

"You know what I think we should do?"

"What?"

"You know how when everything happened with your mom, you and your dad moved way out here?"

I raise my eyebrows. "You think we should move?"

"I don't know. Do you not want to?"

"I kind of want to stay at the same school."

"Well, no. I mean, yeah. We shouldn't transfer or anything. Maybe we could just take a break for a while. Then move out of the apartment. You know, after we both get jobs again."

I nod. "I think that sounds nice."

"Doesn't it?"

We sit quietly for a little while after that. At some point, Val says he wants to go home, so we do. We make dinner back at the apartment, we watch a few movies, then we go our separate ways. I lie on my bed for a few hours just to think everything over. Then I fall asleep. Val doesn't knock on the wall that night, and neither do I. For once, we're both alright.

"The End"

—Mark Hamill

CPSIA information can be obtained
at www.ICGtesting.com
Printed in the USA
FSOW02n2101020417
32643FS